The Lost Letter

After 60 Years, How Many Lives Does This Letter Change?

Clara Jalove

contained within this document, including, but not limited to, errors, omissions, or inaccuracies.

Table of Contents

Chapter 1

March 2005

Sunlight beamed from the cloudless sky above, casting a warmth over our small town, a sign that spring was very much on the horizon. I myself was grateful for that, as I had been itching to get ahead on the yard work for days now, but just couldn't find the time. Any grade school teacher would agree that Friday afternoons were superior for that exact reason, and while I was tempted to head back to the house and use up whatever daylight I had left, I decided a little "me time" wouldn't hurt the family and drove through the streets of Whitefish, Montana.

Cars whizzed through the downtown district, as we were the hotspot for many outdoor tourist attractions. We had it all here—from the sandy beaches to the snowy peaks of the Rocky Mountains. Memories flashed in the back of my mind, of a simpler time, when Justin and I would take the girls on spontaneous day trips, where we would pack a lunch and hike until our feet hurt.

My chin bobbed at the thought of us as one big happy family, knowing in my heart that had not been the case for some time now. I would do anything to go back to those moments in time, and if I knew then what I did now, perhaps I would've held onto their hands just a little bit tighter.

Not all that eager to dwell on the past, I made a quick decision to grab a couple of pizzas for me, Justin, and Brenda for dinner tonight. The scent of cheesy bread wafted from the local pizzeria, making my mouth water. Just as I brushed a hand on the door handle, my cell phone buzzed in my purse on the passenger seat.

That's odd, I thought. *I never get calls at this time unless it's an emergency.* A series of frantic thoughts danced through my mind shortly after, fearing that perhaps it was an emergency.

I pressed the call button and put the phone to my ear, my heartbeat thundering so loud I could barely hear the person on the other line.

"Hello?" I repeated, my voice shrill.

"Hi, yes, is this Marina Wood?" a woman asked. I didn't recognize her voice, and I let out a small breath, grateful it wasn't one of my kids in immediate danger.

"This is, how may I help you?"

"I'm sorry to bother you if you're at work. I'm Dr. Williams from North Valley Hospital. You're the emergency contact for Lucinda Davenport. It says here you're her daughter?"

My throat tightened. My mother was in excellent health for her age, and I had no idea why she would be admitted into the hospital. Was it a heart attack? Stroke? Something worse?

"Yes, what's this about? Is she alright?" I questioned.

"I'm sorry, I guess I should've led with that. Lucinda is fine, she just had a bit of a fall and was brought to the hospital so we could get her checked out. Her x-rays indicate she banged up her hip pretty badly and sprained her right ankle, too. We'd like to keep her at least for a couple of days to keep her under observation and make sure things are healing as they should."

I leaned back into the seat, a hand pressed against my chest. I tried to regulate my breathing but failed miserably and hoped that the doctor couldn't hear my uncontrollable wheezing from her end.

"Thank goodness. I don't know what I would've done if it was something worse." I had already lost my father, I was not prepared to lose my only other living parent, not while my life was in shambles enough as it is. "Is she allowed visitors?"

"Absolutely. I suggest bringing a few of her personal belongings to the hospital if you're available. I find that it helps patients feel more comfortable while they're staying with us. Pillows, blankets, a couple of picture frames of family members, whatever you can think of."

"Of course. Tell her I'll be there as soon as possible; I just have to pop over to her house first but then I'll be there."

"I will tell her, Mrs. Wood. Take care."

The line went dead, and I frantically dialed the house number, praying that either Justin or Brenda was home already. It rang a few times before someone picked up.

"Hello?" Justin's voice brought me a wave of comfort that I desperately needed. While Dr. Williams assured me that my mother was in good health, the thought of her in any sort of pain made my skin crawl.

"Honey, it's me," I rushed. "Mom had an accident. The hospital just called and said she fell and needs to recover for a few days before they'll discharge her. I'm on my way to her house right now to bring her some of her things."

"Is she alright? Where was she? Are you alright? Do you need me?"

"I'm fine," I assured him, though I was still debating it myself, but didn't want him to worry about me either. "I didn't get much detail from the doctor, but I'm sure Mom will tell me all about it when I get there."

"Do you want us to come with you?" he asked. "Brenda just got home from school but I'm sure we can pop over—"

"No, no, no need to fuss," I said. "Order some takeout if you don't feel like cooking, and I'll be home when I can. I'll send her all your love."

"Alright. Drive safe. Love you."

"Love you too."

I sat in the parking lot for a few minutes to regain my bearings. There was nothing worse than driving around with your head in the clouds. That was one sure way to get into an accident, especially with how tourists drove around here. When I was ready, I headed for the family house, grateful that my mother was always adamant about us having a spare set of keys.

It appeared we wouldn't be having a pizza night after all.

***

"Okay, I've got her pajamas, pillows, quilt, what else am I missing?" I muttered under my breath, scouring her house as if something was going to miraculously jump out at me. "Oh! Her knitting!"

I always teased her for her old lady hobbies, but in her defense, she'd crafted things far more extravagant than blankets and scarves in her youth. From the stories she used to tell, her job at the fabric store way back in the day made dressmaking that much easier with all the tools at her disposal; not to mention her mother, my grandmother, had a knack for it too.

Shoving that into the top of her overnight bag, I reminded myself that if I forgot anything, or if she wanted anything else, it wouldn't be much trouble to come back and get it for her. Besides, I had a feeling I would be spending most of my free time at the hospital anyway. There was no way I was just going to abandon my mother and leave her without any sort of company while she recovered; that was not how our family operated.

While a lot of people had a habit of remembering the intense or historic moments of their childhood, for me, it was the way my mother always sat me down and taught me the importance of kindness and humility, that the things we love dearly can be taken from us if we don't hold on tight. I recalled the glossy look in her eyes whenever she'd tell me that, and I couldn't help but feel she was speaking from experience, though I never had the courage to ask what kind of pain she'd endured in her lifetime.

Going over the contents not once, but twice, I clumsily put on my shoes and opened the front door but was surprised to see a young man no older than Brenda with his arm outstretched, as if about to ring the doorbell. His cheeks blushed and he took a generous step back, giving me some room as I shuffled out on the front porch.

He wore a post office uniform and his name tag read "Jamie."

"Are you Lucinda?" he inquired, holding what appeared to be a small parcel in his fingertips.

"No, she's my mother," I confirmed.

"Oh," he sighed. "I was really hoping I could talk to her. You see, I've got something really special—"

"Sorry, I don't mean to be rude, it's just I'm on my way out, and it's pretty important. Whatever it is I'm sure you can just pop it in the mailbox, and I'll grab it later."

I pointed my thumb over my shoulder to the black mailbox fastened underneath the window, preparing to follow him back down the driveway, but he didn't budge from the porch.

"Is there a problem?" I tilted my head to the side, shifting my weight from foot to foot, awkwardly juggling my mother's belongings in my hands.

"Uh, not really, it's just a bit of an unusual circumstance. I think I'd feel more comfortable handing it over to someone than just leaving it to get lost again."

"Again?"

At last, he held up the envelope in question. It was not the bright, white, crisp envelope I was used to seeing from the post office, but yellow, the writing faded to the point it was barely legible. Even so, I could see my mother's name addressed on the front, but I was caught off guard as it had her maiden name on it. Clearly, this letter had been from some time ago—she'd been married for decades.

"Where did you say you found it?"

"At the post office, ma'am," Jamie confirmed. "We're in the middle of renovations right now and some of the contractors had moved things around and well, this was behind some old cupboards. It must've slipped back there years ago, and no one knew the wiser. There's no way of telling what's inside, so I thought the only reasonable option was to deliver it to its rightful owner, though I'd say it's been a while since it was originally sent."

"Yeah, I'd say so," I nodded, flipping it back and forth, but not finding any return address on it. "The thing looks ancient."

"No kidding," he chuckled. "Looks like it could be framed and hung in a museum if you ask me. Anyway, I don't want to take up any more of your time, as it appears you're on your way out somewhere." He gestured to the bags hanging off my shoulders. "I'm just happy it made its way home."

"Thanks again," I smiled.

Stumbling down the porch steps, I tossed everything in the trunk and tucked the letter into my purse, where I knew it would be safe. I couldn't help but conjure up theories of who it was from and what could be written inside.

As tempted as I was to open it up myself, I knew that it wouldn't be right, not with something as rare as this. I couldn't wait to see my mother's face when she opened it herself; surely something like this was going to lift her spirits. No doubt she could use a little blast from the past right about now.

***

With a little help from the lovely lady at the front desk, I followed the purple line through the halls of the hospital until I made it to the proper floor. The smell of cleaning products made me a little uneasy; there was something about hospitals that I was not overly fond of. Maybe it was the bright fluorescent lights, or the thought of people saying goodbye to their loved ones under the same roof, or the simple fact that the strong scent of bleach made my head all fuzzy. Either way, it was a small sacrifice I was willing to make in order to make my mother's stay more bearable.

"Hi, I'm here to see Lucinda Davenport," I told the woman behind the glass.

She glanced up at me from behind her computer screen, gesturing that she'd be with me in a minute. I waited patiently until she was done typing away at her keyboard, and she flashed me her best customer service smile.

"Sorry about that. Mrs. Davenport, you said?"

"That's right."

"You must be Marina. She's been gabbing on and on about you for the past hour. Room 305, just down the hall there. Can't miss it."

"Thank you," I nodded, excusing myself and following the woman's direction. I heard my mother's boisterous voice spilling out into the hall before I even made it to the door.

"Are you giving your nurses a hard time already?" I joked, leaning against the doorframe, a silly smile plastered on my face. My mother's eyes lit up when she spotted me and clapped her hands in delight.

The nurse tending to her also found my comment humorous. "Not at all," the girl said, patting my mother on the foot. "She's an absolute delight. You're lucky to have such a fun mom like her."

"I am," I agreed.

We'd always had the best relationship, even through those rough teenage years when every young girl wanted nothing to do with their mother. She always stuck by me, and now, we were inseparable. Two peas in a pod, or so my husband said. My heart ached a little seeing her hooked up to so many monitors though, and I wondered if it was even necessary given that Dr. Williams assured me there was nothing to be worried about.

"I'll leave you ladies to it," the nurse said. "Visiting hours are 8 p.m. However, you're more than welcome to stay the night if you wish. We can have a cot sent up to the room."

"Oh, nonsense," Mom chided. "I think I can handle a few nights in here by myself. Thanks, Tiana."

The nurse brushed past me, leaving us alone. I plopped her things at the foot of the bed, taking out what I had packed one by one. First, her pillow, which she tucked behind her back and settled into, a look of relief washing over her, then her array of blankets to make her feel more at home. I even took the doctor's advice and snatched a few pictures from her bedside table and set them up for her on the little desk on the other side of the room.

"I even brought this." I held up the knitting bag, and she waved at me to hand it over before she tucked it underneath her arm, patting it for good measure.

"You spoil me."

"I couldn't very well leave you in here with no entertainment. What even happened? Dr. Williams didn't say much over the phone."

"Oh, it was nothing really," Mom grumbled. "I was trying to cover the plants on my porch, and I slipped off the chair. Luckily, the young man up the street was walking by with his dog at the time and called me an ambulance. I tried to tell him that he didn't need to fuss over—"

"I'm glad he did," I replied, settling down into the plush chair and moving as close as I could to the bed without getting in the way of the nurses. "You're not as spry as you used to be. You know I'm just a phone call away."

"I don't want to be a bother, you know that. Besides, I'm more than capable of covering my own flowers, thank you very much."

She gave me that look my mother always had—the one of sheer determination and independence. I had no idea how my father managed to put up with her for all those years. From what he had said, she was a bit unpredictable at times. That spunk must have skipped a generation, as my daughter shared a lot of the same qualities.

"Did they say how long they're keeping you prisoner here?" I asked.

"Not a definite answer. I'm sure they'll know more in a few days once things start to heal. You should see the bruise! It's all kinds of colors now."

"Only you would be amused by that."

"Well, you know I always like to look on the bright side of things. Dwelling on what's come and gone is futile."

"I know. Ah, that reminds me," I blurted, almost forgetting about the letter from earlier. I fished it out of my purse and held it out. "This came for you just before I left your house. The post office is supposedly doing some renovations and they found this behind an old cupboard. Must be from a while ago, that's your maiden name, isn't it? Who would still address you like that?"

She took the letter from me, and it was as if she'd seen a ghost. Her face paled, a hand made its way to her mouth as she let out a little gasp, as if not believing what she was seeing. Running her fingertips over the script on the front of the envelope, she mumbled something under her breath, though not loud enough for me to make out any words.

"Mom?" I murmured, placing a gentle hand on her arm. "Are you okay? You've gone all pale."

"I'm fine," she blinked, a few tears threatening to spill over her cheeks. "I just… this has taken me by surprise, that's all."

"You recognize the handwriting? Who's it from?"

"Someone I never expected to hear from again," she whispered.

Chapter 2

May 1942

The heavenly scent of freshly baked bread, sausages, and eggs wafted from the kitchen, luring me out of my bedroom and down the stairs. It was the same routine every morning, one the five of us had followed since before I could remember. Normally, my father would've been off working his shift at the Micho copper mines at that hour, but his weekend shifts were quite lax, which meant he was about to grace the kitchen table with his presence.

"Lucinda," Mother called, tentatively flipping the last pieces of sausage and piling them onto our plates. "Would you be a dear and get your sister for me? She was supposed to help cook breakfast, but you know Edith."

Her voice trailed off, as she assumed I would follow through with whatever request she had. As the eldest daughter, I had many expectations and responsibilities that hung on my shoulders. To be fair, none compared to that of our eldest and only brother, Leith. He was a hard-working man, but how could he not be, standing directly in our father's shadow for the better part of his life. The only reason he had not been conscripted into the war was because of his occupation, and I knew that our family was grateful for that. With men off protecting the nation, Leith remained at home, working the fields, ensuring that the rest of us left behind had something to eat. It was a tough time for us all, but our mother surely slept better at night knowing her baby boy wasn't somewhere in the trenches fighting to survive.

Our father, the one and only Frank Carney, had also been dismissed from conscription due to a permanent injury he sustained from an accident in the mines. While he was still more than capable of getting up at the crack of dawn each morning and heading on down to the copper mines, it seemed the military could not take the risk of someone so… unreliable, or at least that was what they had said. I could see the disappointment on my father's face when he was told the news that rainy afternoon, and I never quite understood why anyone would want to leave their family behind without any guarantee of coming back.

Regardless of my thoughts and opinions, I was smart enough to keep them to myself. Whitefish was a small war town, one where every eligible man was counting down the days before he was sent off to join the others.

"Edith!" I cupped my hands around my mouth and shouted into the countryside that was our backyard.

If she wasn't inside, it was the only other place she'd be. Among the tall grass, frolicking around, not a care in the world. Oh, how I envied that kind of mindset. It wouldn't be much longer before our mother and father had her smarten up and settle down, just as they had been doing to me for years.

"Yes?" She popped her head out from the far side of the barn, a bouquet of handpicked wildflowers in hand.

"Breakfast?" I blinked, wondering how she could be so clueless. "You know, the first meal of the day, the one our mother slaves over to prepare for her darling children and husband each morning. You're late, as usual."

"Sorry," Edith rushed, the hem of her dress caked in mud, though she clearly was none the wiser.

I rolled my eyes and left it at that, not wanting to get into it with her. It was far too early, and if I were being honest, I simply didn't care. I had far more important things to rack my brain over.

Trailing behind me, we headed for the kitchen, where I narrowly avoided my father's heavy gaze. Mother had just finished slapping eggs, toast, and sausages on his plate before moving to ours, loading them up as if we were soldiers in the war, not delicate ladies meant to watch our figures.

"Where's Leith?" I asked, shoving a piece of bread in my mouth, earning me a swift pinch in the ears for my rude behavior.

"He had to get an early start," Mother explained. "They've got a busy day on the farm, so we probably won't see him until nightfall."

"I have a shift down at the shop, too," I said.

I was one of the few young ladies my age that had a steady job. I was grateful that I not only was able to earn a living to help support my family, but my parents were gracious enough to let me keep a little myself so that I wouldn't be completely dependent on my husband, whenever I went out and found one. I sensed that conversation brewing like a thundercloud overhead, as it was an ongoing topic in our household.

"You know you wouldn't have to work so hard if you had a nice man to take care of you," Father stated.

I could feel his stare burning a hole into my forehead, but I knew better than to cave. As soon as we locked eyes it would be a monsoon of lectures and persuasion. But Edith distracted me with her gentle hum, and when I looked up to scowl her, I was met with all three of them eyeing me from their respective spots at the table. Even my mother, who normally didn't like to get involved in our little spats, was waiting for a reply.

"I don't mind working," I smiled. "It gets me out of the house, and I like it. I even get to meet new people, isn't that a good thing? To present myself as a maiden of society."

"A young girl like you ought to be married off by now," Father continued. "I don't want to have to worry about you if I croak one day. I want to see that my girls are looked after, and Leith can only do so much for this family, and so can that little dressmaker wage of yours."

"What will you have me do, Daddy?" I put my fork down a little too hard and braced myself for the reprimand of a lifetime. "Any eligible man worth my attention has joined the war. Marriage will just have to wait until the fighting is done."

"Having a soldier for a husband is an honor," he said.

"I'll think about it," I conceded. "Take it or leave it."

His mouth twitched, as if he contemplated saying something else, but left it at that. My mother's shoulders settled, and the tension that had built between us seemed to dissipate. My frustration did not; I just wished that my family could understand my heart could not handle the thought of settling down with a man who was destined to pack up and abandon me. I had no intention of getting involved with any soldier, no matter how tempting his hand might be.

***

"He said what?" Gianna gasped, her bite from her sandwich hanging out of her mouth.

The three of us settled on the riverbank not far from town, our dresses hiked up to our knees so we could dip our feet into the frigid water. It was refreshing on a hot day like today, and after a long week of altering dresses for wealthy mothers and sewing up gowns from scratch for their daughters, I needed a little leisure time with my best gals.

"That it would be an honor if I found a husband who was drafted in the war," I scoffed. "As if that sounds appealing to me."

"It is patriotic," Madeline chimed in, sipping her lemonade while basking in the sunlight. "But I do see your point. My mother's been on my case about it too. What's with them and wanting us to chain ourselves in matrimony?"

"It's the way of the world, Maddy," I sighed. "Sooner or later, we're going to have to settle into domestic bliss, just like they had. I'm surprised there's no conscription for wives as well as war."

"Careful," Gianna murmured. "You say it too many times and it might come true."

I pretended to lock my lips and throw away the key into the rushing water at our feet, earning a chuckle from both my friends. I leaned back and closed my eyes, letting the warm light wash over me, and for those few blissful minutes, I could almost forget about all my troubles and worries.

"I would be lying if I said I hadn't thought about it," Madeline admitted. "Finding a husband, that is. Sure, it would be lonely in the house for a while, and I'm sure I'd have to get used to the idea of being someone's wife, but what's worse? Living with my parents until they either die or declare me too much of a burden? Women don't earn enough to support themselves. We don't really have much of a choice."

I knew in my heart that what she said was true, that our lives would always revolve around the notion of marriage, but I was more of a romantic. I wanted to fall in love with someone, get to know them first, learn their passions, dreams, secrets, and share mine, too. Tying the knot and starting a family could come after all that, but there was only so much time a young girl like me would be granted before I became the talk of the town.

"I wouldn't even know where to look for such a man," I started. "The dress shop doesn't get many eligible bachelors across our threshold. I suppose I could talk to Leith and see if any of his friends or coworkers are single and looking for a wife."

"A farmhand, no thanks." Gianna wrinkled her nose in disgust. "I wouldn't want to clean up after that day in and day out. Picture the mud they track in through the halls, not to mention the filth on their clothes."

"My brother always leaves his work boots outside," I said.

"Forget it. You know they're having an officer's dance down at the church next weekend, we should go, the three of us."

"To an officer's dance?" I raised an eyebrow. Had she not been listening to my whole "I don't want to marry a soldier" speech?

"They might not all be heading off to war, and even if they are, they might know someone who's staying in good old Whitefish for a while. But let's not think of it as a pursuit for a husband—when's the last time you got out and had some fun? I know you're just itching for a good time. Lucinda Carney is the essence of pleasure and escapades. It's been far too long since you broke out your dancing shoes."

"Alright, alright," I smirked, though she barely had to convince me to have a night out on the town. "You twisted my arm, I'll go."

***

I will never forget the look of pure joy on my mother's face when I told her that I was going to the officer's dance with Gianna and Madeline. It was as if I told her a man got down on one knee and proposed; and given how much she fussed over the outfit I had picked for the entire week, I feared what would become of me when that day eventually came.

Despite me telling her that it was a girl's night out and that we were just looking for a bit of fun, I saw the wheels turning in her mind, and in my father's too. I was taking an enormous leap into society as a single woman and by standing in the spotlight, at a church filled with people who were bound to stir feelings, they figured this was it—the time I found love, or something equivalent in their eyes.

My only saving grace was that they didn't force me to bring Edith along. They had to break it to her gently that this was a night out for a young lady such as myself, not necessarily a girl who spends most of her time skipping around in the dirt. Her time would come, but only after mine. And so, after a week of anticipation, the night had arrived, and with Gianna and Madeline on each arm, we ventured out in the crisp evening air, not a chaperone in sight.

I promised myself I would make it a night to remember, as I had a sneaking suspicion that I would not get another chance for such luxuries in the future. Even in the past week, more calls had been made for young men to be drafted into the war, that our military was desperate and calling for more trailed soldiers to serve their duty to their country. A heaviness loomed in the air, even in the dress shop, as my boss nearly sewed herself to the radio and listened to the broadcasts all hours of the day.

Things were not like they once were, and this dance was going to offer us all a little solace from what horrors lay on foreign soil.

"Oh, he's scrumptious," Gianna cooed, pointing her chin to a young lad with a freshly shaven face and brown doe eyes. He had an officer's uniform on, but I noticed that it hadn't a spec of dirt or looked like it had even seen the light of day. I would bet all the money I had saved up that he was a new recruit.

"Careful, Gianna," I shushed. "Someone may hear your vulgar mouth and think you're not a proper lady."

"I'm not," she giggled.

"What about him?" Madeline chimed in on the fun, her eyes following a blond man from across the room. He was joined by the younger man that Gianna had pointed out, and the two laughed at some joke one of them made before sucking back a glass of who knows what.

"Another soldier, how convenient. You know I haven't seen a single man out of uniform. I thought you said there would be regular folks here too."

"Give it time," Gianna assured me. "It's still early; the sun hasn't even gone down yet. I'm sure there's stragglers from the farmer's field that have yet to stumble in through the doors."

The three of us standing there must've looked like easy prey to all those men, as the ones Gianna and Madeline had been eyeing made their way over and extended a hand.

"Care to dance?" the blond asked, and Madeline nearly jumped into his arms before he could get any more words out.

Gianna took her claim on the other, letting him lead her out to the dance floor, but not before she winked in my direction.

Merely seconds later, someone brushed up against my shoulder, and when I turned to see who, a tall man with dark hair and a dimpled chin was staring back at me. His hair was styled in a way that his bangs were off his forehead, and he had the whitest smile I'd ever seen.

But I wasn't about to swoon at the sight of him, no matter how much his visage made me weak in the knees.

"Let me guess, you've come to sweep me off my feet too?" I crossed my arms over my chest and dropped my weight onto one hip, showing I was clearly not impressed by his lame attempt to woo me into a dance.

"No, actually," he smiled, "the opposite. I couldn't help but notice you standing alone over her and thought I wouldn't ask you to dance. I'm not very good at it myself. Don't feel like making a fool of myself in front of all these people."

"You don't plan to dance at the officer's dance?" I mused.

"Not unless you beg, then of course I might oblige."

"Don't hold your breath, I'm not the begging type," I remarked. "That is unless you ramble on and on and I grow desperate for a minute of peace."

"A sense of humor, I like that in a stranger." He placed his empty cup down on the table closest to us and held out his hand for me to shake. "Dwayne Anderson, it's a pleasure to make your acquaintance, miss."

"Lucinda Carney," I introduced. "And don't consider it a pleasure yet, you hardly know me. My friends will vouch for my inexcusable behavior once they're done twirling around on the dance floor."

"I doubt that'll happen any time soon. Dustin and Mark may keep them occupied for the remainder of the night."

"You know them?" I questioned, my eyebrows pinching together, and he nodded along as if it were obvious.

"They're my best friends, as I gather those two fine young ladies are yours as well. What an odd coincidence that they might meet each other just like us."

A charmer, I thought. A real good one at that. "Huh," I huffed. "Seems as though you set all this up just so you could come over and talk to me."

"Now what in the world would give you that impression?" His eyes flickered to me, and we stared at each other for a few beats, and my heart danced in my chest, in rhythm with the music. This was it—the moment in time that every girl longs for their entire life—when the world stands still and goes all quiet and nothing else matters except you and him.

The only dilemma was that he was dressed like all the rest in the church hall.

I reminded myself that a conversation was not a lifelong commitment; that I was here to blow off some steam and have a good time.

"So, you plan on standing around all night and watching your friends have the time of their lives?" I asked, swaying to the music, though not daring to ask if he would, in fact, like to take me for a spin.

"It's getting rather crowded in here," he began. "I think I might go outside for some fresh air. Care to join me, Miss Carney?"

He held his arm out for me to take, a grin tugging at the corners of his lips as he waited in eager anticipation. Surely my brother would have a fit if he saw me strolling in the moonlight with a complete stranger, unaccompanied might I add, which was all the more reason I said yes.

"I suppose a bit of fresh air never killed anyone," I beamed.

That was the unforgettable night where Dwayne Anderson tugged on my heartstrings, and it seemed he never let go.

Chapter 3

March 2005

"So," I cleared my throat, feeling as though I should be walking on eggshells solely from the solemn look in my mother's eyes, "Dwayne was a... friend of yours from when you were Amy's age?"

She chuckled a bit under her breath and proceeded to fiddle with the frayed ends of her blanket. I'd never seen her so conflicted before in my life. My mother was fierce by nature, while she would always remain reserved and a polite lady in public, I knew her for what she was behind closed doors—a force to be reckoned with. That wasn't the woman lying in the hospital bed, that woman was holding a sea full of secrets. Anyone who had scars on their heart could tell from a single glance.

"Friend is a charitable way to put it," she murmured. "He's more like a ghost, one I thought was dead and gone."

I tilted my head to the side. "Dead?"

"Were you not listening to the story, Marina?" Mother looked up and forced a smile. "He was a soldier. Most of the men I knew from that time never returned home, leaving their mothers, sisters, and wives to fend for themselves. Though it didn't take long for the girls to find someone new to take care of them."

"So quickly?" I had never fathomed how anyone could just pick themselves up and move on after a loved one died.

"We couldn't afford to sit around and wallow, I'm afraid," she continued. "Only someone who came from true wealth could wait for true love. It was a different time back then, resources were slim, jobs were scarce, and we didn't make enough to support ourselves."

"Oh."

I thought about my father, Russell Davenport, the man who had made sure I had the world growing up. Had he not been my mother's greatest love? I never once doubted in my childhood that my parents didn't love or care for each other, so I felt a bit blindsided learning of this other man in her life. I recalled spending Sunday afternoons out in the backyard beneath the gazebo, sipping on fresh lemonades with my cousins while the adults indulged in something a little sweeter. My memories were fond, and brought me a sense of joy as well as sadness, knowing that we had laid my father to rest some time ago.

"I can see the wheels turning in your head," Mother sighed. "I loved your father; he was an excellent husband and even greater father to you."

"It sounds like there should be a 'but' at the end of that sentence," I said.

"Dwayne was my first love. You know what they say about your first love…" her voice trailed off for a second as she looked out the window, losing herself in what I could only assume was a memory. "It is the most beautiful but painful of all."

I could sympathize with that, every woman in the world likely could at one point or another. Mine was a high school boyfriend. We'd been best friends at first, but somehow, one day, something changed between us. Looking back now, I chalked it up to teenage hormones, but then again, I liked to think of it as something more sweet and genuine than that. He knew me like the back of his hand, I trusted him with my heart, my body, and soul, and even though it didn't work out between us, I was grateful for that relationship and love. It taught me what I needed and wanted in my future relationships, and when I met Justin a few years later, I knew I wasn't settling for him; he was the man I wanted to be with.

"So, what exactly happened between you two?" I asked, my curiosity seeping from my pores as I was desperate to learn more. "He went off to war and then what?"

"That was it," she said with a sense of finality that made me wonder if she was telling the truth or merely protecting herself from it. "Like I said, I thought he died. I never heard from him again."

"You never looked for him? Just to be sure?"

"Why would I?" Her mouth twitched but she brushed it off, her sparkling smile replacing the agony I knew she was feeling underneath it all. "It all worked out the way it was supposed to. I met your father shortly after, and the rest is history. I lived a wonderful life with Russell, and I wouldn't change that."

Something wasn't adding up, and I couldn't be sure if it was because my mother was dodging the questions or if she didn't have all the facts herself. "What's the letter say?" I blurted out, wishing I could take it back.

For all I knew it was intimate and personal. I mean, why wouldn't it be?

"It doesn't matter now," she whispered, "it was a lifetime ago. These sorts of things have little meaning over decades apart."

"It *is* a love letter!" I squealed, clapping my hands in delight. I shimmied closer, wanting to catch a glance at the contents of the letter myself, but she quickly folded it back up, keeping it away from prying eyes.

"Hush, Marina," Mother blushed herself, waving her hand as if to swat at me. Despite her efforts, there was no hiding the growing smile tugging at the corners of her lips. If I didn't know any better, I thought she was going through the motions of a crush, feeling those giddy sensations in the pit of your stomach, no matter how hard you tried to force them away. "I don't need the entire hospital learning of my former scandals."

"Scandal!" I wheezed. "I thought it was just an appropriate courtship that never went anywhere, but not—"

"Whatever impure thoughts you have bouncing around in that head of yours I don't want to hear them," she grumbled. "I just meant that mutual feelings for one another, that's all."

"You know if someone brought me an old love letter from a previous boyfriend, I'd think I'd have more of a reaction than this," I pointed out.

If he truly was the first epic love of her life, why did it seem like something awful or tragic happened between them?

"I married someone else," she reminded me. "Or have you gone and forgotten the man who helped bring you into this world?"

"I never thought of Dad as the jealous type. Are you worried what he might think if you went down this road of long-forgotten emotions for another man?"

Mother scoffed but brought the blanket up to her chest as if it could offer her some sort of comfort during this delicate conversation. "I'm worried about my own heart, Marina. It is a fickle thing, and it's already been broken once before; I doubt I can go through that again."

I slouched, my shoulders dropping a bit as I leaned back into the chair, bringing my knees to my chest. "That's why you never looked him up," I said softly, "you were worried what you might find."

She nodded, unable to form any words.

"Was it his possible death that frightened you so much or something else?"

"Something else."

She didn't need to go into detail for me to be able to work out what she meant; at least if he died that would be a valid reason for why they never ended up together. On the other hand, if he was one of the lucky few who made it out of the war alive but never sought her out once he came home… it meant that he had made that choice himself not to be with her, and that would surely be far more painful than being separated by death. Even with that in mind, I couldn't help but wonder if he was still out there somewhere, and that this was all just a matter of miscommunication between the two of them. If he had sent this letter while he was deployed but she never got it, maybe he thought she was not going to wait for him, or something along those lines. Maybe it was just because I was an idealist, but I couldn't go the rest of my life without knowing the truth, even if it would cause me a great deal of pain.

"So that's it then?" I asked. "You're just going to pretend like you never got his letter and continue on with your life?"

"What else would you have me do, Marina?"

I shrugged, surrendering to this topic entirely, not wishing to cause her any more grief on an already stressful afternoon. But if I was in her position, I didn't think I could give up without a fight.

***

Despite all my efforts to stay with my mother in the hospital, at least for the first night to make sure she was comfortable, she sent me on my merry way, and so I headed home, my head lost in the clouds.

It was not exactly how I had pictured my Friday afternoon turning out, with my mother falling and needing recovery time in the hospital, nor a young man handing over a precious piece of history that had been lost for some time. It stirred an array of emotions to say the least, things I had not thought about for years. I was in a happy marriage, one filled with love, compassion, trust, and respect. Sadly, I couldn't say that was the same with all the relationships in my life, and as much as I tried to ignore it, I couldn't for much longer. The weight of my failures was grinding down like the rocks in the sea, slow and almost nonexistent at some points, but the longer time passed, the sooner the scales would tip, and everything would come crashing down.

Pulling in the driveway, I sat in my car for some time, not even accompanied by the sound of the radio, just sinking into my thoughts until there was a small knock on the window. I blinked out of my weary daze and spotted my daughter staring back at me through the foggy glass.

"Mom?" Brenda inquired, her eyebrows furrowed, and I could sense she feared something was the matter.

Like any mother, I put on a brave face and flashed her a tender smile, quickly grabbing my purse and stepping out. "Hello, darling," I greeted. "How was school?"

Always the go-to question when your brain was a jumbled mess. She tucked a few strands of light brown hair behind her ear, following behind me as we made our way up the porch and into the foyer. The smell of Chinese food wafted from the kitchen; at least Justin went ahead and ordered food since I wasn't going to be around for dinner.

"I joined a study group for exam season," Brenda said. "That's where I just came from actually, I was working on some—"

"Did your father tell you about your grandmother?" I interrupted.

"No?" she replied, her face draining of all color. "What's wrong? Is she alright?"

"I didn't want her to worry," Justin appeared out of thin air, holding a plate of food in each hand before planting a kiss on my cheek. I always loved him for his intuitive mind. "I thought it would be best to wait until you were home."

"What happened to Grandma?" Brenda repeated.

I rested my hands on her shoulders so she could look me in the eye and know I was being truthful. "She's fine, she just had a little fall is all. She's in the hospital for a little while, but that's because they just want to make sure everything is healing properly. It might be nice if you picked up a card for her and brought it sometime over the weekend," I suggested, taking my seat at the table and digging into the plate. I hadn't realized how hungry I was until that very moment.

"I'm sure I could find the time," Brenda nodded, helping herself to her plate, too. Justin, although he had long since eaten, joined us, his hand resting on the back of my chair.

"I was thinking I should probably find a way to tell Amy," I continued.

Brenda snapped her plastic fork in half, her face turning an unnatural shade of pink. I should've known better than to bring up her sister at the table, as the mere mention of her name was almost like tossing a live bomb into a room full of people. It had been so long since she'd been with us that it left a bitter taste in my mouth. I blamed my little slipup on the day I had, but it was too late to take it back now.

"Why bother?" Brenda snapped, leaning so far forward her hair almost touched her food.

"She is a part of this family just like you or I," I explained. "When these things happen it's best to let everyone know. It's common courtesy, honey."

"Amy doesn't care about us!" Brenda shouted. "She hasn't been a part of this family ever since she ran off with that dumb boyfriend of hers. When are you going to give up and move on?"

Brenda didn't understand a mother's love, and she never would, only if and when she had children of her own. I didn't bother diving into it; even if Amy had packed up and left in the middle of the night all those months ago, she was and always would be my daughter.

"You know your grandmother loves you girls very much," Justin intervened. "I'm sure she would be happy to hear from you both."

"No, you mean Amy," she fired back. "She and Amy get along better than we ever have. Everyone in this family seems to care about Amy more, and she's not even here!"

Standing up, Brenda's chair squeaked against the linoleum floor, and she stormed up the stairs, slamming her bedroom door for good measure. I let out a deep exhale, rubbing my temples as if that might somehow help this god-awful situation we seemed to have found ourselves in. I didn't like talking about Amy as much either, but I just couldn't help myself sometimes. Even if she never wanted to see us again, she would always be in my heart. The letter drudged up those feelings I had locked away, and now it was as if the flood gates had opened, and everything came pouring out.

"Maybe I should go talk to her," Justin suggested, though I could tell by the way he held his jaw tight that he wasn't sure it was the right thing to do.

"Give her some time." I patted his hand with mine before giving it a gentle squeeze. "This whole thing with Amy can't be easy for her to deal with."

Not that I would know anything about the bonds of siblings myself, as I was an only child. I had dreamed about having a younger brother or sister, but it never happened, and as I grew older, that wish slipped out of my fingers and disappeared like all the rest.

"What do I know about the hearts of teenage girls anyway," he joked.

"Funny you should mention that," I remembered. "Someone dropped something off for Mom at her house before I went over to the hospital. Turns out it was an old love letter that was lost at the post office, back from when she was Amy's age."

"Really?" Justin gasped. "That must've been weird for her to read."

"Why weird?"

"Well, no offense, but that's sort of like a lifetime ago for your mom," he explained. "I think anyone would be thrown for a loop if they got something like that out of the blue."

"I was thinking about trying to find him," I confessed. I knew my mom was unsure if she wanted to know of his fate, but I couldn't help myself. I had even convinced myself that she would thank me in the long run for doing this for her.

"She asked you to do that?" Leave it to Justin to see right through me.

"Not exactly," I hesitated, trying to find the right words to pitch my argument. "But I just thought that since Dad has passed it really wouldn't hurt anyone to go snooping around. For all we know this man could be the one who holds the key to her heart."

"Marina, darling," he murmured, placing a hand on my cheek, "I don't think this is such a good idea. It's like you said, your mother already lost her husband, I doubt she wants to lose anyone else right now."

"Is that what you truly think?" I thought for sure my husband would vouch for true love, but he seemed to be on the fence about the whole debacle.

"I just think this family is going through enough rough patches as it is; I'm not sure digging into your mother's past and unveiling some long-forgotten romantic suitors is something any of us needs right now."

I supposed he had a point, but I had long since thrown my rational thinking out the window. Regardless, I gave a small nod, and he sighed with relief, pulling me closer to him so I could rest my head on his shoulder.

"I love you," he whispered, brushing the hair off my forehead, putting me at ease.

"I love you, too."

Chapter 4

March 2005

"Welcome to Dunkin' Donuts, how can I help you this morning?" I flashed my best customer service smile, hoping the old man on the other side of the counter didn't notice I was running on four hours of sleep.

It seemed my boyfriend and his college buddies had such important matters to attend to in the early hours of the morning that they simply couldn't wait until everyone in the house was awake, but what did I know? I was just the dumb girlfriend who wasn't even smart enough to finish high school.

The old man's wrinkled face scrunched up as he studied me sharply before letting out a deep huff. "Well, Amy," he eyed the name tag pinned to my shirt, "I don't see any more of your specialty donuts, you know, the ones with the colorful sprinkles on top and jam in the inside?"

I exhaled slowly through my nostrils, having given the same speech over and over again for the past two days. "I'm sorry, sir, those were part of a promotion the company was doing, and they're no longer available. Perhaps I could interest you in something else? Our regular sprinkle donuts are a huge hit with the crowd."

He groaned once more, shaking his head in disappointment. "You youngin's don't know a thing about keeping your customers happy."

"I'm really sorry, sir," I repeated. What I really wanted to say was that the staff had absolutely no say when it came to what products were available and what donuts were discontinued, and that if he has such a problem with it, maybe he ought to call up the owner and give him a stern talking to.

As expected, he settled for just the regular sprinkle donut, as all the others had before him. The rest of my shift was uneventful, save for the handful of elementary school kids I had to kick out for splattering wet toilet paper all over the bathroom mirrors. Not a single customer came in during my last hour; the minutes seemed to drag on longer than they ever did in class.

I couldn't help but think of my time in high school, the friends I had, the clubs I was curious about joining but never had the courage to follow through with it out of fear of not looking cool, and the day my best friend's older brother introduced me to Tommy, or Ace, as everyone else knows him as. He'd told me the story about how he earned such a nickname more times than I could count, and apparently it was because whenever he and his buddies ever played a round of poker, he somehow always got a pair of aces. I didn't want to say it at the time, but it sounded a lot like he had rigged the deck, but what did I know?

The timer went off in the back, meaning that the store had closed, and just as I was about to finish up with the register, the bell over the door chimed.

"Sorry, we're closed!" I hollered, hoping whoever it was would turn back around and leave without making a fuss.

"Hey, Ames," a gentle voice said.

I popped my head from behind the counter and saw one of my old high school friends standing on the carpet that separated the dining area where she gave me a small wave.

"Liv?" I gasped.

Olivia was my best friend once upon a time. After I dropped out, we sort of fell apart too, though I did see her brother at the apartment quite often. He had fallen victim to Tommy's many gambling tricks, and I couldn't help but feel bad. Olivia didn't care much for the bad boy crowd, and I didn't blame her. Sometimes, when I was lying in bed at night, unable to sleep because of his irritating snoring, I wondered how my life might've turned out had I followed her advice in the first place.

"In the flesh," she smiled. In those few seconds I was transported back to a time when she was the most important person in my life, who knew all my dark secrets. Now, I was afraid I didn't know her at all.

"How did—I mean—what are you doing here?" I fumbled over my words, untying my apron and hanging it up on the hook before joining her on the other side of the counter.

"Ace said I might find you here," she explained. "I'm not stalking you if that's what you think." We both laughed, knowing that I wouldn't put it past her. She always did try to steer me on the right path, though it seemed not enough to persuade me. "Anyway, I was kind of hoping you could help me out with something for school, if you're not too busy though."

I pursed my lips, weighing my options. She knew that school was a sensitive subject for me, but she was my oldest friend, and I didn't want to disappoint her. "What's the project?"

"It's for home economics," she admitted. "Lame, I know, but the guidance counselor said it'll look good on my college application. Anyway, we're supposed to be sewing a dress from scratch, but we're not supposed to just slap things together. We have to do some research on colorology and patterns, and whatnot. I figured that since your grandmother was a dressmaker and you're pretty handy with that sort of stuff yourself that you might be able to help."

"I'd be honored," I grinned, placing a hand on my chest for good measure. "Just give me a minute to grab my coat and lock up, and we can head over to the library downtown."

Olivia squealed. "You're the best! I knew I could count on you."

I figured it was the least I could do for all the trouble she'd gotten me out of during our youth. Locking up the shop, we headed for the library, which I knew had lots of patterns and sewing stencils that she could use for the dress she planned to make. My heart fluttered a little, a pang of jealousy bouncing around in my mind that Olivia was still experiencing all the joys of the education system while I was slaving away at a place like Dunkin' Donuts to contribute to the bills.

"So, is adult life all that you wanted it to be?" Liv asked, nibbling on a granola bar she pulled out of her backpack. "How's Ace treating you?"

"Yes," I lied. "And like a queen."

"Good. That's good. We all miss you," she went on, refusing to make eye contact with me. "I know the others—"

We had just rounded the corner, the library standing tall before us, when I ran smack into someone heading the opposite direction. I cursed, but remembered my manners and offered them a hand, though luckily, they hadn't fallen on the sidewalk.

"So sorry," she said, flipping her hair out of her face and we locked eyes. My heart fell into my stomach. "Amy?" Mom whispered.

"Mom?"

"Oh my," she stammered, "Hi! It's so nice to see you."

"I'm sorry for nearly trampling you," I replied.

I didn't know what else to say; I was in complete and utter shock. The last time I had seen my mother was when I was running out the door in the middle of the night a few months back. She had tried to call me since then and left countless voicemail messages on my phone begging me to come home, and that we could fix whatever was broken between us, and I shamefully deleted them all.

"I didn't know you two were hanging out again," Mom beamed, her eyes flickering between me and Olivia. I knew she was trying to cling onto whatever morsel of my childhood was left, and it broke my heart to disappoint her.

"Oh," I began, "We're not. I'm just helping her with a school project, that's all."

"Speaking of," Liv interrupted. "I think you two have got more to catch up on than we do." She rested a hand on my shoulder and gave me her famous look I knew all too well; the "don't mess this up" eyebrow raise that frightened me when we were kids. "It was nice to see you, Mrs. Wood."

"You too, Olivia. Tell your parents I said hello."

We stood awkwardly on the sidewalk for a few beats, waiting for the other to say something else. I thought for sure she would initiate, but when I looked up from my boots and saw tears welling up in her eyes, I knew that while she might've had a million things to say, she couldn't find the words.

"There's a coffee shop just back that way." I pointed my thumb over my shoulder and gave her an encouraging smile. "Want to grab a cup of coffee with me?"

Her face lit up, and it made everything hurt on the inside, but I pushed all my sorrow beneath the surface, not too keen on tapping into that at the moment. We didn't share a word the entire way until we sat down at a little table outside the cafe, our steaming cups in hand.

"How's Dad?" I asked.

"He's good," Mom said. "Busy at the bank, but you know him. Brenda's good, too. She's getting ready for exam season so she's a bit all over the place right now."

I nodded, secretly wondering if this was such a good idea after all. We didn't do this sort of thing, catch up over coffee; I hated her, hated the life in that suffocating house where I wasn't able to be who I wanted to be.

Well, hate might be a strong word, but I certainly felt it at the time. Now it just left a bitter taste in my mouth, but the more time that passed, the less it hurt.

"I'm fine," I blurted out even though she didn't ask. "Ace and I are great. We live with his two other roommates, college friends. It sucks being the only girl," I laughed, and she did too, before falling silent once more. "How's Grandma?"

Mom's face changed, and I knew that it looked well... something happened. "She's in the hospital right now, but before you freak out," she held out a hand as I prepared to launch myself out of the chair, "she's fine, Amy, I promise. She just had a fall, and she's recovering but she's fine."

"A fall? When? Where? Why didn't you tell me as soon as it happened?"

"I wanted to," Mom continued. "I left you a message a few days ago but I never heard back from you. I figured it was just another one you deleted before even listening to it."

Guilt caked the back of my throat; she knew me all too well. Of course, that was what I had done. But if I had known it was something serious, I never would have.

"She's at North Valley Hospital," Mom explained. "I'm sure she'd love to see you. I'll even let you go alone so the two of you can talk without me or Brenda hovering around making you uncomfortable."

"Alright," my voice cracked, a sign that the wall I had built so long ago was on the verge of breaking. "I don't even know what I'd talk about."

"You can ask her about the mysterious love letter she received the day of the accident," Mom winked. "A suitor from her past, before she ever met your grandpa."

"What?" I gasped.

"I'll let her tell you herself." She reached over and placed a hand over mine, giving it a light squeeze. "It was really nice to see you again, Amy. I've missed you more than I could ever string it into words."

"I know," I breathed.

***

I was ashamed to admit how long I had lingered outside the hospital, contemplating whether or not I was going to go inside.

While I loved my grandmother very much, it had been so long since I'd seen her, and out of everyone, I cared about her opinion the most. I didn't want her to think any less of me from the decisions I made in my life, nor did I have any desire for her disappointed lectures. I could handle the discontent from my mother and sister, but not her, not the great Lucinda Davenport.

My grandmother was as fierce as an unforgiving forest fire. I remembered all the tales my grandfather told us as children, how she was unlike any woman he'd ever met, from her outlook on life, her attitude, and the way she carried herself in formal society. Back then, it was unusual for a woman to present herself in such a forward manner, but my grandmother didn't hold anything back. I wanted so badly to be like her when I grew up, but it seemed that fate had different plans.

I cleared my throat and the nurse behind the desk glanced up from the computer screen, letting out a low grumble as she looked me up and down. "Can I help you?"

"I'm here to visit a patient," I explained, holding my chin up so she knew I didn't care what she thought of me. "Lucinda Davenport."

She typed furiously, no doubt looking through the long registry to find the name I had offered. "Floor 3, Room 305," she said. "Follow the purple lines on the floor and you'll find it. Is that everything?"

"That's it, thanks."

Avoiding eye contact with anyone who walked past, I made my way deeper into the hospital until I reached her room. Just as Mother promised, she had not come, which I was grateful for. My grandmother's voice carried out into the hallway as she sang to herself, and when I poked my head around the corner, I was not at all surprised to find her working away on a new knitting project.

I knocked twice on the open door and let myself in. Her eyes flickered in my direction and a bright smile spread across her face. "Amy, darling!" she cried, tossing her knitting needles aside and holding her arms out, waving me into a hug. "My darling girl, I swear you've grown since I've seen you last!"

She always said that, even when I stopped growing a few years ago. I never corrected her, as the familiarity of her words brought me a sense of comfort nothing else could. "I heard you had a bit of a tumble," I remarked. "What did I tell you about wearing your shoes on the wrong feet?"

We both chuckled at my lame joke. Plopping myself down on the end of her bed, I kicked my boots off and crossed my legs, making myself more comfortable.

"I take it that this unexpected visit means you've seen or spoken to your mother," she pointed out, giving me a sympathetic look.

While I had not ever gone into great detail about the fallout between me and my parents, my grandmother was no fool, and I had a feeling she managed to piece it all together herself.

"We bumped into each other earlier," I confessed. "She had some other interesting news to share that afternoon."

Her eyes landed on an envelope on the end table. I squinted, trying to make out the cursive handwriting, but the ink was faded, making it rather difficult. She let out a deep exhale before folding her hands in her lap.

"Your mother's always been a helpless romantic. It's those movies she watched growing up, made her yearn for a tragic love tale that ends with a happily ever after."

"Not you though," I answered. "You're more of a realist, like me." I believed that love was not something that happened because of fate's design; it was just merely chemical responses in the brain when you met someone you were attracted to. No man had ever convinced me otherwise.

"I wasn't always," she sighed. "When your heart shatters into a million pieces and you're left to try and glue them back together," she paused, twitching her mouth, "you do whatever you can to protect it from happening again. But I was one of the lucky ones when I met your grandfather. He would never cause me any harm."

"So, who was this other fellow?" I leaned back on my elbows, cracking my knuckles. "He broke your heart, did he? Want me to break his face?" I smirked.

"You're a cheeky little thing, aren't you?" she mused. "But I'm afraid it's far too late for that. Besides, God may have already taken him from this world. I fear your mother intends to find out."

"She wants to find him," I replied. Knowing my mother, she would chase after anything that resembled a love story, and she didn't always have your best intentions in mind.

"She thinks it couldn't hurt to know what happened."

"But you do. You think that you could have your heart broken all over again. I gotta admit, Grandma, I didn't take you for a chicken."

I tucked my hands under my armpits and squawked like a chicken, earning myself a smack in the face with a soft pillow. I laughed so hard my stomach ached.

"Didn't anyone tell you to respect your elders," she teased. "Besides, I never said *no*, I just said that I wasn't sure about it."

"Tell me about him," I asked. "Tell me about your Romeo."

She paused for a moment, looking out the window, a tender smile on her lips. If I didn't know any better, I thought she might still love this man, somewhere deep down in her guarded heart.

"He was handsome," she began. "The real bee's knees. He had such a way with words, I always felt we could have a real and honest conversation, and whatever my opinion, he'd never judge me for it."

I let her go on and on for what seemed like hours, diving deeper into the charms and grace of a man named Dwayne Anderson.

Chapter 5

The week after the officer's dance I had a bit of a pep in my step. Even Edith, who, bless her heart, was often lost with her head in the clouds, seemed to notice.

"You're different," she squinted.

It was just us girls at the breakfast table, my brother and father off to work in the early hours of the morning. I too had business to attend to this afternoon, but luckily it wasn't at the crack of dawn.

"No, I'm not," I replied.

"Yes, you are," she insisted. "Ever since you came back from that dance, you've got a perpetual smile plastered on your face. Doesn't she, Mama?"

Mother smiled behind her teacup, choosing not to get involved in our little spat over breakfast. I shoved a hardboiled egg in my mouth and nearly choked before excusing myself, practically sprinting to the front door. Edith trailed behind me, twirling the ends of her hair between her fingertips.

"So, who is he?" she continued. "I know a boy has something to do with this, it's the only reason the rebel child in you is in brighter spirits."

"Can't a girl just be happy without needing a reason?"

"A regular girl, maybe, but not you." Planting both hands on her hips, she stood in the doorway, acting as if she were made of stone, and it wouldn't take a simple nudge to get her to move over. "Come on," she whined. "I promise I won't tell anyone about your secret crush."

"Hush," I warned, eyeing the kitchen where no doubt our mother was tentatively eavesdropping. "Listen, it's not a big deal. He was just a nice gentleman, and we had a fun time together, that's it. Nothing else, nothing more to dissect. Just two young people who were hanging out with other young people, listening to music and dancing the night away."

"Dancing, huh," she snickered. "I never thought the day would come where you went out and found yourself a husband."

"You need to get a life of your own, Edith," I said. "And I'm late for work. Remember, if this gets back to Mother and Father, I assure you that you will regret it."

My sister pretended to fasten her lips as I walked out into the crisp morning air of our town, grateful that the walk to work wasn't that much of a trek. To be honest, I wouldn't mind if it were, as I took that precious time alone to be one with my thoughts. A sense of dread washed over me that I had given in to Edith's pleas, knowing she didn't have the best history of keeping secrets. Then again, what younger sister did. My only saving grace was how nonchalant I had been about the whole thing; if she truly knew how I felt when I returned home that fateful night, I would bet she and my mother would be taking my measurements to the finest seamstress in town.

Dwayne had managed to grab ahold of my heart and run away with it in the night. The only issue was that I was pretty certain he had absolutely no intention of doing anything with it. It was like I had said, we were just two people looking for a good time and that was that. Almost a week had passed since that night, and not once had I heard even the faintest of whispers about him being interested, so why would I bother wasting my time thinking about him? I vowed that I wasn't going to, that I was going to focus on my work and worry about the impending threat of marriage some other time.

The bell to the shop chimed above my head and I spotted Mrs. Nelson hunched over the long table, her glasses balanced on the bridge of her nose.

"Good morning, Mrs. Nelson," I greeted, hanging my coat and scarf on the rack by the front door.

She lifted her gaze momentarily, her eyebrows pinching together. "My, oh, my," she gasped. "I think this is the earliest you've ever come in, Miss Lucinda."

"I'm afraid Edith was in one of her moods," I confessed. "My only solace was escaping the house entirely. Besides, I have a few orders jotted down that I'd like to get a head start on. You know how Mrs. Gibbons can be when she doesn't get her dresses back within the same week."

Mrs. Nelson nodded along, scribbling something down in her notebook. We had a lot of regulars come into the shop: widows, wives, daughters, you name it. We even had a few men who required specific tailoring for suits, and ever since the soldiers in town were preparing to depart overseas at a moment's notice, we had more young men stroll through the door than ever before.

"I need to take a trip to the fabric store to stock up our supplies here, not to mention we're running low on buttons and fastens. I shouldn't be too long, no more than an hour. Think you can handle things here until I get back?" she asked.

I did my best to remain calm, as she had never trusted me with such a responsibility before, and I didn't want to mess it up. "Absolutely! I'll be working away at the table, but should someone come in, I know how to assist."

"Excellent," she acknowledged. "I am trusting you, Miss Lucinda, don't disappoint me."

"I wouldn't dream of it."

Wrapping her shawl over her shoulders, she grabbed her coin purse and tucked her notebook under her arm before slipping through the shop door. Counting to ten, I figured the coast was clear and twirled around the room, my heart feeling like it might very well explode. Once I composed myself, I got to work, starting with the easy task of sewing up a few hems for a customer who was much shorter than her older sister whom she inherited the dresses from.

I was so enraptured with my work I didn't even hear the bell, only the distinct sound of someone clearing their throat. Expecting to see one of the older ladies that usually came in around this time, I was instead caught off guard when I saw *him* standing there, looking as prim and proper as ever.

My heart skipped a beat; my mouth was suddenly dry of all saliva, making it difficult to swallow the lump in my throat.

"Mr. Anderson," I breathed, fumbling to straighten out my skirt, hoping I didn't look like a complete mess. "What are you doing here?"

"Gianna said I might find you here," he confessed, wringing his fingers together as if he were somehow nervous to be in my presence. "I'm sorry to bother you at your work, but I just had to see you."

I scoffed, regretting it the second it happened. "*Had* to see me? That's strange, because not once had you come to call on me this week. I don't believe I am that hard to find."

"It wasn't that I didn't want to see you," he stammered, which seemed wildly out of character for him. While I had only spoken to him for a few hours that night, I didn't once think of him as the shy type. "I just wasn't sure if you..."

This time I heard the bell, and of course, it had to be Mrs. Gibbons. I gave her a small wave, indicating that I would be with her in a moment.

I lowered my voice just enough so she wouldn't be able to hear me. "Look, I have actual work to do, so if you don't mind, I must get back to it." I brushed past him, but he placed a hand on my forearm, halting me in my tracks.

"A tie!" he declared, holding his finger up in the air as if he had just come up with a glorious idea. "I'm in need of a new tie."

"We sell those off the rack," I giggled. "They don't require any alterations, so just pick one and you can go."

"No, no, I'm afraid that just won't do." Taking a step toward me, I could've sworn I caught him taking in a deep breath of my perfume, making my insides twist. "I have a rather large head; I'm told it's because I'm so inquisitive, but that means my neck must compensate for the extra weight. A custom tie is the only thing that'll do."

I snorted, earning myself a stern look from Mrs. Gibbons, who had apparently never laughed once in her entire life. "Just give me a few minutes, and I'll get you your tie."

"Miss Lucinda," she smiled, pleased that she now had my full attention. "You wouldn't happen to have those dresses for my daughter ready, would you? She begged and begged for me to come and see; you know how young girls can be," she went on, rolling her eyes in disdain.

"You're in luck, I just finished," I confirmed. "I'll wrap them up for you so I don't take up too much of your time."

"That would be wonderful, dear. Where's Mrs. Nelson? Normally she's here buzzing around like a little bee."

"Oh, she just stepped out to run an errand, but she'll be back soon. I have the receipt book here though, so I'll be able to take your payment for the adjustments."

"A real working lady now, aren't you?" she chimed, glancing at Mr. Anderson for a few beats before wrapping herself tighter in her shawl. "And you are?"

"Dwayne Anderson, ma'am." He extended out his hand to shake but she turned her nose up at him.

I hurried up, not wanting the awkwardness to linger a moment longer than it needed to. Tying our signature bows around the box, I slid it across the counter, and she already had her coins at the ready.

"We appreciate your swiftness, as always, Miss Lucinda," she said. "Do tell Mrs. Nelson I say hello when she returns. Have yourself a lovely afternoon."

"Take care," I called after her, though she was already halfway through the door, her box under her arm.

Letting out a deep sigh, I rubbed at my temples, praying that I didn't totally mess things up. Mrs. Nelson was a bit of a gossip, so I had a funny feeling she would be talking all across town about how I was wasting my time talking to a young man when I was supposed to be tending to paying customers such as herself.

"I apologize if I caused you any grief," Dwayne murmured. "I'll see myself out."

"Why'd you come all the way down here?" I blurted out. We were already this far down the rabbit hole; I wasn't about to let things slide without at least getting a proper explanation for his absence. It was the least he could do after leaving me high and dry for the past week.

"I know what you must think of me," he began, his eyes staring into the depths of my soul. "That I'm some kind of flake. I promise you, despite my shortcomings, I would never treat a lady like that. If I'm being honest, I thought that you might not want to start anything, not after what you said about starting things up with a soldier."

I stood there for a few beats, unsure of what I was supposed to do or say. Of course it had been my fault that he had not called on me. He thought that I wanted nothing to do with him.

"For you, Mr. Anderson, I am willing to make an exception, should you so earn such an honor as to spend whatever time you have left in Montana with me."

That cheeky smile that had made my knees weak the night of the dance pulled at the corners of his mouth. "And how might I do that?"

"Make your intentions clear, and not just to me. I have no desire to start something up without it going somewhere, and the only way to do that is—"

"To meet your parents," he finished. "I would be more than happy to oblige, all you need to do is tell me when, and I'll be there."

"Tomorrow night," I declared. "You may come over for dinner and you can tell them yourself."

***

I curled up in the cushioned armchair in the front sitting room, my eyes peeled on the front porch, waiting impatiently for Dwayne's arrival. The clock ticking away irritated me to my very core, and I genuinely contemplated dismantling it. But that meant looking away from the window, and there was little chance of that happening.

"I've never seen you so wound up before," Leith chuckled, leaning against the doorframe, a half glass of whiskey in hand. During his time off he rather enjoyed a glass or two. He said it made him feel old and sophisticated.

"Please don't think any less of me."

"I would never. I just hope he's worth it, that's all."

"He is." I couldn't help but smile as his face popped into my head. "I don't think I've ever met someone like him before. It's rather scary now that I think about it," my voice trailed off for a moment. "The power he holds over me."

"Dare I say you are already in love?" he hinted.

"I don't know," I admitted. "You'll just have to wait and find out like everyone else."

"He's here!" Edith squealed from the top of the stairs. "I caught him walking up the street."

"Relax, darling," Mother hollered from the kitchen. "He's just a nice young man coming over to join us for dinner. I expect you all to be on your best behavior, and *calm*," she reiterated, cupping Edith's chin and forcing her to agree.

There was a knock at the door, and we let Leith answer, being the other man in the house. Despite my efforts to listen to their conversation, they kept their voices low, but my brother waved him in all the same. I was pleased to see both of them smiling when they came into the kitchen.

"Hello," Dwayne nodded, handing over a bouquet of flowers to my mother. *Nice touch*, I thought, smiling like a fool. "Thank you so much for inviting me, Mrs. Carney."

"Oh, it's our pleasure," she cooed. "It's not every day that Lucinda brings over guests. Well, except for those two, uh, eccentric friends of hers."

"He knows Gianna and Madeline," I chimed in. "He's familiar with their antics."

"I hear a new voice," Father interrupted, the door to the back porch swinging open, and he stepped into the kitchen. He too had a glass in his hand, and I hoped he hadn't guzzled back more than that on an empty stomach. "You must be Mr. Anderson."

"Dwayne," he confirmed, "I was just thanking your lovely wife for having me."

"She's a saint," Father beamed, kissing her on the side of the forehead. "As are my two girls. Lucinda, you already know," he gestured, "and the other is Edith. That strapping young man lurking in the corner is Leith, he's their older brother, so watch out for him."

"He's already been warned," Leith teased.

"It's so refreshing to be in a house with so many family members under one roof," Dwayne pointed out.

"You don't have any brothers or sisters?" I asked. While we had talked about many things that night at the dance, we cautiously avoided the topic of family, which I greatly appreciated. I wanted to escape them that night, just for a little while.

"Just one brother, but he's not around all that much. He's a soldier, too."

"Oh," I blinked. That was another topic of conversation I hoped to avoid. It broke my heart to think of him leaving me behind for God knows how long, with no guarantee that I'll ever feel the touch of his hand or look upon his smiling face again.

Tension built around us, and I didn't know whether or not I should acknowledge or ignore it. Before I could, I was saved by my dad, who pulled out his chair at the table and sat down.

"Well, let's eat before this delicious meal goes cold!" Father clapped his hands together, and Mother jumped up to serve everyone.

I let out a slow exhale between my lips, hoping that meant Dwayne had his blessing to start something, even if it meant he would be leaving shortly after. I knew he would be honored to have a soldier for a son-in-law if it ever came to that, but he would need to win such gracious affections before I ever offered my hand.

I felt his eyes on me, and when I looked up for a brief second, he was gazing at me as if I were the moon in the night sky. The same feeling from when we first met returned; the lightness in my chest that snatched my breath right out of my throat. I knew from the bottom of my heart that it wouldn't take much for him to sweep me off my feet.

Chapter 6

March 2005

My grandmother had talked my ear off for hours that night, and although my mother and I rarely saw eye to eye on anything, I had a feeling that she was right; there seemed to be something special about their love story. I knew from the very second she started to rave about him that it was real. Her eyes lit up like the Fourth of July, and although I sensed she was neglecting to tell me everything, there was no hiding the cheeky smile, no matter how many times she brought her hands to her lips. A relationship without that kind of love surely would've faded over time. The way she had acted was as if she were a young lady again experiencing the highs of tender infatuation.

While many people saw me as cynical or cold-hearted, I couldn't deny the warmth I felt stirring inside me when she talked for the better part of the evening. If that had been me all those years ago, I doubted I would've let the man slip through my fingers—not one who was supposedly able to change my entire perspective on settling down. To be fair, war was a fickle thing back then; I hoped that it tore him to pieces to leave my grandmother behind.

She even let me read the letter that had been lost. I had been careful not to be too rough with it as the paper was fragile and the ink faded. His declaration of his love was perfectly conveyed with such a genuine string of words, where he went to great lengths to tell my grandmother how much their short time together meant, and that if she would do him the greatest honor of waiting for him to return to Montana soil, that he would spend the rest of his life showing his appreciation, starting with getting down on one knee.

His absence afterward made absolutely no sense to me, not that I had much expertise in the romance department myself. Sure, me and Tommy were together and things were more or less functional between us, but I wouldn't go as far as to say he was my soulmate or one true love, not after reading the love letter from Dwayne. They had only been together for a few short weeks and had already felt a lifetime's worth of passion and adoration; we'd been going out for almost a year now and not once had he ever said anything like that to me. A part of me hoped that he just wasn't a man of sophisticated words, and that didn't mean he didn't feel it on the inside, but I was not my mother. I was no hopeless romantic.

The familiar jingle of his keys yanked me out of my reverie, and I quickly scrambled to turn on the television so he wouldn't think anything was off. He most definitely would've questioned what on earth I was doing curled up on the sofa in complete darkness. Laughter echoed in the apartment hallway, and I grumbled to myself, figuring that he and his friends were just coming back from yet another eventful night at the bar.

"Are you sure it's alright if I stay over?" a female's voice asked. If I didn't know any better, I thought she sounded hesitant about whatever plans they had arranged. "I don't live far from here; I don't mind walking home."

"Don't be silly," Jason, Tommy's roommate, coaxed. "There's more than enough space for you. Besides, Amy makes a mean egg breakfast."

"Who's Amy?"

The three of them stumbled into the living room, flicking on the light to find me buried beneath a ratty old blanket. "I am," I waved.

"Amy," Tommy slurred. "I thought you'd be passed out by now. Sorry if we woke you up, I didn't think we were being that—"

"You didn't," I interrupted. "I was just watching some TV and lost track of time. Did y'all have fun?"

"A blast," Jason winked. "This is Martha. We met her at the bar. Do you have any pajamas she could borrow for the night? She didn't bring anything with her."

I eyed her up and down, wondering if it was my place to say that she didn't look all that thrilled to be there. My guess was that at the time when she agreed she had been all liquored up, but the walk back had sobered her and now she was second-guessing such a rash decision.

"Sure," I smiled, standing up and tossing the blanket on the back side of the sofa. "I'll leave it for you in the bathroom, just give me a minute."

"Thanks," she nodded.

Tommy followed me down the hall to our bedroom, plopping down on the bed without even bothering to take off his clothes. It was a pet peeve of mine, but I held my tongue, exhausted from the day's events to get into a fight now. All I really wanted was to fall into a dreamless sleep for a few precious hours before getting up for my morning shift at work.

"Are you pissed at me?" he blurted, having the decency to at least kick off his boots so they didn't get mud on our sheets. "You seem... snappy."

"I'm not mad, just had a long day, that's all."

"Anything I can do to help?"

I knew that tone of voice; he was asking more of me than I was of him, but I was in absolutely no mood to get tangled in the blankets; not tonight.

"I'm on my period," I fibbed.

He scrunched up his nose in disgust, rolling to his side of the bed and letting out a huff. I couldn't help but giggle at his childish attitude and left him there to sulk while I went to the bathroom to drop off the pajamas for Martha. I was surprised to find her lingering in the hallway, her arms wrapped around herself as if it were a shield. She dropped her arms by her sides when she spotted me, but it was too late for that.

"Here," I offered, handing over the shorts and T-shirt. It was all I had that was clean enough for a stranger. "You can just leave them in the hamper before you leave tomorrow."

"Thanks," she mumbled, but didn't so much as budge. I wondered if she had any intention of unplanting herself from that position at all.

"Is everything alright?" I asked, lowering my voice just in case Jason was eavesdropping from his bedroom. "You don't look…"

"I just prefer to sleep in my own bed, that's all," she began. "Can I ask you something?"

"Sure."

"Is he a good guy?" Martha whispered. "I mean like, is it safe to be here? You'd tell me if I was in any kind of danger, wouldn't you?"

"You won't end up a missing person on the news tomorrow if that's what you're worried about," I chuckled. "They're college guys. What do you expect? I'm afraid they're only after one thing."

"Then why are you here? You look like you're just a kid. I bet you're not even old enough to get into a bar."

She had a point. "I have nowhere else to go; nowhere I want to be anyway. I make it work."

"Maybe I should go."

"Be quick about it," I said. "Don't tell him you talked to me about it or I'll never hear the end of it."

Before she could say anything else, I turned on my heels and slipped back into our bedroom only to find Tommy fast asleep. Sprawled out on his back, he snored profusely, leaving me little space on my side of the bed. I yanked and tugged with all my strength to get the blankets out from underneath his body, but he didn't move even an inch. I was tempted to hit him in the face with the pillow but refrained.

Trying to make myself as small as possible, I hung off the edge of the mattress, praying that I wouldn't fall off the bed in the middle of the night. It didn't take long for me to float away into dreamland, where I was a young girl in the 1940s, and a charming young man was determined to sweep me off my feet by any means necessary. It was a wonderful notion indeed.

***

After an awful night's sleep, I was far less pleasant to customers than I usually was on my shift, earning me a few sneers from my boss, who always seemed to pop out of nowhere at the most inconvenient times. Luckily for me, it was just a short four-hour shift, which flew by with the morning rush.

I was home before I knew it.

I contemplated taking a nap, even though I knew it would make me groggy for the rest of the day, but decided against it. With the boys gone either at a class or who knows where else, I had the apartment all to myself, which was a rare blessing. Powering up the computer, I tended to the dirty dishes in the sink while it roared to life.

We shared it as best we could, although Jason and Tommy always took precedence over me since they claimed to need it for school. Not once since I lived here did I actually see either of them work on anything for college, but what did I know. Any time I walked by, I caught them frantically switching browsers to hide the fact they were deep into a video game. Like everything else that happened in the apartment, that was just another thing I didn't bother to complain about. I feared if I had, it might give them a reason to kick me out, and I couldn't let that happen, no matter how many times my family had asked me to come back home.

Whipping together a quick lunch, I nestled myself in the computer chair, sifting through my emails first. I only looked at them every once in a blue moon, as they did more harm than good. I had pages and pages of emails from old high school friends asking me how I was doing even though most of them turned their backs on me when I dropped out. There were a couple from Mom and Dad sprinkled throughout the horde, again, just looking to check in on me. I felt a pang of guilt reading one of them from my dad, who had asked me to join them for a family dinner last week. I must've missed that one, and although there was a slim chance I would've gone, I still felt bad.

Logging onto MSN Messenger, a chat popped up in the corner before I had the chance to set my profile as away. Olivia's picture stared back at me as I hovered the mouse over the chat.

Don't open it, a little voice in my head chimed. *Just log off and pretend you didn't see it. She won't be offended.*

Against my better judgment, I clicked.

Olivia: Hey! How did it go with your mom yesterday?

I almost forgot she had been with me when we ran into each other on the street. At least it had been her and not someone else.

Amy: Pretty good. She wanted to tell me that my grandmother was in the hospital.

Olivia: OMG. Is she alright?

Amy: Yeah! She's totally fine. Just had a fall. You'll never guess what else happened.

Olivia: What?

Amy: She had a lover before my grandfather. We just found one of the last love letters he wrote to her.

Olivia: OMG. How scandalous! You should track him down so she can write back. How cute would that be?

It wasn't the worst idea in the world. Mom had just wanted to track him down just to see where his life ended up, and maybe reunite them somewhere down the road, but a letter in return sounded just as romantic, if not more. That was, after all, their main form of communication, or so it seemed. She never exactly told me how long they had corresponded for when he went off to war.

Amy: Very cute. Maybe I will. I am a master of the internet. Who better than me to help bring them together after all this time?

Olivia: You always did have a soft spot for Lucinda. Let me know how it all goes. Class is over, G2G. Chat soon. Love you.

The little icon beside her name turned red, indicating that she had logged off. I stared at it for a few seconds, a wave of envy washing over me, threatening to pull me into its unforgiving waters.

I was just about to turn the computer off completely but stopped myself at the last second. I did have some extra time before the guys were going to be coming back, and the thought of finding Dwayne was sounding more fascinating by the second.

Typing "Dwayne Anderson" into the search engine, I held my hands together in anticipation, waiting for the results to come pouring in. Several news articles popped up, and I filtered through them, one by one, feeling somewhat like a detective as I connected the dots. There were several Dwayne Andersons, but a few newspaper clippings that had been posted online captured my attention the most. It was not the connections to the war, and by the looks of it, he had been declared a war hero, but the young fellow that seemed to be in all his pictures. Reading the bottom script beneath a message from a community center in a place called Twin Falls, Idaho, it read "from left to right, Kemp Stewart, Dwayne Anderson, and Michael Roberts." That wasn't the only picture of the two of them together, and I wondered if they were somehow related. I wasn't the best when it came to geography, but I knew that it wasn't that far from Montana. There was a chance that he was the one I was looking for. This young mystery man Kemp might be the ticket to getting to meet Dwayne.

My heart fluttered in my chest, excitement making my leg bounce up and down. I was getting ahead of myself. I couldn't just up and leave on some spontaneous road trip to Idaho looking for someone just because they have the same name as the man as the one from my grandmother's past. There was a very good chance that he was just some man with the same name, and it would all be for nothing.

I thought about it for a second, and a part of me wondered if maybe I would have a better chance if I roped in my mother, but that thought vanished as quickly as it came. She would tell me to mind my own business, even though she was likely doing the same thing I was, scouring the internet for any sort of clue or information that might lead her down a promising road.

The only way to truly know this man was who we wanted was going there and asking him myself. Mom had obligations as a wife, mother, and a schoolteacher, it wasn't like she could just pack up her life and travel to another state at the drop of a hat. But I could. I was a high school dropout with nothing to lose, and I also had access to a vehicle, it would just take a bit of... convincing, and I knew how to play my cards right.

"Amy?" Tommy's voice echoed throughout the apartment.

I must've lost track of time reading articles that hours had passed, and dinner time was encroaching. I cursed myself for getting sidetracked.

"In here!" I shouted, frantically closing all the articles I had open, but not before clearing the browser history. It was a force of habit from when I lived at my parents' house, not wanting them to snoop on my personal life.

He stood at the threshold of the room, and I studied him closely, hoping to gauge his reaction. His expression was soft, his shoulders were relaxed and not tense around his ears. I hoped that meant he had a good day and didn't come home to take it out on me.

"Sorry, I was wrapped up in emails after work," I explained. "Why don't I order us a pizza? My treat."

Tommy's face lit up at the notion of greasy food. He nodded eagerly, practically drooling. "Make sure you order enough for Jason too."

After a quick phone call to the local pizza place down the street from us, I joined him on the sofa, cuddling up to him real close. He was a simple man who loved affection and attention of any kind. He wrapped his arm around my shoulder and pulled me in close, planting a fat kiss on my cheek.

"How was work?" he asked. It was an empty question that he asked every single day when he came home that had little meaning over the last few months. Still, I answered the same as I always did.

"Good. How was class?"

"Meh," he shrugged. It was either that or awful, so meh was good in retrospect. "You hear from your mom at all?" He nudged his chin toward the computer, inferring to an email I might've read.

"I always do," I replied.

We didn't talk about my home life that much, mostly because I didn't want to. He respected my privacy enough not to pry, which I appreciated. It was one of the reasons our relationship worked as well as it did; he was perfectly content with leaving the past in the past if it meant he didn't get berated for not asking more about my life. Apparently, he had many girlfriends who nagged and whined over his lack of communication. It was one of his finer qualities in my opinion.

"Actually, I had an idea, something I kind of hope will piss her off."

It was a little white lie, but I knew he'd be on board with anything that might cause my parents trouble. To be fair, I wasn't sure if she would be upset with me going on an excursion to hunt down the man behind the love letter, but I didn't really care. I was doing it with or without her permission.

"Oh?" he queried. "Go on."

"It's just a little road trip," I confessed, searching for the right words to make it sound like something he'd want to do. "You're just about to be on your reading break, no? It's the perfect time. We can drive down there, spend some alone time together," I paused, pressing my chest up against him to seal the deal. "It could be fun."

"And our destination?" Tommy asked.

"Idaho."

Chapter 7

I found it terribly difficult to try and concentrate on teaching my students, as my mind was elsewhere. Luckily, they were at that age where rolling the TV up to the front of the class was like hitting the jackpot—in a matter of seconds, I had become their favorite teacher.

I planned to use those precious hours of the school day to come up with a plan to find out all that I could about the curious Dwayne Anderson.

The lunch bell rang, and I quickly gathered my things and headed for the staff room, eager to discuss what had happened to me over the weekend with some of my colleagues.

"Marina," Tabitha waved me over to her table, "you look rough. Are the girls keeping you up all hours of the night again?"

My heart ached a little; I had not divulged my home life with the other teachers, as a large part of me was embarrassed I had let things get so bad. If I could not control or take care of the children I brought into this world, what sort of qualifications did I have to teach and nurture 30 others?

"Oh, no, nothing like that," I shrugged, plopping myself down into the hard plastic chair and nibbling on some carrot sticks I had thrown into a bag earlier. "It's just my mom. She had a fall over the weekend but she's alright. Just caught me a little off guard, that's all."

"That's terrible!" Tabitha gasped, holding a hand to her chest. "Send her all our love. Lucinda's a terrific woman, she won't let this hold her down for long."

My mother had a bit of a reputation in town; she was beloved by all who knew her, and even those who didn't said the same things. I was just about to tell her about the lost love letter when Mr. Chapman walked in, a steaming cup of coffee in hand. It was almost as if a lightbulb went off in my head the second I laid eyes on him—he was a history fanatic, not just because he taught it for years in the old high school up the street, but it was just one of his many interests. He took pleasure in walking through the halls of museums and using his summer vacations to travel across the world to take in all the magnificent sites. While I didn't exactly have an interest in those sorts of things myself, I loved listening to the stories of his adventures to Peru, Athens, and Egypt.

"Hello," he acknowledged us with a nod before taking a seat at one of the empty tables.

"How was your weekend?" I asked, engaging in a little small talk before I went into any sort of favors.

"Same as it always is, nothing too special. You?"

"A little chaotic, but nothing I can't handle. Listen, I have a history question to ask, who would one talk to if they wanted to get some information on a soldier who fought in World War II?"

He snapped his book shut and turned his body to give me his full attention. "It would depend on his rank. Some soldiers wouldn't have any information written about them unless someone came across a journal and submitted it to a museum or library for the archives to keep. Now, if he was someone of great importance, such as a corporal or sergeant, he might pop up more in history books, especially if he directly contributed to any successes in the war," he rambled on, his leg bobbing up and down from excitement. "Why do you ask?"

"My mother, well, it's a bit of a weird story now that I try to put it into words," I began, feeling my cheeks turn hot. "Someone found an old letter that a special friend of hers had written decades ago while he was deployed overseas. They lost connection after he served in the war, and we're just a bit curious about where he ended up or what happened to him. I was kind of hoping I might be able to do some research myself, but I haven't been able to come up with anything promising just yet. Unfortunately, it seems like technology is against me on this one."

"Yeah, it can be a bit tricky when you don't know what you're looking for," he agreed. Taking a scrap piece of paper out of his briefcase, he scribbled a name down and handed it over. "I highly recommend talking with Albert Fitzgerald. He knows much more than I do and even specializes in war history. He holds lectures and events down at the library; in fact, I think he even has something scheduled there this week. You can tell him I sent you. He'll be able to help you find whatever's out there about this soldier."

I tucked the paper into my purse, patting it a few times for good measure. I was one step closer to discovering some real family history, and even though my mother was hesitant about the whole thing, I knew she would come around eventually. As long as we did things delicately, everything would work out. If things got too real or too complicated, I would pull the plug, or at least that was what I told myself.

"Thank you," I smiled. "You have no idea how much this means to me."

I just prayed that after all of this hunting and sleuthing was over, I would go back to getting a decent night's sleep.

***

After doing a little research of my own on upcoming events at our local library, I saw that Albert Fitzgerald was scheduled to speak. Luckily I only had to wait two days, since my anxiety and anticipation to learn more surely would've all but consumed me had it been any longer.

"It's a school night," Justin said, lifting his gaze up from the book he was reading long enough to give me a perplexed look. "I thought I only had to point that out to the girls."

A smile tugged at the corners of his mouth, making me blush. While we had been married for years, he never ceased to give me butterflies, no matter how many days breezed past. I couldn't help but wonder if Dwayne had been, or could've been, that for my mother. What if she had merely settled for my father? What if he was her one true love all along?

"I promise to return home well before curfew," I teased.

"Where are you off to?"

"The library. Don't make a big deal out of it, but I'm meeting a historian who might be able to guide me in the right direction regarding our Mr. Dwayne Anderson."

"Marina," Justin sighed, dropping the book in his lap, "I really don't think it's a good idea for you to be getting so caught up in all this."

"It's harmless curiosity, that's all," I countered. "It's very likely that tonight will just lead to dead ends or nothing at all. I just have to see it through to the end. You understand that, don't you?"

I was much more of a romantic at heart than my husband was; in fact, he and Amy were almost one and the same. To be fair, he did have a soft spot for the woman in his life, and he showed his love in many ways, though they weren't always outright and apparent.

He walked me to the front porch and planted a soft kiss on my temple. "I will be here waiting for whatever outcome arises. I love you."

The warm and fuzzy feeling returned in the pit of my stomach. "I love you, too. I'll see you tonight."

"Go on now." He patted my behind, nudging me toward the van. "Let your imagination run wild."

I arrived at the library well before Albert's lecture was scheduled to end, giving me plenty of time to wander around and collect some findings of my own.

I sat down at one of the plush sofas in the history section, silently watching as people would come and go. Most of them were students, Amy and Brenda's age, scrambling to do research on their papers for school, or so I assumed. Brenda had been up to her eyeballs in studying for exams, and my heart ached that Amy was not. I tried so hard to give her the life she deserved, the life I wanted when I was her age, but she had other plans for herself. Had she not dropped out and left everything behind, she would be preparing for college applications right about now, just as her friends were. It was nice to see her hanging around Olivia the other day, though I had a feeling it was more of a spontaneous affair than anything real or concrete. She was captivated by the allure of adulthood from that boyfriend of hers—Ace or something like that—though I would hardly say that was a real reflection of what life had to offer. All I could do was let her make her own mistakes and decisions, and should she find her way back to us, I vowed to be there to help glue back the pieces.

But that was a matter of if, not when.

"Is there anything I can help you with?" An older woman's voice asked from behind. I turned in the sofa chair and spotted the librarian hovering over me like a bat. "Oh, Mrs. Wood, I didn't realize it was you."

Families who had been living in Whitefish for generations were easy to recognize, but I figured she knew me through the school.

"Janet," I greeted, scrambling to shake her hand, fearing her judgment if I were not polite to her standards. "Nice to see you."

"Are you here to pick up something for your class?" she questioned, pushing her glasses further up her nose.

While the school was more than adequate for doing all my printing, photocopying, and laminating, I did make use of the library's resources too, as it was often less crowded here. Besides, the faculty members received a discount, and I was a proud representative of the library. I had organized numerous fundraisers over the years to support their reading programs throughout the summer months.

"Oh, no it's nothing like that." I waved my hand, assuring her that she didn't forget I was coming to alleviate her rising guilt. "It's more of a personal errand."

"Oh," she blinked. "I see. I suppose I'll leave you to it."

"I could use a bit of help," I urged, holding a hand up to stop her before she walked away. "Do you have anything on World War II veterans? Specifically, those who might've been from Whitefish or the surrounding area."

"Local war heroes," she acknowledged, turning on her heels to scan the dozens of shelves behind us. "Yes, we might have something like that. Follow me."

I trailed behind as she muttered under her breath, scanning shelves one by one. It wasn't until we zigzagged through the first three rows of bookshelves that she settled on the one she had been looking for. It was titled *True Tales: Stories of Soldiers from World War II*.

"This may have something in it that could be worth your while," Janet explained. "Do you want me to try and hunt down anything else for you? It's a bit of a slow night, I don't mind."

"No, that's alright. I'm really just trying to buy time until I can speak with Mr. Fitzgerald."

"Albert?" Janet's eyes lit up. "He's a wonderful gentleman, very intelligent. He most certainly would be a valuable asset to answer any of your burning questions. I'll be sure to send him up here once he's done his lecture downstairs."

"Thank you," I beamed. "That would be great."

She fluttered away toward the front desk while I helped myself to one of the bigger tables in the seating area. I skimmed the table of contents, hoping I wouldn't have to read the book from cover to cover just to find a sentence or two about Dwayne. Sadly, nothing of great importance popped out, so I was left to start from page one, though my mind must have been elsewhere, as I had not retained a single word, no matter how many times I reread the same sentence, over and over.

It wasn't until someone cleared their throat that I nearly jumped out of my own skin, and I quickly realized how much time had gone by. I looked up to see an older gentleman standing with his hands clasped in front of him, giving me a friendly smile. He had a name tag pinned to his blazer; it read Albert Fitzgerald.

"Greetings," he said. "Janet mentioned that you were hoping to have a little chat."

"Yes!" I exclaimed, waving to the chair across from me. "Please, have a seat. I don't want to take up too much of your time, so I promise I'll make this quick."

"Nonsense." He brushed off my courtesy like water on a duck's back. "I don't mind talking about history with a fellow educator. She mentioned you were a teacher."

"Yes, yes, I am, but I'm not here for any school research. It's more of an inquiry than anything else, a thread I was hoping to pull to learn some family history."

"Did a relative of yours serve in the army?" he asked.

"He's not my relative, no," I replied. "Just someone my mother knew during her adolescence."

"It sounds like you at least have a name."

"I do. Dwayne Anderson."

His face shifted, almost as if he recognized the name himself. At first, I thought it was impossible, as there were likely hundreds of thousands of names he came across during his career. But the look in his eyes said something completely different.

"Do you mind if I see that?" He gestured toward the book Janet had found me earlier, and I slid it across the table without hesitation. He fluttered through the pages, taking a pad of sticky notes from the inside of his jacket and flagging a few chapters before closing it shut.

"Dwayne Anderson was called to action in June 1942. He was just a young man when his platoon set off across the sea, and he was accompanied by his older brother, Ethan Anderson, and father, Henry Anderson," he recited off the top of his head.

I leaned as far forward as I could, drinking up every last word that came out of his mouth. "And he was from around here?"

"Indeed. He came from a working-class family. Before the war, Henry worked as a repairman. It was said that he did odd jobs to help take care of his wife and children, and their mother worked as a seamstress to also bring in some extra income. Anything was better than nothing. Unfortunately, that's about as much information as I have about his parents. His father didn't make it back. He died during his service, only a few short months after his deployment."

My heart sank. I knew the pain of losing a father, but mine had passed away from an illness, something we had prepared for, and we were able to say all of our goodbyes before we laid him to rest. I couldn't imagine what Dwayne must've felt learning of his father's passing while fighting a war for freedom and justice.

"That's awful. What about his older brother?"

"We believe he made it home, too. There's not much on him either. Historians suspect he didn't move back to Whitefish after they returned, just like Dwayne hadn't."

"He didn't?" I questioned, my eyebrows pinching together. "How do you know so much about him then?"

"Dwayne Anderson is well-known among the history buffs," Albert explained. "He is a decorated war hero. He served his country with honor, and he moved through the ranks quickly because of it. There are many journals written about him, from other soldiers who witnessed his success and his dedication to the military. But he did it selflessly, or so they recounted, not because he was adamant about receiving any fancy metals or titles. That was just the kind of man he was."

"What did he do that was so great?"

Albert paused for a second, twirling his thumbs around each other, trying to find the right words to tell his tale with the honor and integrity it deserved.

"The archives painted the picture with far more finesse than I will, but I'll do my best," he started. "It had been a cold winter's night. Frost covered the uneven ground, and more men were dying from the elements than enemy fire. But Dwayne always did everything he could to keep them in high spirits. It was his belief that a healthy mindset was going to help them win the war, not bullets or guns. His position in the military meant he didn't have to lay in the muck with his fellow brothers, but he did anyway. He was always in the thick of it. At this point, the allies were beginning to gain momentum, and there was a shift in the atmosphere, giving the men courage and stamina to see it through to the end. But this night there was something different—it wasn't quiet, and they weren't waiting out a storm. Their compound was raided from above, and had Dwayne not stepped up when he did, his men surely would've all perished."

"He put himself in the line of fire?" I breathed, holding a hand to my chest as I immersed myself in the monumental historic moment.

"Without a flicker of hesitation," Albert confirmed. "They thought for sure he had perished. When the dust settled, his men ran out of the trenches to collect his body, with the hope that they could give him a proper burial, and when they found him, he was clinging to life. They managed to get him to one of the pop-up hospitals, where he recovered for months until he received an honorable discharge for his efforts that day."

"Wow," I blinked, at a loss for words myself. "I had no idea. I couldn't imagine going through what he went through. To be standing on the threshold of life and death itself..." my voice trailed off in utter disbelief.

"You'd be surprised what a man is capable of when given the opportunity for greatness," he mumbled. "Some crumble before it, others rise to the occasion. Mr. Anderson was one of those people."

"Thank you," I blurted. "Thank you for taking the time to tell his story."

"It was my pleasure," Albert concluded. "Your mother should feel a certain sense of pride in knowing him. I know I would."

He was absolutely right. She should feel proud that she was part of his history, and if luck was on my side, this knowledge would tip the scales in my favor. "Thanks again, Mr. Fitzgerald. I will certainly pass along the message to her next time I get a chance."

I stood up and tucked the book under my arm, promising myself I would read the sections he flagged when I got the chance. He shook my hand and went on his way. I grabbed my phone from my purse and dialed the hospital's number as I ventured out to the parking lot.

"Hello, North Valley Hospital, visitors desk, how may I direct your call?" a polite voice chimed on the other end.

"I was hoping you could connect me to Lucinda Carney's room," I requested, nibbling on the skin around my fingernails. "That's if she's still awake."

"Please hold."

The line beeped several times until someone else clicked on. "Hello?" I recognized my mother's voice. I was happy she didn't sound groggy, which meant I hadn't woken her up. "Marina, is that you?"

"You'll never guess what I just learned," I squealed.

Chapter 8

June 1942

While it had only been a few short weeks since the dinner at my parent's house where we got my father's approval on our courtship, it felt as if we had spent a lifetime together. Not because time seemed to drag on, but rather, because I felt as though we knew each other in and out.

I had become a master at reading Dwayne's facial expressions, knowing that when he had that little crease between his eyebrows, he was deep in thought and wished to be left alone, or when he adjusted the collar of his shirt it meant he was uncomfortable or didn't know what to say or do. It didn't happen often, as he was quite skilled at the art of conversation, but the odd time it did, I would reach over and lace my fingers with his, giving his hand a gentle squeeze. And just as I had become undoubtedly familiar with all his quirks, he had become acquainted with mine. He teased things out of me I didn't even know were there, pieces of myself I had either buried as a coping mechanism or simply had yet to discover.

A love like ours was fueled by the fire in our hearts, but a fire needs to be well tended and taken care of. If we weren't careful or took our eyes off it for only a few seconds, it would either consume us or devastate us. Dwayne assured me that it would never happen, but he had yet to strip me of all my realistic outlooks on life. Even with that thought looming in the back of my mind, I ignored it as best as I could and focused on living in the moment, knowing that our days and weeks of innocent bliss would come to an end.

"Have you decided what you wish to do tonight, my love?" Dwayne brushed a few soft kisses against my clavicle before wrapping his arms around my waist and holding me against him.

I closed my eyes at the touch of his lips, a smile growing from ear to ear. Most of the time he left our date nights up to me, not because he didn't care to plan anything himself, but because it was difficult for him to keep up with my moods on any given day. One minute I would be up for a night out on the town, with all the bright lights, the loud music, and the dancing, while others I would much rather have a quiet night indoors where I could hear myself think.

Tonight was one of those nights. I had something special in mind, but with a summer storm rolling in, I hoped the rain wouldn't spoil it.

"You'll find out soon enough," I purred. "Would you excuse me for a moment?"

"Of course."

I left him alone in the front sitting room and made my way upstairs, feeling my heart race in my chest. I just hoped that I didn't look as anxious on the outside as I felt on the inside. My nerves settled when I spotted Mother sitting in front of her white vanity, tentatively dabbing on some blush with the tips of her fingers before she blended it out for a more natural look. I watched her for a few seconds in silence, not wanting to disturb her. She glanced at me through the reflection and smiled.

"Should I be worried about you lurking around?" she asked before selecting one of her red lipsticks and applying a thin coat.

She was not much for fancy makeup as a housewife, but since this was a special occasion, she had made the exception. It was their wedding anniversary, and I had put aside some money I had made working at the dress shop so they could do something together. It had been so long since they got out of the house, just the two of them. They were frugal, for good reason, as jobs were few and far between, and it didn't take much for the bills to start racking up. It was one of the reasons why Leith and I were happy to pitch in as much as we could; I couldn't bear the thought of my parents swimming in debt.

"Not at all," I chimed. "I just wanted to see if you needed any help getting ready. What time are you two leaving for your date?"

Mother glanced at the delicate watch on her wrist and pursed her lips. "In the next ten minutes or so. Your father said he made reservations at that new French restaurant downtown. Oh, what's it called again?" She paused, her nose twitching as she thought too hard about it.

"*Le Clair de Lune*," I said. "It's beautiful. The entire ceiling is skylight windows, and tonight is a perfect night. The moon is bright, and it'll be romantic for sure."

"How do you know what it looks like?"

"Dwayne took me there for one of our first dates," I blushed. "He had to bribe the Maître d' to let us in. It's very sophisticated; they don't just let kids in from off the streets. They don't want to ruin the ambiance for the rest of their guests."

"You've really gone and spoiled us, haven't you," she mused. Getting up from her vanity, she disappeared into the closet, trying to find the right coat to go with her outfit, though she had limited options. "I hope there's no ulterior motive behind this little ruse to get us out of the house."

I might've been able to pull the wool over my father's eyes, but I knew that it would be a lot harder to trick my mother. In my defense, she was the woman who raised me, so if anyone was going to discover my plan, I was not surprised it was her. Still, that didn't mean I had to come clean about it.

"Not at all," I gasped. "Can't a young woman do something nice for her parents?"

She poked her head out of the closet and raised an eyebrow at me. "And what will you and Mr. Anderson be doing this evening? Perhaps meeting up with some friends, I hope."

"Maybe," I lied. "I think we're just going to see where the night leads us. I think Gianna and Madeline are out on their own dates tonight."

"Falling in love with soldiers too, I see."

Mother emerged from her closet with a long black coat and a clutch tucked beneath her elbow. She placed two fingers under my chin and forced me to look her in the eye, though she didn't look like she was about to give me one of her many lectures. "I want you to be careful. The heart is a fragile thing, it doesn't take much to break it."

"I'm afraid you have to have one in order to break it," I chuckled, though she didn't find my comment at all humorous.

"I mean it, Lucinda. I've seen the way you look at that young man. You cannot hide how you feel from me. Promise me you'll be careful."

I wasn't exactly sure what I was agreeing to, but I nodded nonetheless, hoping that it would suffice enough to get her out the door.

It had been, since five minutes later they were shuffling out the front door, and the house suddenly fell into eerie silence. Leith was off at the billiards with some of his friends, and I had even managed to convince Edith to vacate somewhere else—anywhere, I didn't care—so long as I could be alone with Dwayne for a few hours. It didn't take all that much convincing on my end, just a promise she could borrow one of my dresses the next time she went out, which I was more than happy to oblige.

I lingered in the hallway for a few beats, gripping the candle holder with my finger to the point where my knuckles turned white. My throat was suddenly dry, making it both difficult to swallow and breathe, but I couldn't stand there forever. Sucking in a deep breath, I walked into the front room to find him standing by the window, his hands clasped behind his back. He looked almost regal, with his tailored jacket and fitted pants. It wasn't until he turned to the light and the military insignia was illuminated that my heart sank into my stomach.

If only you didn't have to go, I thought.

"There you are," he whispered, though he might as well have screamed it. The silence was deafening, though not nearly as much as the blood pumping through my veins. I could hear the steady rhythm of my heartbeat. "I thought you'd gone and abandoned me."

"Never," I smiled, meeting him in the middle of the room and brushing a hand across his cheek. "Come, I want to show you something."

I guided him up the stairs, though I sensed his uneasiness. This was a forbidden part of the house, at least unaccompanied by a chaperone. It was unladylike to have an eligible suitor in your bedroom all by yourself, but I was not much of a girl who followed all the rules. In my eyes, they were more like guidelines, or suggestions, if you will, and more times than not, I bent them to suit my needs.

Like it was for many girls, my bedroom was my oasis, my place of escape and solitude, the one place where I could truly be at peace with myself. He had not had the pleasure to step within its confines until that evening, and although I felt as though my skin might ignite, I let him into my world, giving myself to him the best way I knew how.

Biting my tongue, I let him observe at his own pace. He ran his fingers across my duvet, which I had meticulously tucked so not a corner was out of place. Books lined my shelves, and he stopped for a few seconds to read the spines, likely hoping it might give him a chance to see even further into my soul. He lingered at the mannequin with the half-sewn dress, the corners of his mouth turning up into a smile.

"What is it?" I asked, feeling a wave of embarrassment and anxiety wash over me. I was more than proud of my skills as a dressmaker, but for some reason, his scrutiny made me nervous.

"Nothing," he mused. "Just thinking of the first time I saw you after the dance, that's all. I wasn't a very good gentleman disturbing you at your place of business, but I'm sure glad I did." He paused, turning his head just enough to look at me over his shoulder. "Why did you bring me up here?"

I could tell by the look in his eyes that he knew why, he just wanted me to say it out loud.

"I love you," I breathed. "I want you to always be with me, and me you, no matter where you are in the world. Mind, soul, and... body."

He took careful steps toward me, gently tucking my hair behind my ear before gripping the back of my neck. "Have you thought this through?" he asked. "We have lots of time before we take that next step. I don't want you to have any regrets, and I don't want you to feel like I expect anything from you."

"I want to," I rushed. "And you and I both know that our time is limited. You could get called away a week from now, and we have no idea of knowing if or when we'll see each other again."

Tears pricked my eyes, and he cupped both my cheeks and planted a hard kiss on my mouth. I sank into him, grabbing him as tight as I could, desperate to never let go. I couldn't be sure how long we had stayed like that, lost in each other's tender kisses, but before I knew it, he guided me toward the freshly made bed and laid me down on my back. We broke apart, his face hovering only an inch over mine, and I could feel his warm breath on my skin.

"Are you sure—"

"Yes," I interrupted.

My hands found their way to the buttons of my dress, and although they were shaking slightly, I managed to unfasten them while he worked on his own. Both of us didn't have a clue about what we were doing exactly, and I was grateful for that because it meant I didn't have to adhere to any expectations he might have in his head. I had never seen a man shirtless before, save for maybe some childhood friends growing up when we went for a swim in the creek, or my older brother working out in the backyard during the hot summer months. None of those occasions were intimate, but this certainly was, and it made my cheeks burn as I took him all in.

Letting my dress crumple to the floor, I decided to leave my undergarments on, not because I was shy or modest, but rather because I wanted to give him a chance to take them off if he wished.

His eyes narrowed, and there was a hunger in them, something I had never seen before. He kissed me again, much harder than the last time, trailing his mouth down my neck until he reached my breasts.

I couldn't recall much after that, as my head was so far up in the clouds., It wasn't until the late hours of the night that I came back down to earth, long after he had left my bed. His side of the mattress was cold, but I was not, and if I closed my eyes, I could still feel his hands against my skin, in places no man had ever touched me, and I vowed none ever would.

I was devoted to Dwayne Anderson, and tonight had sealed the deal between us, that we would always be one.

***

I felt the heavy weight of Mrs. Gibbons's gaze, even from across the room. I hoped she would get the message that I was in no mood for idle chatter, but those sorts of things tended to go right over old ladies' heads.

Still, she must've known something was up, for she didn't offer any useless commentary on things I was well aware of. Just last week she had reminded me how one should properly attach a button to a garment as if that wasn't one of the first things I learned as a little girl.

The night I had spent with Dwayne was absolutely magical in every sense of the word. He was tender, gentle, and I felt as though my love and affection for him had doubled in the blink of an eye. It had been everything I thought it would be and more. Perhaps he had started to sway my heart to the romantic side of things, because I was almost certain that a proposal was on the horizon. I mean, why wouldn't there be, after such an act of true love. I wouldn't have offered my body to just any man walking down the street, and he had to have known that.

It didn't explain why I had gone the last week and a half without hearing a single word from him. Not a letter in the mail, not a message left here at the shop or with my mother at home, not even Gianna or Madeline had heard from him. It was as if he had simply disappeared into the night without a trace.

I loathed the desperation stirring in the pit of my stomach. I had to stop myself on numerous occasions from walking across town to where I knew he lived in fear I would make a complete fool of myself.

Maybe I had been wrong about his intentions this whole time; maybe I misread the signs and signals, and now that he had what he wanted, he had left me to pick up the broken pieces.

"Joke's on you, Mr. Anderson," I grumbled under my breath, simultaneously pricking my thumb with a needle, making me flinch. "I am not such a fragile little flower."

"Did you say something, dear?" Mrs. Gibbons asked. She was busying herself with replenishing our shelves with our most popular products, as it was a bit of a slow afternoon.

"No," I blushed, shaking my head. "I mean, yes, I did, but it's not important."

We exchanged a look, and if I didn't know any better, I thought the old woman might've been taking pity on me.

"We're supposed to be getting another one of those summer storms tonight," she declared, peeking out the window at the clouds rolling in. "Why don't you head home before you get caught in the rain and catch a cold. I was thinking about closing up early anyhow. Might go home and read a good book."

I wasn't opposed to the idea of curling under the bedsheets myself and falling into a dreamless slumber, where I didn't have to think of all the possible reasons why Dwayne had not come by to see me.

"Thank you," I said. Packing up what I had open at my workstation, I wrapped a thin shawl around my shoulders and headed out.

The streets were desolate, no doubt because of the impending weather. I quickened my pace, feeling a shift in the air. Just as I rounded the bend of my street, I spotted a young man nestled beneath the giant oak tree. I wouldn't have given him much thought had he not been wearing the soldier's uniform I had grown so fond of. My throat tightened and my palms started to sweat. I slowed my steps, giving myself a few extra seconds to regain my composure before standing in front of him, my heart on my sleeve.

"Miss Carney," he bowed, reaching for my hand and giving it a small kiss, just as he always did. "I was hoping to catch you on your way home from work. I'm glad I got here when I did, otherwise I may have missed you."

"Where have you been?" I questioned, narrowing my eyes at him, crossing my arms for good measure. Patience was not one of my strong suits, but he knew that.

"I know what you must think of me," he sighed. He shifted his weight from foot to foot, unable to hold my gaze for more than a beat or two. "I promise that my absence has nothing to do with what happened between us. It's just..." His voice trailed off, and he cleared his throat before holding his head up high. "When I got home that night there was a letter waiting for me. It was from my commanding officer. It seems that my platoon has finally been called into action."

Tears pricked my eyes within an instant. "When?"

"You know this doesn't change anything—"

"Dwayne," I growled, letting my emotions get the better of me. "How long do we have together until you leave?"

He sighed again. "A week."

I let my head hang low as the tears started to fall, just as the sky opened up around us, soaking us to the bone. It seemed the tree could not protect us from the storm, just as I had failed to protect myself from such heartache. He pulled me into a hug, and I wept uncontrollably, sinking into his arms. My knees buckled, but Dwayne did not falter, and we stayed there for a while, despite the ferocity of the rain.

"I love you, Lucinda Carney," he whispered in my ear, sending a shiver down my spine. "We're going to get through this, I promise. This is not where our story ends. Do you hear me?"

"I hear you," I said.

I'm just not sure I believe you.

Chapter 9

March 2005

"How many times have I told you about putting your feet up on the dashboard," Tommy muttered, swatting at my legs.

"What's the matter? Afraid I might break my legs if we get into a car accident?" I fired back.

I readjusted myself in the passenger seat, though I longed for a break so I could properly stretch my legs. Tommy had been adamant about making the trip to Idaho in one straight go, which meant only stopping to go through the drive-through or taking a bathroom break.

He scrunched up his face in confusion. "No. I just don't want your dirty toe prints on my windshield."

I couldn't help but roll my eyes at his blatant disregard for my safety, even if I had been the one to put myself into danger. To be honest, I didn't know why I was so shocked. It wasn't like he had such a shining track record for being Prince Charming. I knew what I had signed up for when I left home, and that meant fending for myself, in all aspects.

"How much longer?" I changed the subject.

"Less than an hour," he replied, though he didn't sound all that confident.

It had taken us longer than we anticipated, as I might've steered us in the wrong direction a handful of times. In my defense, it was difficult reading a map in the dark, where my only source of light was from the odd streetlight we passed.

"Great. We should stop and get food from somewhere once we get into town. And find a cheap motel to stay at. I'd prefer one with a pool, but I'm not all that picky, as long as it's not grungy on the inside."

"You'll settle for whatever I can afford," Tommy sneered. "But you're paying for lunch. You've got all kinds of money now, don't you?"

He glanced at me for a few seconds before turning back to face the road. He was testing me, or rather, challenging me to start up an argument. It was one of his faults, always looking to antagonize me so he could put his foot down and let me know he was the one in charge. Little did he know the only reason I *let* him win was because it benefited me in the long run.

"Fine," I agreed. "But I get to pick the place."

We drove in silence the rest of the way there, which, as it turned out, had been longer than an hour, though I kept any and all comments to myself.

In a lot of ways, Twin Falls reminded me of Whitefish, despite the glaring difference of its massive waterfall, which was no doubt a hot tourist attraction in the summer months. It was rustic and peaceful, the streets were quiet at this time of day, but I was sure by the weekend it would be bustling with people. I felt a bit queasy driving over the massive bridge that overlooked the water, but once we were safe on the other side, I started to relax a bit.

With my hand out the window, I lost myself in my thoughts for a few minutes, that was until a delightful scent wafted up my nostrils. I spotted a diner that overlooked the scenery and nudged Tommy's shoulder.

"There," I instructed, not giving him a whole lot of time to signal and turn, but he managed to follow my direction without causing an accident.

He pulled into one of the empty parking spots and turned the car off, and I immediately jumped out, eager to stretch my limbs from hours of sitting. Tommy followed suit, though his was to light a cigarette.

"Let's sit on the patio," I suggested, hauling him toward the diner, despite his obvious objections. He tossed what was left of his cigarette and trailed behind me, muttering something incoherent under his breath.

"Welcome to Rickie's Diner, booth or table?" the hostess asked.

"Actually, I was hoping you could seat us outside. It's such a beautiful day, it would be a shame to waste it," I beamed.

The young lady nodded, waving for us to follow her through the restaurant and out the side door onto the patio. She seated us close to the door, probably because it would be easier for our waitress if she had other tables to assist inside, but I didn't mind. I closed my eyes for a few seconds and relished in the warmth of the sun, nearly forgetting the whole purpose of this trip.

"Aurora will be by in just a second to take your orders," she explained. "Here's a couple of menus for you to look over. Can I get you started on something to drink while you wait?"

"Iced tea would be great," I said.

"And for the gentleman?"

"Same."

He didn't even have the courtesy to look at her when he gave his order, which made my skin crawl. As someone who worked in the food industry, there was nothing worse than a rude customer. I gave her a sympathetic smile before she disappeared back inside. I was just about to lecture him about manners when the door swung open again, but this time it was a brunette.

"Hi," she greeted. "I'm Aurora, I'll be taking care of you today. Have you had a chance to look over the menus or do you need a couple minutes?"

"We're still deciding," I admitted. "But I love your name. It's so unique. I bet you get that a lot though."

Aurora laughed, the kind of polite, awkward laugh you do around strangers when you're not really sure what to say. "I've heard weirder."

She looked like she couldn't be more than a few years older than me, if that. With the small-town vibes I was getting from Twin Falls, I hoped she might be able to solve my little dilemma.

"Speaking of, I'm looking for an old friend of mine. We knew each other when we were kids, but I'm afraid we lost touch. His name is Kemp. Ever heard of him?"

Aurora's face lit up in recognition, which I hoped was a good sign. "Kemp Stewart," she nodded. "Yeah, I went to high school with him. He's still around, like the rest of us unlucky folks who never got out. I hear he works over at the rec center a few days a week part-time if you're looking to run into him. I'm afraid I don't know where he lives though, sorry."

"Oh, that's alright," I chirped. "Where's the rec center again?"

She raised an eyebrow at me, and I realized that someone from around here surely would know that, but thankfully, she didn't question my lack of knowledge of local landmarks. "It's about five minutes down the road. Take a right on Main Street, and you'll see it."

"Great, thank you."

Aurora waited a few beats before shoving her notepad and pen back into her little apron. "I'll be back in a bit to take your orders. Take your time."

***

Tommy wanted to fold in the towel for the night and start fresh in the morning, but I couldn't wait that long. This trip was the most exciting thing that had happened to me in a long time, and I wasn't about to just spend the rest of the afternoon and evening holed up in some dingy motel room when I could be finding a way to talk to Dwayne myself.

"He's probably not even here," he protested. "That chick said he only worked a few times a week."

"Today might be one of those days. The only way we'll know is if we go inside and find out for ourselves."

"Maybe I'll just stay here."

"You're right, maybe you should." I readjusted my tank top, and applied a thin layer of lip gloss before rubbing it in. "He might be intimidated by you, and we wouldn't want that. Besides, I give off a friendlier aura."

"Friendly isn't the word I would use." He yanked my shirt up higher over my chest, covering as much of my cleavage as he could. I hid my smirk as best as I could, knowing he had just walked right into that trap. "Let's just get this over with. I'm tired and just want to go to the motel, have a hot shower and sleep."

"We can do all that *after* we talk to our new friend, Kemp."

The rec center was open to the public, though some of the staff members did give us some suspicious looks as we wandered up and down the hallways. I figured it was because we were two young adults that not only were dressed for a midnight rock concert in the city, but that neither of us were all that keen on smiling at old people as they walked by. I forced myself to act like I would if I was around my grandmother and that seemed to work a bit better in our favor.

I stopped in front of the giant bulletin board that had multiple schedules for different activities they offered. Some were for daycare programs for kids who weren't old enough to be in school yet, while others were for senior citizens, and sounded a bit degrading if you asked me. Did old people really care about arts and crafts? Or did no one know how to entertain them anymore?

Running my finger across the pages, I realized that a lot of the activities were hosted by volunteers, and after a bit of searching, I found Kemp's name alongside bingo, which was scheduled to finish up in the next couple of minutes. Memorizing the room number that was holding the activity, I headed further into the rec center, not even bothering to see if Tommy was following or not.

I waited outside the door until old folks started pouring out, most of them had a personal care worker offering a helping hand. I smiled politely, saying hello to those who were brave enough to acknowledge my presence, and once the coast was clear, I slipped inside, spotting a young man collecting papers on the desks.

Our eyes met, and I was ashamed to admit I felt a little spark flicker inside. He was attractive, there was no point in denying it, but it was less in the bad boy type that I was used to chasing, and more in the "good guy you bring home to meet your parents" kind of way. He had a kind smile, perfect teeth, combed brown hair that swooped over his forehead, and a nice set of clothes that made him look older than I guessed he was.

"Can I help you?" he asked.

My eyes flickered to the handwritten name tag pinned to his sweatshirt. I grinned before tucking my hair behind my ears. "Yes, yes you can. My name is Amy, this is Ace," I pointed my thumb over my shoulder, and Tommy remained stoic, as usual. "You're just the guy I've been looking for."

Kemp shifted his weight from foot to foot as he eyed us up and down. I wondered what thoughts were running through his head at that very moment, if whether or not he thought he was about to be jumped or assaulted. Even if he was afraid, he didn't show it on the outside.

"I hate to sound like a broken record, but is there something I can help you with? Are you looking to sign up for some programs here? Or are you doing, uh, community service?"

"Neither." I jumped up on the closest desk and crossed my legs, getting comfortable. I felt Tommy's eyes burning a hole in the back of my head, but he let me take the lead on this, which I appreciated. "Do you by chance know a man named Dwayne Anderson?"

Kemp's face shifted, and I could've sworn I saw him breathe a sigh of relief. He remained quiet for a few seconds, tossing the soiled bingo sheets into the trash can before wiping his palms on his pants.

"I suppose that depends on who's asking," he replied.

"I am."

"Yes, I kind of figured that," he chuckled. "I know you're not family, so who are you?"

I took a moment to try and find the right words to win my case. "Let's just say I'm related to someone he knows."

He leaned against the front desk and shoved his hands into his pockets, studying me closely. It made me antsy, but I shoved my nerves as far down as I could and held my ground.

"I've worked for Mr. Anderson for a few years," he admitted. "My official title is his caretaker, but he would object otherwise. He always says that makes him sound old. I'm more of a companion though, I spend time with him, drive him where he needs to go, and run errands for him when he's too busy to do it himself."

"So, you'd say you know him quite well then," I began. "I was hoping you could introduce us. I have a lot I wish to discuss with him."

"You've never met him before?" Kemp hesitated, and I realized that was a poor choice of words. "What's this all about? He's not really keen on talking to strangers at the moment. He's still grieving his late wife and can be a bit grouchy on his off days."

"He knew my grandmother once upon a time," I confessed, sliding off the table and walking down the narrow aisle until we were standing face to face. I heard Tommy approach from behind, though he didn't join me by my side.

"I'm going to need more than that," Kemp said.

"He wrote a letter to my grandmother, a really long time ago, and it's been lost for decades. I just wanted to clear the air for them, in case either of them are holding onto any grudges and whatnot."

"Nope." Kemp shook his head and moved away from the desk, acting as if that was going to somehow dismiss me. Clearly he didn't know me, as I wasn't about to just fold when things didn't go as planned.

"I don't think it's your decision to make," I argued, clinging to him like a shadow as he collected his personal belongings.

"Did you not hear me?" Kemp stepped forward, so close I could smell the gum in his mouth. "He's mourning his dead wife. He doesn't need some random blast from the past to come and turn his world upside down. Mr. Anderson might come across as a strong, charismatic man who is unfazed by these sorts of things, but that's just a coping mechanism, to protect himself. He feels and bleeds just like the rest of us."

"Just hear her out, man," Tommy interjected. I hadn't expected him to speak up on my behalf, mostly because I wanted to handle this myself, as it was family business.

"I'm just trying to look out for Mr. Anderson, which I'm sure he would appreciate. You have no idea what he's been through, and frankly, I think the expiration date for this little, what did you say it was, a love letter?" he waited for confirmation before continuing his rant, "has come and gone. I apologize if you expected a different outcome, but I'm putting my foot down on this one."

I understood where he was coming from; if the roles were reversed, I would want to make sure I was doing everything I could to protect my grandmother's heart. Though they had different surnames, I had a feeling that Kemp and Dwayne's relationship was a lot like grandfather and grandson, or something equivalent.

He grazed past me, and in a moment of spontaneity, I latched onto his forearm, pleading with my eyes for him to change his mind.

"True love doesn't have an expiration date." It felt strange hearing those words come from my mouth, as I wasn't entirely sure I believed them myself. He hesitated, his eyes looking into the depths of my soul, as if he were searching for a glimmer of truth.

"It was nice to meet you, Amy," he nodded, refusing to acknowledge Tommy's existence altogether.

I released my grip, watching him go, knowing that I was going to have to change my tactics the next time—if there was a next time.

"Well, as my pops always used to say, I guess you gave it the ol' college try," Tommy said. "I guess we'll just stay the night and head back tomorrow."

"We're not going home," I huffed.

"Did you not hear the guy? He said he's not letting you anywhere near that old man. Come on, Amy, you gave it your best shot."

"That was not even close to my best. I just need to regroup, and before the week is through, I'll have Kemp whistling a different tune."

Chapter 10

March 2005

"Sweetheart? Did you hear what she said? Marina? Is everything alright?"

I could hear Justin's words echoing in the back of my mind, but it was as if I were paralyzed, stuck in time, no matter how hard I tried to pull myself out. For a few agonizing seconds I was consumed with white noise until suddenly, I was back in my own kitchen, my husband and daughter staring at me with confused looks on their faces.

"Sorry, what?"

I cleared my throat, trying to play it off as no big deal. Brenda was easily convinced, though Justin was not. He knew me like the back of his hand, and therefore, knew that something was up. I just hoped he wouldn't confront me about it in her presence. The last thing any mother wants is for her child to think she's going insane.

"I was just going to tell you how my first exam went," Brenda started. Her eyes flickered at Justin, looking for some sort of non-verbal confirmation that she could proceed with her story, and with a gentle nod, her face lit up. "The teacher marked them superfast. We only took them yesterday, but she knows that a lot of us were really nervous about the scores. Guess what? I scored the highest in the entire class!" she shrieked. "A 98%. Mrs. Barnaby said she's never had one of her students test that high. She says I'll be looking at a full-ride scholarship no problem as long as I keep it up for the next two years of high school."

"Wow, congratulations honey," I smiled, resting my hand on hers and giving it a quick squeeze. "You must be very proud of your accomplishments."

Brenda's eyes glistened, and I swore I saw her bottom lip tremble. I couldn't help but feel like a terrible mother; clearly that hadn't been the response she was looking for. Unfortunately, it was all I could offer at the moment.

"I say this is a cause for celebration," Justin piped in, saving me from making a total fool of myself. "Why don't we go out to dinner tomorrow night after school? You can even pick the place."

"I'll try to get a hold of Amy and see if she wants to come."

She scratched her utensils against the plate and the sound made my skin crawl. "No?" I continued. "I thought you'd want your older sister to be there. Sorry, I take it back."

The damage had already been done, and there was no amount of backtracking I could do to change the defeated look on Brenda's face. Tears streaming down her face, she tossed her napkin in the center of the table and fled upstairs, slamming her door for good measure. I let out a deep sigh, defeated that I had once again ruined my daughter's life with only a matter of a dozen words.

"People always say the first five years of a child's life is the hardest," I mumbled, rubbing my temples in gentle circles. "That's bull. It's the teenage years that test you each and every day. What's wrong with me, Justin? Why am I failing so hard at this?"

My husband frowned and shrugged his shoulders. Getting up from his seat across from me, he stood behind my back and proceeded to massage my shoulders, which was his way of calming me down. For the most part, something like that would take the edge of my nerves, but not tonight. Tonight, I was a simmering pot of hot water, ready to boil over at a moment's notice.

"You're not a failure," he mused, resting his chin on the top of my head. "Things are just… a little rocky at the moment. Brenda's just going through some stuff right now, and Amy's out there in the real world trying to find her place. All we can do is be there for them, however they may need us, whether it's just to be present and listen to what's going on in their lives, or—"

"I'm not giving up on our daughter," I snapped, sensing where he was going with this conversation. "She's our child, our first born, the greatest love I had ever known the second she came into this world. I will love her for as long as I shall live, and there isn't anything she can do to change that."

"You know that's not what I was going to say," he replied. "I just don't want you to suffocate her, that's all. She's always been like this, the wild child who is independent and does what she wants without a care of the repercussions. She left because she felt like she was being squashed beneath your thumb, and now, your other daughter is desperate for the same attention, and you refuse to give it to her."

"I'm not refusing to give her what she wants or needs," I said defensively. "I just don't want to make the same mistake twice."

"You won't."

Letting out a defeated sigh himself, Justin walked over to the other side of the cabinet and retrieved a bottle of whiskey from the liquor cabinet. Only on rare, special occasions did he ever have a drink, and it seemed like now was one of those times. I wanted to believe him, wanted to believe that I wasn't messing things up and tearing our family apart, but what else could I think, when I was witnessing it happen before my very eyes? It didn't matter what I did, somehow, it always ended up being the wrong thing. Sometimes I wished I could be more like my own mother; through all her quirks, I hardly thought she'd ever done anything wrong in the realm of parenthood.

"I think I might just go have a hot bath and call it a night," I murmured.

"That sounds like a lovely idea." Justin took a generous sip of his drink, his eyes glossed over as if he were deep in his thoughts. "Hey, you never said if that night at the library was a success? Find out anything good about our mystery suitor?"

My husband was not as subtle as he wanted to be; he was phishing for something—an excuse, a reason, something to justify why I had been acting the way I had. He would have to do a lot better than that.

"Dead end," I lied. "Seems like whatever happened between them in the past will just have to remain there," I paused, holding out on saying the last few words until my back was turned, "until I found out what it is."

***

I'd received a call from the hospital that my mother was making some pretty good progress and that they suggested a bit of exercise might be beneficial. With sunny skies overhead, they asked if I could come by after work and take her for a short walk outside, not only to stretch her legs and see how much weight she could put on her injury, but to also get some fresh air in her lungs. I could only imagine how much she was suffering from cabin fever by now, it was the least I could do.

Before I drove over there, I made sure to leave a voicemail at the house to let my family know that we'd be going out to dinner as soon as I got back, and that I would give my mother all their love. I promised myself I wouldn't be long, that way I could devote the rest of my night to celebrating my daughter's accomplishments. I was extremely proud, after all, even if I struggled to show it.

I was told a nurse would be meeting me in the courtyard outside of the emergency entrance, and as I walked up the brick path, I spotted my mother from a mile away. She had on a floppy hat, a pair of giant sunglasses, and her knitted sweater that she made herself. She must've been telling a story to her nurse, as her hands were flying in all directions, emphasizing whatever it was she was saying.

"Look at you!" I grinned, clapping my hands in delight. "I think you might be outshining that bright ball of fire in the sky."

"How cheesy of you," Mom snickered, planting a fat kiss on both cheeks before linking our arms together. "Hurry, take me as far away from this place as they'll let you. I'm sick of the hospital stench burning my nostrils."

"It would be my pleasure."

"I'll only be a few steps behind you," the nurse chimed in, though she didn't look entirely thrilled to be on babysitting duty. I wanted to tell her there were worse things she could be doing on her shift other than following a couple of chatty Cathies around the hospital grounds, but it wasn't my place.

"Listen, this is your time to get out and enjoy the sunshine, so I promise, until you're back inside where you cannot escape, there will be no talk or letters or lovers." I crossed my heart and mimicked zipping my lips for good measure.

She laughed again, which was music to my ears. No matter how old I got, there was nothing like a mother's love, and I hoped that she might offer me some much-needed wisdom about how I might get through this little rut myself.

"Giving up so soon, are you?" she questioned. "I thought after the other night when you called that you'd be knee-deep into historical documents to try and find out more."

"The historian said there isn't a whole lot more to tell, just that he's a decorated war hero and that he moved out of Montana at some point when he returned home."

"That explains why I never saw him again," she said.

"Did you want to?" I asked without hesitation, despite my promise to drop the subject for the time being. I didn't know why, but I knew there was more here, I just had to keep digging.

"Yes and no. By that point I had already gone and healed from the heartbreak, so even if he had shown up on my doorstep after he came home, it wouldn't have made a difference. I was with your father at that point."

"And if the letter hadn't been lost?" I whispered. "Would that have made a difference?"

Her nose twitched as she remained quiet for a few beats, and I wondered if she was going to respond at all. "I don't know; it's hard to say. It was such a long time ago; I was a completely different girl back then. I suppose it doesn't really matter. We cannot rewrite the past, regardless of how hard we try."

"Were you always this wise?" I laughed, guiding us toward one of the iron benches in the garden, noticing that she was getting a little winded.

"Of course not, I was just as brazen and brash as our darling little Amy is," she confessed. "My friends would even call me a bit of a hothead, and I'm sure your grandmother would've agreed with them, too. Life changes you though, all the trials and tribulations it has to offer, it shapes you for the rest of your days."

"You mean marriage and having children?"

"That, and other things as well. I was luckier than most when it came to marriage; your father and I got along just fine. Our romance blossomed into true friendship, and that's rare indeed."

"And motherhood?" I pried.

She must've caught on to my desperation, for she leaned her arm over the back of the bench and rested my head against her shoulder. I closed my eyes, transporting back to a time when I was just a little girl without any shred of responsibility; to a time where I was shielded from the harsh realities of the world.

"Go on," she urged. "I can't give you any motherly advice if I don't know what I'm working with."

"It's not really anything specific, it's just," I groaned, trying to make sense of it myself. "They're at that age now where it seems like the only thing I can do is make things worse."

"That's just your perspective, Marina. I've seen both of those girls, watched them grow up into beautiful young ladies, with a strong head on their shoulders, and enough love in their hearts to make the flowers bloom after a hard winter. Cut yourself some slack, won't you?"

"Didn't you ever feel like a failure though? Was there never a time during my childhood where you questioned whether or not you were good enough to raise a child?"

"Just you asking that question means you're more than capable. It's the ones who are so afraid they're going to do a bad job that are good parents. And yes, I had the same thought cross my mind from time to time, it just comes with the job."

"But at least you only had one kid to deal with," I grumbled, tucking the stray hairs behind my ears as the wind started to pick up. "I've got two girls who are yanking me apart."

My mother's mouth opened, ready to say something, but her eyes darkened, and she clamped her jaw shut. It was the first time I had seen her so distraught, though I had no idea why.

"I'm a bit tired, perhaps we should head back," she suggested.

"Of course," I rushed, offering her my arm once again as we ventured back to the front entrance of the hospital.

"Tell Brenda and Justin I say hello," she said, giving me one final hug goodbye. "And Amy too, whenever you get the chance to speak with her next. I was so happy when she came to visit. I've missed her terribly."

I felt my throat tighten, though I fought to keep the tears at bay. "Me too."

"I love you, Marina, more than the stars love the moon. You'll figure things out, you always do."

"Thanks," I smiled, hoping she was right. "Try not to have too much fun in there. Only a little while longer, and you get to go home."

"I can't wait."

***

"Well that was fun, wasn't it?" I exclaimed, discarding my coat onto the bench in the front hall.

Dinner had been a success, or at least no one left the dinner table out of anger, so I was counting it as a win in my books. The waitress had even been kind enough to give us our dessert on the house, which I thought was awfully generous of them. I'd made sure that just this once I didn't bring up Amy, and instead, focused all of my attention on Brenda.

"It was," Brenda nodded, hovering by the staircase. "I think I'm gonna go upstairs and study for a bit before bed. Thanks again for dinner."

She bolted to her room, but she didn't slam the door this time. I didn't think anything of it until Justin cleared his throat. When I looked to see what he wanted, his arms were crossed over his chest, and he was leaning against the kitchen counter.

"What?" My eyebrows pinched together, and I instantly felt defensive, though I wasn't sure what I had done. "Did you not enjoy yourself? We didn't have to cook tonight, or wash up, and they even took the cake off our bill. What's got you so upset?"

"I thought you said you were dropping the whole Dwayne Anderson search?"

"I was—I am," I shook my head, trying to get my words to come out the way I wanted them to. "What are you talking about?"

He opened one of the drawers in the cabinet and held a book up in the air. It was the one I had checked out of the library the night I spoke with Albert Fitzgerald. I cursed under my breath at my foolishness for leaving it out in the open for him to find. But then I remembered it had been in my work bag with all my other school stuff—that meant he had snooped through my personal belongings.

"Where'd you get that?" I fired back, planting both hands on my hips.

"Does it matter?"

"It does, because it means you were sneaking around behind my back looking for *something* to argue about."

"I didn't want to find anything," Justin started, "I just wanted to make sense of why you've been acting so weird lately."

"I'm not acting like anything. This is who I am, Justin, I'm the same Marina you agreed to marry all those years ago. Nothing's changed."

"You might not think so but I do. You'd never get so wrapped up in this kind of stuff. Sure, you'd cry at romance movies, but you were always pragmatic. Now, I don't know where your mind is half the time. Why are you so desperate to dissect every single aspect of this letter and secret romance? Are you so dissatisfied with your own life that you need to lose yourself in some fictitious—"

"It's not fictitious!" I screamed. "And how dare you make assumptions about whether or not I'm dissatisfied with our relationship. Have I ever given you such an impression before?"

He blinked, and within a few seconds he realized that he backed himself into a corner that I wasn't going to let him out of. "No," he said, "of course not. I didn't mean—"

"How about next time instead of jumping to conclusions, or judging why I'm doing the things that I am, you just support me? Like a husband should?" I sniffled. "I don't know what's going on, I'm trying to make sense of it myself. I can't explain it, but something deep inside my soul is telling me to see this through, that despite my mother's hard exterior, she's desperate and curious to know the truth, too. I'm going to do whatever I can to give that to her, even if you don't agree with my choices."

"Marina..."

"I'm going to bed," I blurted. "I just need some space for a while."

"I'll grab some extra blankets from the hall closet and crash on the couch down here," Justin suggested. "If that's what you want."

I looked at him for a few seconds and nodded before disappearing into the bedroom, where all the walls I had built up simultaneously came crashing down.

Chapter 11

July 1942

I sat at the desk for hours, my only light source coming from the flickering candle, but even that was on the verge of burning out. The sun had long since gone down, but still, the paper in front of me remained blank. I had done everything I could to will my words into existence, but try as I might, they remained hidden within the shadows of my heart. I knew as long as they stayed there, I could never fully be at peace with Dwayne's departure, nor myself, by telling him how I truly felt.

"You're still awake," a voice startled me. I whirled around in the chair to find my older brother lingering in the hallway, only a sliver of him visible from where I forgot to shut the door all the way. "Mother said you never came down for supper tonight."

"I wasn't hungry," I whispered back, though it sounded as if I had shouted the words into the void.

"Are you now?"

He pushed the door open and held a tray in his hands, where he balanced a steaming bowl of soup with a piece of buttered bread. My mouth watered, and my stomach growled in unison, but the thought of eating just made me nauseous. I blamed it on the heartache, but I feared it might be something else. I motioned for him to set it down on the side table beside my bed, indicating I would eat it at some point before I went to sleep.

I figured he was going to leave after that, but he stayed, making himself comfortable on the edge of my mattress. He stared at me for a few seconds before he spoke. "I'm not going to bother asking if everything is alright because I know it's not."

"I'll be fine," I breathed.

A small part of me feared I never would be, that I would never be the same again. Colors had started to lose their vibrancy as the days went by, sleep had almost become nonexistent, mostly because I always saw him, and it hurt more knowing that it would be a long while until we were together again. I'd lost pleasure in the simple things of life—not even taking a walk down my favorite paths had cheered me up. It was as if I were slowly losing parts of myself, and one day, I wondered if I was going to wake up and be someone completely different. If this is what love did to a person, I didn't understand why some would fight so hard to get it.

"Nobody expects you to just move on as if it doesn't bother you that he's gone. We're not fools, Lucinda. You don't have to hide from us, we're your family."

"I said I'm fine," I rushed, though my voice cracked, an ultimate betrayal. Tears pricked my eyes, and I furiously wiped them from my face, more angry than sad that I felt like this.

"Don't worry about writing the perfect letter," Leith said, his eyes flickering to the empty page sitting in front of me. "Just speak from the heart."

"Have you ever felt like this?" I croaked. "It hurts so much it feels like I can't breathe."

Leith frowned and leaned forward to cup my cheek with his hand. His calluses were rough against my skin and brought me little comfort. If anything, it reminded me of Dwayne. He too had rough hands, thanks to his rugged upbringing. Neither of us came from particularly wealthy families, which meant sons were expected to pitch in from a young age. I liked that we had that in common; the working mentality, the lifestyle expectations, we were so compatible, it was as if a greater force was at work to bring us together.

"Time heals all wounds, or so I'm told. This too shall pass, and one day you'll wake up and realize that the pain hurts a little less. I can't promise it'll happen tomorrow, or the next day, or even a month from now, but it will happen."

He stood up, kissing the top of my head and walking quietly across my bedroom and pausing at the door for a few beats. I couldn't help but notice he failed to answer my question about whether he'd ever been in love. Perhaps he too was working through it, in silence, while the rest of us were just going about our days without giving it a second thought.

"Try and get some sleep," he said. "And eat something, before you start to make Mother worry."

"I will."

He left me to sit with my thoughts, and as I turned back to face the empty paper taunting me, I found myself reaching for the pen:

> You've been gone for weeks now, and I'm sorry it's taken me this long to write to you. I'm not ashamed to admit that I was having a hard time trying to figure out what I wanted to say to you, and what could wait until you come home. The truth is, neither of us really know when that will be. I'm trying not to think about the "if" part, but it's a reality we have to acknowledge at some point.
>
> Great men have lost their lives to this war, and there's a chance that could be you, too, which is why I want to say everything I need to say now. The last thing I want is to carry any regrets around with me. I love you, Dwayne Anderson, I love you more than I'll ever be able to show, but I hope you know that you have captured my heart and soul. It's yours, forever, if you still want it. I know we made promises to each other the night before you left, and I know that people tend to say those things when they're afraid they'll never see the other person again. It's never real, but what I feel is. So, I'll wait. I'll wait for you until the sun rises in the west and sets in the east. I will never love another again, not as long as you tell me now, once and for all, that you meant every word you said to me that night. You'll

have to get down properly on one knee once you come back to Montana, but until then, a love letter will do.

I pressed my lips against the bottom of the page, signing it with a kiss. I had no way of knowing how long it would take to reach him, wherever he was in the world, nor how long I would have to wait to hear back. I prayed that it would be sometime soon, as I had so many other important things I had to tell him.

***

Signed and sealed, I had dropped the letter off at the post office the next morning and waited. And waited. And waited.

I blamed it on the circumstance for the lack of response on his end and tried not to picture him elbow-deep in muck, fighting to survive. Those kinds of nightmares haunted me when I went to sleep; I didn't need them plaguing my thoughts when I was awake. But it was the only logical reason to explain why he had not written back, not after I had poured my heart and soul into that love letter. I had come to the crippling realization that it was one thing to utter promises, and another to actually keep them.

"Lucinda!" Mother called from downstairs, her voice echoing throughout the house. "You have a guest."

My heart fluttered in my chest, and for a split second, I thought it might be Dwayne himself. *That's impossible,* I reminded myself, *he's halfway across the world right now.*

Throwing a shall over my shoulders, I padded downstairs, only to find Gianna pacing in the front room, one hand on her hip, the other clutching a picnic basket of some kind. When our eyes met, I felt the guilt oozing from her pores. I didn't want nor need her pity, but I supposed it was a best friend's rite of passage to feel such things when their other half was down in the dumps. Without saying a word, she pulled me into a tight hug, and I nestled my face into the crook of her neck, closing my eyes for a few seconds. The scent of her shampoo put my anxieties at ease, if only for a moment, enough for me to pick up the broken pieces of my heart and put on a smile.

"I'm sorry I haven't been around much," Gianna pouted. "I'm such an awful friend. But I've been busy up to my eyeballs in work, not to mention my dear old mother has been breathing down my neck—"

"You're not a bad friend," I interrupted, placing both my hands on her shoulders and shaking her about. "We all have our own lives; I understand that more than anyone. We're not kids anymore, it's time we grew up."

"What do you say we go back to that childlike wonder, just for an afternoon?" Gianna offered. "I was thinking a picnic down by the creek would be a great way for us to just unwind and forget about the world for a little while."

"That sounds like a great idea," I beamed. "Let me go raid the kitchen for some food. Something tells me if I opened that basket all I'd find is a couple of sodas and silverware."

Gianna snickered. "It's the thought that counts."

Luckily, my mother kept a well-stocked fridge. I gathered up some cucumber sandwiches that were leftover from yesterday, and some cheese and meat to nibble on. I even managed to snag the last piece of coffee cake, which I was sure Leith was saving for when he got home, but I left a note saying I'd make it up to him tomorrow. With our wares in hand, we set off into the hot summer sun, heading for our special spot down by the creek. It was away from the road, so we wouldn't be bothered by the crowds that ventured down to cool themselves off after an afternoon of walking through town. It wasn't that I didn't *like* getting splashed by children, but I tended to only go there when I needed to get away from all the chaos, not because I wanted to go out and look for some more.

I threw down a knitted blanket on the small sandy beach, and we both kicked off our shoes and hiked up our dresses to our knees. It was the perfect day, not too hot, not too cold. There wasn't a cloud in the sky, but a gentle breeze that cooled our skin. Even so, I knew we would have to find refuge in the shade soon enough, or else we might get seriously burned.

"This is just what I needed," Gianna sighed, dipping her toes into the water and walking around a bit. I watched her from the blanket, not wanting to move quite yet. "I've just felt so… overwhelmed lately, and I'm not exactly sure why. It's like one morning I woke up and all of a sudden—"

"You're living a totally different life," I breathed, nodding my head in agreement. "I know what you mean. Mother said it was bound to happen and counts us as the lucky ones. Girls in much more delicate situations have no choice but to face the world head-on before they're our age. At least we got to cling to our youth for as long as we did."

"Now all anyone wants to talk about is marriage and babies."

My throat tightened, and tears pricked my eyes, threatening to spill over my cheeks if I made any sudden movement. I looked down at my fingernails, noting that I was in desperate need of a manicure, as they were a bit rough. But I couldn't muster up the urge to care about my outward appearance, not when my heart was dangling on a very fragile thread.

"Gi!" A woman shrieked from somewhere, and the two of us looked around for the source. Madeline was sprinting down from the hill, holding two envelopes above her head. "You'll never guess who it's from!"

Just like that, I watched my best friend's face light up like the sun. All that talk about growing up, marriage, starting a family, and how she wasn't ready for it, vanished within seconds. I didn't blame her; I had no doubt in my mind I would react the same way had I received a love letter of my own.

She sprinted out of the creek, kicking up water on the blanket before nearly tackling Madeline to get her hands on hers. They rejoined me on the beach, nestling beside each other, staring at their envelopes, though neither of them opened it.

"Go on," I murmured. "Don't hesitate to spare my feelings."

"Are you sure?" Madeline asked. Her eyes flickered to Gianna before settling back on me, where she gnawed on her lower lip.

"Of course! You've been waiting weeks to hear back from the boys, there's no sense waiting a minute more when you have those letters in your grasp. Go on," I urged once more, putting on a brave face for the sake of my friends. "I want to hear all about their adventures overseas."

Madeline tore into hers first. She read it as quickly as possible, to herself at first, in case there was anything private written in there that she wasn't supposed to share with us. Her face changed a number of times, her smile widening, and then frowning all of a sudden, before she burst out into a fit of laughter. When she finished, she held the piece of parchment to her chest, shedding a few tears.

"He says he misses me," she began. "That not a day goes by where I'm not on his mind. That I'm the first thought he thinks of when he opens his eyes, and the last thought before he lays his head down to rest."

"Wow," Gianna chuckled. "Who knew Mark was such a romantic at heart?"

Madeline gave her a little slap on the wrist, but they laughed it off. "He's just shy around people he doesn't know; he can't help it."

"Did he say anything else?" I was curious to know all that I could about what was happening so far away; any glimpse into what Dwayne might be going through would make me feel just a smidge closer to him, even if I couldn't hear it from him.

"Just that it's nothing like what he expected. He didn't go into much detail about what he's been seeing or doing; I don't think he wants to scare me. He said there are more dark days than good, but that they've all got high spirits that the war will end soon. Right now, his platoon is just waiting to be stationed elsewhere, but that was weeks ago, based on the date of this letter. Anything could've changed by now."

We fell silent for a few beats, processing her words. For them, it meant that the loves of their lives took whatever opportunity they could to reach out. For me, it meant that Dwayne hadn't. They were all in the same platoon, luckily enough, and now that they both had letters, it was clear as day that he must've gotten my letter and had simply chosen not to respond. It was a harsh reality that I had prepared for, but it didn't make the sting hurt any less.

Clearing my throat, I rested a hand on Gianna's knee, nudging for her to go next. She was much gentler with her envelope, and I figured she planned to keep every single correspondence she received while Dustin was gone. I leaned forward, trying to get a glimpse of the letter myself, but it was difficult to make out his rushed scribbles.

"Oh my." She held a hand to her mouth, her eyes so wide I feared they might fall right out of her skull.

"What is it?" Madeline and I said in unison. My brain jumped to the worst possible scenario, that someone we knew must've died in battle to cause such a reaction out of my best friend.

"Dustin, he... uh, he proposed! Look!" She turned the letter around to show us, pointing her finger at the last line of the letter.

Sure enough, there it was, in awful cursive script, the words, *"Will you marry me?"*

"He did not!" Madeline squealed, falling onto her back and kicking her legs like a happy child. "I didn't think he had it in him!"

"We talked about it before he left, but I had no idea that he'd actually ask me to be his wife, not when all of this was going on!" Gianna gasped. "I mean, it's crazy right? For him to propose in a letter?"

"I think it's kind of sweet," I said, wanting desperately to feel included. "He must've talked to your father before he left. No wonder your mother has been hounding you about marriage. She's probably been waiting for this letter just as much as you have."

"You think so?" Gianna glanced at me, her eyes glistening with joy and happiness.

As much as I wanted to crawl into a dark hole and pretend like none of this had happened, I couldn't steal this moment from her. "Absolutely."

"Maybe you've got something waiting for you back home," Gianna whispered, though I sensed a hesitation in her words, as if she doubted them herself. "You might have your happily ever after, too."

"Maybe," I smiled, and left it at that.

But just as I had expected, when I returned home later that afternoon, sun-kissed and exhausted, nothing had come in the mail. And the more days that had come and gone, I knew nothing ever would.

Chapter 12

March 2005

I knew I couldn't leave Twin Falls without having at least *met* Dwayne, but the only problem was the fact that Kemp was hell-bent on preventing that from happening. I supposed I should've prepared for such hiccups along this unexpected journey; not everyone was as friendly as the folks in Whitefish.

Back home, everyone knew everything about everyone, even if you didn't want it. I could sympathize with Kemp's desire to keep Dwayne's life private. I wasn't much of a fan of how many old women in town looked at me with pity in their eyes—it was as if they wanted to say, *"Poor girl, you had your whole life ahead of you and now you've gone and ruined it."* I didn't see it that way. I saw it as my first real taste of freedom, and now that I had wind beneath my wings, I was not about to give it up.

Tommy was not so enthusiastic about us staying in Twin Falls, especially after how things went down with Kemp. He'd chalked it up as a complete waste of time and would much rather pack up and head home with our tails between our legs, but I was not ready to accept defeat. These people were my own kind; I just had to think as they did, and then I just might be able to slip through the cracks without any issue.

The first step to my master plan was getting some fresh air and something to eat. The motel's continental breakfast was pathetic, and I needed a lot more than just stale bagels and burned coffee to fuel my body. I'd spotted a small diner on the corner as we were checking in yesterday, and I hoped that they would have a much more appetizing selection to choose from.

While the sun had only just come up an hour or two ago, the streets were already crawling with people. It brought me an unusual sense of comfort as it reminded me a lot of home. I wondered if that was why Dwayne had chosen to settle down here after the war. I added that to the ever-growing list of questions I had thought of over the past few days. The last thing I wanted to do was overwhelm or upset him by basically interrogating him, but my curiosity had a tendency of running wild sometimes. I just couldn't help myself.

A bell chimed above my head, and a short old lady popped her head up from behind the counter, a dirty rag in her hands. I was happy to see that the breakfast rush had settled down, and although there were only a few patrons seated in booths, there wasn't a single person in line at the counter.

"Hello," she greeted, and I spotted the name "Anne" pinned to her uniform. "What brings you to Twin Falls?"

I pinched my eyebrows together. "How'd you know I'm not from around here?" I didn't think I looked that much like a tourist, but perhaps I was wrong about that.

"Darling, I know every young face that walks through those doors," Anne chuckled, "and you sure ain't one of them. Shouldn't you be in school? You don't look old enough to be out of high school."

"I'm just on a short vacation for senior year," I lied, not interested in confessing my whole life story to a complete stranger. "We're just passing through."

"You picked a great place. What can I get for you?"

"How about two of your grand slams—scrambled eggs, sausages, toast, the works. Can I also get two black coffees with that?"

"You got it," she nodded, scribbling frantically on her notepad as she took my order. "It'll be about a fifteen-minute wait, is that alright with you?"

"Yeah, take your time. I'm in no rush."

"Take a seat anywhere," Anne offered. "I'll come and bring you a coffee while the cook whips up your breakfast."

I took a seat in the closest booth, hoping none of the other customers could hear my stomach growling. The sweet and savory aromas wafting from the kitchen were making me even more hungry. I'd been tempted to grab one of the tasty pastries at the front counter, but I decided against it. We didn't have a whole lot of cash to spare, so we had to be smart with our purchases. That meant refraining from all the sweet and delicious treats, no matter how good they looked.

While I waited, someone else walked in. It was as if the stars above had granted me a wish.

"Good morning, Kemp!" Anne beamed. She tossed her rag to the side once more before pushing through the swinging doors into the kitchen. When she returned, she had two brown bags in her hand. "Got it all ready for you, piping hot. You tell Mr. Anderson that I say hello."

"Always do," Kemp nodded, handing her a few bills before shoving a couple more in her tip jar. "I'll see you at the same time next week."

He turned to walk out, and our eyes met, forcing him to halt in his tracks. I flashed him a cheeky smile and even went as far as to flutter my fingers together as a way to say hello. I could've sworn I watched him suck in a deep breath, as if he didn't expect to see my face ever again. Still, being the gentleman that I suspected he was, he took a seat on the opposite side of the booth, placing his food on the bench next to him.

"You're still here," Kemp bleated.

"Surprised?" I tilted my head to the side, sipping on the steaming cup of coffee that Anne had brought over only moments earlier. "I thought I had made my intentions clear yesterday."

"As did I," Kemp remarked. "Look, I know that you probably mean well, but I meant what I said. Dwayne is just not in the right headspace to entertain ghosts from his past. He just lost his wife not too long ago."

"I'm not a monster, but shouldn't that be all the more reason for me to meet with him? I mean, he's not getting any younger, and neither is my grandmother. Time is a fickle thing; it creeps up on you when you least expect it."

I could see the wheels turning in Kemp's head. He knew deep down that I was right, that the two people we cared about most might not have long left on earth. Now that I knew about Dwayne, I doubted I would ever be able to forgive myself if I didn't at least try to bring them back together, even if it led nowhere.

"I don't know, Amy," he sighed. I felt a weird sensation arise in the middle of my chest. Maybe it was because I didn't expect him to remember my name after our brief conversation yesterday, or the fact that it sounded much different coming from his mouth. "I need to know that this isn't going to completely crush his heart and soul first."

Suddenly, I had a brilliant idea. "Alright, I'll play along. How about we don't tell him who I am? It can buy you some time to do some digging to see what he'll tell you about my grandmother, and you can see if he has any hard feelings, or if you think that he might want to see her again if given the chance. I'll still be able to meet and talk to him, but it'll save him from getting hurt. What do you say?"

He tapped his fingernails on the table, mulling it over. The plan was foolproof. There was no way he could object to it—at least that was what I hoped. I feared that it was my last option to finally meet the infamous Mr. Anderson.

"I can't believe I'm saying this, but I think that might work. We're in the middle of doing a kitchen renovation right now, but we're kind of at a standstill for the interior decorating part of it all. We don't really have a knack for picking the right paint colors, knobs, or trim…"

"I can help with that!"

I wasn't one to brag, but I quite enjoyed the entire scope of interior design, no matter if it was for a piece of art or putting an entire room together. It had been far too long since I'd let my creative juices flow, and the possibilities started bouncing around in my head. The color combinations, the wood stains, the cabinetry—I'd of course need to see the layout of the room first before making any final decisions.

"I can tell him I outsourced a designer to help complete the project. I doubt he'll suspect anything nefarious is going on. Something tells me you're good at lying."

I didn't know whether I should be offended by his comment, but I let it slide. The last thing I needed was for him to revoke his offer.

"So, when can we get the ball rolling?" I asked, hoping I wasn't coming across as too eager, but it was difficult to contain my excitement.

Reaching into his pants pocket, he slid his phone across the table. "Give me your number, and I'll try and set something up for tonight. As far as I know, he doesn't have any plans, but I'll have to double-check when I get there."

I quickly typed it in and handed it back. That was the easiest a man had ever received my number, though I doubted he cared all that much about getting to know me on a personal level. I had a feeling I was far from his usual type.

"I will await your call," I said.

"One last thing," Kemp held a finger up as he stepped out of the booth and gathered his breakfast. "Will your boyfriend be joining us?"

I'd almost forgotten that he was looped up into this little scheme.

"Unfortunately, where I go, Ace goes."

Kemp's face twisted in disapproval. "We'll work around that. Maybe he can be an assistant or a builder."

I nodded, bidding him farewell, and right on cue, Anne waved me over, signaling that my breakfast was ready. My heart sank a little knowing that there was no chance in hell that Tommy would ever let me get all buddy-buddy with this new handsome stranger without him being there to keep a watchful eye.

***

"Something's just not adding up," Tommy grimaced, steering us down a winding path to Dwayne Anderson's residence. "You remember how dismissive this guy was yesterday? And what, now all of a sudden he's had a change of heart? I don't buy it."

I understood his hesitation; in all fairness, Kemp had been adamant about us not meeting with Dwayne, for the sake of not wishing to cause any unnecessary pain and suffering. He'd been through so much in the last few months, it would be cruel to put him through something that easily could've been avoided. But we'd come up with an alternate solution, a way for us to all get what we wanted. And who knew, by the end of it all, maybe something good would come out of it. I was just as much of a cynic as Tommy was when it came to matters of life and the heart, but the little love story I had tangled myself in was somehow growing on me. What once would've made me gag at the mere thought of reuniting lovers separated by time now brought me a certain sense of excitement and pleasure. I'd found myself daydreaming about it during those quiet moments when Tommy was occupied, and I was alone.

"I know you may find this hard to believe, but people can change their minds about things," I remarked.

"All I'm saying is don't get your hopes up too much. I know much more about life than you do, Amy, I've seen things that you've yet to experience."

I couldn't help but roll my eyes at his comment. He was only a couple of years older than me; it wasn't like he had decades of knowledge to make his statement truthful. Besides, I bet I had seen and done far more things than he had, but I refrained from pointing it out. I let him have this one.

"Have a little bit of faith, will ya? And remember, this is a bit of a stealth mission. We're not telling Dwayne that I'm Lucinda's granddaughter. In fact, don't mention her at all. Not until we know there's no real bad blood between them."

Tommy gave a single nod, acknowledging that he'd keep his mouth shut. We remained silent for the rest of the drive, following the directions on his GPS that Kemp had provided. It didn't take long for us to pull down a long narrow driveway surrounded by tall pine trees, which offered a great deal of privacy. Though there was a gate at the front, it was left wide open, and I couldn't tell if Kemp had done that for us or if the gate was simply for show.

The property was absolutely mesmerizing; the lawn was immaculate, and there were several tall trees guarding the house. It was painted white and had light blue shutters and a wrap-around porch. Two rocking chairs sat on the front, facing the small forest that divided the property from the main road. Hundreds of flowers in every color decorated the two front gardens, and I couldn't help but wonder who had been maintaining it all. Was it Kemp? Dwayne? Or did they have a gardener come in and tend to the outside of the house? Surely someone with a house of this magnitude could afford such a luxury. I'd thought about my mother suddenly, as she had a green thumb herself. She'd spend hours in the spring and summer tending to her flowers, trimming, and pruning until they looked absolutely perfect.

There was a detached garage at the end of the driveway, and the door was wide open. I spotted Kemp inside, working away on something, though he appeared to be alone. Tommy parked behind the pickup truck and turned the car off, for once looking at me to take the lead.

"I have one request," I murmured, reaching over and grabbing his hand. "Please try to refrain from the bad boy attitude? At least in front of Mr. Anderson. I don't want him to get the wrong impression of us."

Tommy's face scrunched up as if he were offended by my words. "You really care what this old guy thinks of me? Or you?"

As a matter of fact, I do, my voice echoed inside my head. "Just do it for my sake, please?"

"Fine," he groaned.

We approached the garage, but Kemp met us in the driveway, yanking on the rope and pulling the door shut. He tossed a dirty rag over his shoulder, and I was curious to know what sort of project he was working on inside there but didn't want to pry.

"Welcome to the Anderson estate," Kemp greeted. His wide smile was contagious; it was as if he were a beacon of light, and I was a moth, completely and utterly drawn to his presence.

"It's beautiful," I breathed. "You don't typically see this much land back in Montana, not unless you're a farmer. I would've loved to have grown up here."

"He and his wife settled down here," Kemp explained. "They didn't have any children; it was just the two of them."

My heart ached a little at the thought of having this much space and no family to share it with. I grazed a hand across my stomach for a few fleeting seconds before composing myself once more.

"Is he here?" I asked, a bit foolish since Kemp had invited us for the sole purpose of meeting him. "I mean, is he inside?"

"Yes." Kemp looked at his watch for a second before waving us toward the front door. "It's teatime now, so I hope y'all don't mind having a cup while we sit down and get to know each other a little bit."

"What do I look like, a senior citizen?" Tommy muttered under his breath. I gave him a quick slap on the wrist, earning myself a sneer. "What? I should be having a beer right about now."

"*Quiet*," I hissed.

Kemp glanced at us over his shoulder, and I figured from the look on his face he was beginning to wonder if he was doing the right thing. Fortunately for my sake, there was little he could do about it now.

"Dwayne!" Kemp hollered as he stepped inside. He took his boots off, and we followed suit. "I have some people I want you to meet!"

"In here!" An old man's voice echoed throughout the house.

I took a quick glance around, but I was rather overwhelmed that I was finally getting to meet the man who was my grandmother's first love. I could hardly retain anything I laid my eyes on. It didn't exactly have the same warm, cozy, vibe as her house, and I realized it was because it lacked a woman's touch.

We rounded the corner into the half-built kitchen, and I took a good look at him. He was what I expected of any older gentleman—properly dressed, even though he probably had nowhere to go at this hour, salt and pepper hair that was pushed back, not a strand out of place, and thick reading glasses perched on the end of his nose.

He took one look at me and his face paled as if he'd seen a ghost. The plate he had in his hands slipped through his fingers and smashed against the linoleum tile. Kemp sidestepped in front of me, shielding me from any flying debris that came in our direction. Awkward silence filled the room, and I couldn't help but feel somewhat responsible.

"Are you alright?" Kemp asked, reaching for the broom nestled in the corner. He got to work at cleaning up the mess, while Dwayne continued to stare at me in confusion.

"Yes," he nodded, finally peeling his eyes off me long enough to realize what had just happened. "Oh, my, I'm sorry Kemp, my hands were slippery from just washing the dishes."

"Don't worry about it," Kemp said. "This is the interior designer I was telling you about earlier. She's going to help us make this place look like a home again."

"Amy," I introduced myself, extending my hand out for him to shake. "It's a pleasure to meet your Mr. Anderson."

"Please, call me Dwayne," he urged. "And I do apologize for that, I didn't mean to startle you. It's just…" he paused, looking me up and down once more before practically burning a hole in my retinas. "You look like someone I used to know."

"I'm told I have a familiar face," I lied. "Probably someone from a movie. I get that a lot."

"Why don't we take this little party into the living room?" Kemp suggested. "You can tell them all your ideas, and we can work out a game plan. How does that sound?"

"Good idea," Dwayne stated, leading the way down the hall.

Tommy followed, but Kemp grabbed me by the wrist at the last second, holding me back. "That was close," he whispered.

I could see the fear in his eyes, but I couldn't help but feel it was a reflection of my own. "As you said, I'm a good liar."

Chapter 13

I'd made several promises to Kemp, promises that I had every intention of keeping, but that didn't mean I couldn't work around them. While I was not going to confess that I was Lucinda's granddaughter and that I was here to see if he wanted to reconnect, I would, however, ask about other aspects of his life, if he was so willing to share.

More times than not I found that the older generation were dying to share their life stories with youth; I had lost track of how many war veterans had stumbled into the Dunkin' Donuts and went on and on about the things they'd done and seen when they were my age. I didn't have much interest in such tales, but I certainly did now—mostly because I was desperate for any glimpse into Dwayne's life. The only information I had been going on thus far was the short story from my grandmother, and it seemed that even she had only spent a short time with him before his departure.

I was most interested in what came after. When did he return after the war ended? Why had he not reached out? His letter was quite detailed in his love for her, but his actions were not as equally matched. There was a missing piece to the puzzle, and I was going to connect the dots, even if it was the last thing I would do.

Lost in my thoughts, Kemp nearly scared the daylights out of me when his voice cut through my daydreams. "I think that cup is washed enough," he chuckled.

I flinched, splashing soapy water all over myself and the counter, nearly dropping the teacup in the process. Luckily, I had a good grip, and I managed to regain my bearings before flashing him a disapproving stare.

"Why are you sneaking around here like that?" I lectured, aggressively breathing a few stray hairs away from my face as I finished up the last of the dishes. "I could've broken something valuable."

"Anything that means anything to Mr. Anderson is tucked away in the china cabinets. The cups in the cupboard are just things he'd purchased to survive on a day-to-day basis," Kemp explained.

That made me feel a little bit better, but not by much. "When did you get here?" I changed the subject.

"Just a few minutes ago, I was running late at the rec center. Old people are slow," he joked, leaning against the kitchen counter and crossing his arms over his chest.

It was still a disaster in here, as we had yet to really sit down as a group and go over what plans or ideas he had for the design aspect. I'd been thinking of some concepts on my own, though Tommy didn't care much to listen to what I had to say. Whenever we left here and went back to the hotel, he'd spend most of his time at the pub down the street and wouldn't wander back until the late hours of the morning. If it was anyone else, I thought perhaps he was having an affair with some local girl in town, but that was the one good thing I could count on, he didn't care much about looking or drooling over other women. In fact, he barely had any care to show me such affection or attention at all. More times than not he'd have kicked back a few beers or shots before he showed any interest in being intimate… which I supposed was almost all the time. But things had become so routine between us, for once I just wanted something spontaneous and fun. It would be easier to pull teeth than ask him to do something romantic for me.

"Dwayne said he was a bit tired this afternoon, so he's gone down for a nap," I said. "He wanted me to tell you he needed you to pick up a few groceries for the week. He left a list on the table."

"Wow," Kemp murmured, eyeing me up and down. I didn't know how I felt about his scrutiny, so I hugged my arms around my chest, mimicking some sort of security blanket. "He must really like you."

"Why's that?"

"He's weird about his sleep. He thinks it's when a person is at their most vulnerable state. If he didn't trust you, he would've fought to stay awake long enough until I arrived."

"I doubt he thinks I have any secret intention of killing him in his sleep," I snorted. "To be honest, it's probably because Ace isn't here. He tends to make people uncomfortable. He's a good guy and everything, but not many people can see past the tattoos, the leather, and the snarky attitude."

"Ah, Ace," Kemp sneered, and I rolled my eyes in response. "That's two days in a row he has not graced us with his presence."

He'd made his thoughts abundantly clear on the first day the three of us met, and it's been the same ever since. He didn't trust Kemp, nor did he like him. Tommy barely tolerated him for that matter, but at least it was reciprocated. Neither of them felt the need to pretend when they were around me, but a small part of me wished they would.

"He's not feeling well," I lied. Kemp tilted his head slightly to the left, reading my face, and I could tell by the sour look in his eyes that he knew I was not telling the truth, but didn't call me out on it.

"I recall only a few short days ago that you said he wouldn't be too keen on having you come around the house by yourself. What changed his mind?"

A raging hangover that has yet to be cured from sleep and hydration.

"I told him that he has nothing to worry about and left it at that. I doubt that Mr. Anderson is looking to sweep me off my feet," I giggled, pausing long enough to feel Kemp's heavy gaze. "And you, well, you made up your mind about me from the moment we met. Didn't you?"

He lingered just a little too close. I felt his warm breath on my cheek, and when I glanced up at him, his eyes were narrowed, his facial features somewhat dark and haunting. I'd never seen him so wary before, not that I knew him all that well. We'd only been in town for just over a week, but it felt like months had already passed. I blamed it on the fact that I was in a new town and that I had been so open with these strangers, but my heart had told me it was something else.

"I wouldn't say that. You... have surprised me. I fear I may have misjudged you."

I couldn't hide my smugness even if I tried. "Well, well, well," I murmured. "It sounds to me like Kemp Stewart is not as wise and all-knowing as he claims to be."

"Hey, now," he teased, flicking a bit of soap remnants in my face. "I never said that; you made it up."

"Care for some company to the grocery store?" I inquired, switching gears on our conversation since it bordered on flirting, and I didn't want him to get any impressions about our newfound friendship. "Ace is going to be asleep for hours, and I don't want to wake Dwayne up with me puttering around the house."

"Yeah, sure, why not. I've got a couple other things I want to do first, if you don't mind spending your entire afternoon with me," he said.

I smiled. "I'm sure I can handle that."

***

We had indeed spent the entire day together, and it was the first time in a long time that I truly felt at ease with another person. I'd felt terrible for thinking that, as I had been with Tommy for so long that I *should've* been comfortable with him by now. It wasn't that I couldn't find myself able to relax in his presence, but more like... I was constantly trying to maintain something, a persona, one might call it, and that required my constant attention.

With Kemp, I could just be Amy Wood—no changes, no alterations, no new versions of myself. I chalked it up to him being a complete stranger in a new city, new state, new life, but that wasn't entirely it. Then I wondered if he was one of those empaths that made people feel warm and safe, but something deep inside told me that wasn't quite it either. Whatever the reason, I didn't dwell on it too long, I couldn't, not since I knew that there was a very slim chance that I'd ever see him again once this was all said and done.

He was a good boy from Twin Falls, and I was a bad seed from Whitefish. Our paths were simply not meant to cross, or at least that was what I had convinced myself; it made the pain of eventually leaving this place behind bearable.

"Can I get you anything, Mr. Anderson—I mean Dwayne?" I corrected myself, earning a sly grin from the man himself. "Sorry, my grandmother always taught me to be polite when talking to my elders."

Kemp shot me a fierce glance from the other side of the porch. The three of us had gathered out there and basked in the warm, afternoon sun, drinking lemonade and eating sandwiches I had prepared once we returned from the grocery store. We were supposed to be doing work on the house, which was the sole purpose of my being there the past couple of days, but Dwayne mentioned he was in no rush. I figured he liked the change in companionship, not that Kemp was such a bad choice. Not once in the hours we'd spent running all over town did I stop and think "*I wish I was somewhere else right about now.*"

"Tell me about your family," he breathed, placing the newspaper down on the wicker table to his left and readjusting himself to give me his full attention. "Where are they from? Idaho?"

I didn't have the heart to lie straight to Dwayne's face, even if I technically had been for the past few days. "Montana, actually," I admitted, and something in his eyes flickered for just a few seconds.

I wondered if it was just the trick of the light, as the sun was passing over us, but I'd seen that expression before, in my grandmother's eyes when she spoke of the man sitting across from me. It was love.

"Oh, really? I knew a few folks from there, in fact, I grew up there myself, in a little town called Whitefish."

"Never heard of it," I gritted through my teeth, and watched as Kemp slowly exhaled a sigh of relief. This was certainly not part of the plan, but I never promised to not bend the rules just a bit. "We're from

Livingston," I blurted, recalling the first city name that popped in my head.

"And you, are you an only child or do you have any siblings?" Dwayne asked.

"I have one sister, Brenda. She's still in high school."

"And you're in what college? University?" He knitted his fingers together, and I could tell he was genuinely interested. I feared this part, where I would have to come up with some elaborate story to make my life seem far better than it actually was, but for some reason, I couldn't think of anything, no matter how hard I tried. As much as it pained me to admit my faults and follies, I really didn't have much of a choice.

"Well, no, not exactly, but I'd like to get there someday I suppose. I'm uh, what do they call it…" I cut myself off, picking at the skin around my fingernails, when he cleared his throat, making me look up.

"No need to feel ashamed, my dear," Dwayne affirmed. "There's nothing wrong with trying to find your way in life. We all do it differently; life has no defined path for every single one of us to follow. Some will stay the course that they think is designed for them, others… others like you and me, well, we go a different route."

I'd never heard it explained like that before, but in the blink of an eye, it was as if everything I'd ever been searching for suddenly made sense.

"I suppose you're talking about fighting in the army?" It was my turn to ask the questions, and I hoped that Dwayne was up for a little back and forth. "I've seen all the medals around the house, and your uniform hung up in the closet. I don't know much about what they all mean, but I have a feeling that having so many must mean *something* in your world."

Dwayne took a few beats to absorb my words and find his own. "It was June 1942. It was one of the hottest summers we'd had in a while, and I'd been spending most of my time with, uh, close friends who meant a great deal to me." I recalled what my grandmother had said about when their love affair took place and wondered if she was one of the special someones he'd been referring to. He continued, "I'll never forget the day I received my letter. Several of us had, my brother and father, as well as some of my best friends who joined the same platoon as me. We were called away urgently, which meant I only had a few days left of my old life before taking the grand step into my new one."

"Were you scared?" I found myself leaning forward in my seat, as if getting closer was going to make his story come out any faster.

"Of what? The war?" Dwayne crossed one leg over his knee and let out a deep sigh. "Any man that tells you he wasn't, is a liar. It's like nothing you've ever known, and nothing I pray the two of you will ever have to endure, either from home or overseas. I remember just laying in the muck some nights, unable to sleep as the world was caving in around me, and I'd just force myself to close my eyes for as long as I could and picture the faces back home. For those few peaceful moments, I could almost forget that people were dying around me, that things were being blown to smithereens just to my left, and that my body was not aching, tired, and being pushed to its limits."

"That's what they say," Kemp joined in. I wondered how many times since he's started working for Dwayne that he heard all the tall tales of his adventures overseas. "They say the elements are what kill more soldiers than guns do."

"You're not wrong about that. Hunger, dehydration, frostbite, infections, you name it. But you'd be surprised how much you can withstand if your mind and heart are in the right place. The second you start to let either slip is when you're in trouble."

"Your wife... Connie, that was her name, right? Was she one of these faces that you thought of when you were afraid? She's the reason you made it out of there alive?"

"Well, no actually," Dwayne muttered. "I didn't know her before I fought in the war; we'd only met after I came home and settled in Twin Falls. She was a wonderful woman, you really would've liked her, the both of you. I'd consider her more my best friend than my wife, that was just the type of relationship we had."

"That was like my grandparents too," I acknowledged. "They just had this mutual understanding that I'd never seen in a couple before, it was like they could read each other's minds. I don't remember them being quite as affectionate growing up, not like my parents," I chuckled, "but they had love and respect for each other, something that didn't need constant hugs and kisses. I don't know how else to describe it."

"Yes, I know what you mean. That was what I had with my Connie. I'm blessed to have spent so many years with her by my side. I hope I'll be able to see her again someday, so I can thank her for putting up with me," he laughed.

"She was your true love, wasn't she?" The seconds the words fell off my lips I wished I could take them back, not just from the fear in Kemp's eyes, but the pain in Dwayne's. It was what I wanted to avoid at all costs—hurting his already broken heart.

"Connie was my beloved wife, but true love?" Dwayne lifted his chin up to the sky and his eyes fluttered shut for a few beats. "That title is reserved for someone else, I'm afraid. I... I don't think I've ever talked about it to another person before, not since we parted."

"We don't have to—"

"It's alright," Dwayne insisted, patting the empty space on the porch sofa next to him. I eagerly jumped to his side and nestled in the corner, anxious to learn all that I could. "Her name was Lucinda Carney, and she was a bit of a firecracker. Intimidating, independent, and had a strong head on her shoulders. She was the eldest daughter of her family, and she often felt the burden of taking care of the household, even though she lived with her parents. They were blessed to have such a strong family connection, but they were not exactly as well off as some of the others in town. But that didn't stop Lucinda. I was quite frightened by her when we first met at the officer's dance. I'd wanted to introduce myself some time before that, but I hadn't mustered up the courage. That night, well, something must've come over me, and I just waltzed right up to her, and we started talking, and the rest was history after that."

He'd perfectly described my grandmother in so many words. "She sounds like someone I'd like to meet."

"She was incredible. I'm honored to have been a part of her life, even if it was only for a few short weeks. You know, it's funny you should say that because when I first met you, she was the first person I thought of. You could almost be twins."

My eyes flickered toward Kemp, who had clenched both of his fists at his sides. "Well, isn't that something?"

"A coincidence, I'm sure," Kemp forced out of his pursed lips.

"Lucinda wasn't just my first love, but the truest love I've ever known. I don't think there's been a day that's gone by that I haven't thought about her."

Chapter 14

August 1942

I didn't know what I expected when I was to be sent overseas to fight in the war, but what I had endured during those first couple of weeks would change my life forever. I was no longer the simple, idealistic man from Whitefish, Montana, but someone else… a soldier in the U.S. army. While I did not care for violence, death, and blood myself, it was an honor to be fighting alongside so many noble men, in the hopes that we would have a better world when we came out the other side.

If.

If we came out the other side. We had yet to truly face the horrors of war, but I knew it was coming soon. Training took up most of our time as our superiors prepared us for the front. We'd been told it could come any day now; it didn't matter if we weren't ready, or even if we hadn't fully passed our training. If our platoon was needed, we'd be fired off like all the rest, and the only thing that was keeping my head on straight was the fact that I wasn't going at it alone.

Ethan, my older brother, was helping me adjust to soldier life. While we'd been serving the same length of time, he had adapted much more quickly; I figured it was because he was the eldest of us, and he'd been used to taking on that leadership role our entire lives. He shared his rations, even though they were barely anything to begin with, and often reminded me of what was waiting for me back home—Mother, of course, but also my one true love, Lucinda.

Our father had also arrived with our platoon, but he'd been stationed somewhere else within a few days. I couldn't help but wonder if his age and mobility had something to do with it. Everyone else in our camp was young, spry, and had a bit of spring in their step, at least they had when we first got here. Now, half of us were walking zombies, barely conscious, as we waited for further instructions.

For the fourth day in a row, I'd volunteered for guard duty. I needed time away from the tents, from the camp, from the boys, even though they'd become my brothers in arms in a matter of minutes. I needed time alone with my thoughts, to process everything, but mostly, so I could wallow in my sorrows in peace.

It had been almost two months since I last saw or talked to the woman who had stolen my heart, and I longed to hear from her again, even if it was only a few simple words. We'd promised we'd write to each other, that she would initiate contact, that way we wouldn't get our correspondence mixed up or lost in transit. The postage was not as reliable out here than it was back home, and I'd hate to miss something just because our letters had come out of order.

"Dustin said I'd find you up here," Ethan's voice echoed through the torrential rain pouring down on us.

It had been raining for over a week, and I'd barely had the chance to get dry before my next shift on guard. Pretty soon, If I wasn't careful, I'd be at risk of catching a cold, and that was a deadly sentence for a soldier. With limited resources in the field, something as simple as a fever or a cough could cost a man his life. I made a mental note to take the day off from volunteering tomorrow so I could dry my uniform as best as I could in the humidity.

"It's quiet," I said. "I like the quiet."

"You always have." My brother helped himself to the narrow space beside me, his legs dangling through the rails of the tower. Guard duty was pretty boring in itself, as in all the time I'd been stationed up there, not once had I seen anything suspicious on the other side of the wall. "Even when we were kids, you were the one who stood back in the shadows to observe rather than being in the thick of it."

"What can I say, I don't like being the center of attention all that much. I'll leave that to the guys with thick heads," I chuckled, nudging my chin toward some of the soldiers working out in the middle of camp.

It didn't take long for those ones to set themselves apart from the rest of us. They had different motivations than us when it came to serving in the army; they craved bloodshed and longed to have one of the enemies on the other side of their rifle. They relished in the thought of taking another man's life, which I found concerning, though I kept such opinions to myself. I promised myself that I'd never become like them, that I'd never find joy in being a harbinger of death. I left that up to a higher power, someone much more qualified than I would ever be.

"I have something to tell you," Ethan confessed. I looked sideways at my older brother and recognized that face all too well. He had bad news. I'd seen it many times before, though those were much different circumstances than they were now.

My heart pounded in my chest as I thought of all the things he could tell me that might permanently change or crush my life as I knew it. "What is it?"

"Sergeant Matthews called me down to his office this afternoon, said he had a telegraph for us. It was from the front lines. It's about our father, Dwayne."

I closed my eyes for a few seconds in an effort to prepare myself for what came next. I already knew, or at least I had my suspicions that he'd gone to a better place. In fact, I had a dream about it the night before. He came to visit me at camp, though there was something different about him, almost ethereal. He told me to never lose sight of who I was, to never lose hope, and that I was a far better man than what this place asked of me. I didn't think anything of it when I woke, but now that my brother was sitting beside me, with tears in his eyes, I couldn't help but feel that was his spirit speaking to me, one last time.

"You don't need to say it," I murmured, patting his knee with my hand. "I think I already know."

Despite my words, Ethan shared all that he knew. "The telegraph said that he didn't suffer. They didn't go into details about what caused his death, just that it was quick. They're sending his body back to Montana so that he can be buried with the rest of his family."

"Have they told Mother yet?"

My heart sank into my stomach knowing that she would be completely and utterly devastated when she heard the news. They'd been married for almost 30 years, and I couldn't imagine the pain and heartbreak one would feel when they woke up one morning and found out that the love of their life had perished. It was a reality she must've prepared herself for, as her three boys went off to war, but that didn't mean it would hurt any less.

"They never said," Ethan confirmed. "They did however offer something for the both of us. They're giving us the opportunity to go home if it's what we want, so we can be there for the funeral, but also to help Mother during this dark time. I told Sergeant Matthews I had a feeling of what you would decide, but still thought I'd run it by you first."

"I'm not going anywhere," I blurted, not giving it an ounce of thought.

It didn't matter how much I desired to be in my warm bed again, to know that Lucinda was only a few blocks away from me and that I could simply walk a few miles and see her beautiful face again. I'd sworn an oath to my country that I would serve it with honor, dignity, and grace, and I had every intention of seeing that through, even if it meant I'd end up with the same fate as my father.

Ethan nodded, and we fell into silence for a few minutes, save for the sound of rainfall all but consuming us.

"So, what did you tell Sergeant Matthews? Are you going home?" I was afraid of his answer, mostly because if he was going to take the deal, I would truly be alone out here.

"That I'm not going anywhere without my baby brother."

***

"Dwayne! Dwayne! The mail has just come in, you better get your ass out here now!"

I scrambled out of the cot, nearly smashing my face against the ground. You'd think that as a soldier I'd get used to being woken up in such a violent manner, but that was one of the ways I had yet to adjust. I was a heavy sleeper, so when I finally managed to succumb to my slumber, I was out like a light.

Forcing my feet into my damp boots at the end of my bed, I rushed outside and was surprised to find the sun shining over camp. It had been so long since I felt warmth on my skin, I relished in it for a few seconds before joining my group at one of the benches.

Ethan was there alongside Dustin and Martin, my two best friends I had grown up with. Brad was there too, a younger fellow that we'd sort of taken under our wing. He was the runt of the platoon, but he was loyal and had a good heart. I feared what long-term side effects he might face from all the hardships we'd had to endure so far. He had his whole life ahead of him, as did many of us, and I couldn't help but feel he should be somewhere far away from this place, embracing what life had to offer. Instead, he would only know death and destruction for who knew how long. The war could end in weeks, months, or even years. None of us really knew how long we were pledging our lives for. That was the worst of it; the not knowing part. My mind reeled over how long a girl like Lucinda Carney was willing to wait for someone like me.

"What's all the shouting for?" I asked, yawning so big I thought my head might cave in. *What I would do for a steaming cup of coffee right about now,* I thought to myself.

"Did you not hear what I said?" Dustin gasped, sliding over a delicate piece of parchment across the wooden table. "The guys just delivered a crate of mail to camp, and guess whose was sitting on top?"

No. It can't be. I'd been waiting for what felt like a lifetime for this letter, and now that it had arrived, I didn't know what to do or think. What if it wasn't all that I had hoped it would be? That she was writing to tell me that while we had our fun back home, she was moving on, or worse, that she had already found someone else to keep her company at night?

I felt bile rise in the back of my throat but forced it back down. I couldn't think like that. Lucinda was an honorable woman; we'd made promises to each other that I knew in my heart she would keep. It was the only thing I had going for me out here, and if there was even the slightest hint that she was pulling away from me, well… I didn't know what that would do to my sanity. I foresaw a lot of volunteering at the guard post in my future if that were the case.

"Well?" Martin urged. He leaned forward across from me, raising his eyebrows in suspense. "What are you waiting for? Open the damn thing!"

My hands trembled as I fought to open the seal of the envelope. I did my best not to rip it too much, as I planned to carry the letter with me wherever I went.

Tears pricked my eyes as I recognized her handwriting on the paper. Sucking in a deep breath, I read:

> You've been gone for weeks now, and I'm sorry it's taken me this long to write to you. I'm not ashamed to admit that I was having a hard time trying to figure out what I wanted to say to you, and what could wait until you come home. The truth is, neither of us really know when that will be. I'm trying not to think about the "if" part, but it's a reality we have to acknowledge at some point.
>
> Great men have lost their lives to this war, and there's a chance that could be you, too, which is why I want to say everything I need to say now. The last thing I want is to carry any regrets around with me. I love you, Dwayne Anderson, I love you more—

I paused, holding the letter to my chest so none of them could sneak a glance at the rest of it. "You know what, I think I'm just going to read this myself if y'all don't mind. I don't think she'd want me revealing all our secrets and confessions to a group of stinky men."

"Oh, come on!" Dustin protested, throwing his hands up in the air as if this was a life-or-death situation. "You can't just start and not finish! We want to know how it ends!"

"It's not some fictional tale, this is our lives," I reminded him. "Besides, I'm sure you have your own correspondence to swoon over, or has Gianna changed her mind about you?"

"Don't you worry your little heart about our love affair," Dustin winked. "I've secured her for when I go back home."

"Poor girl," Ethan teased.

Dustin reached over and gave him a quick smack on the cheek, but that earned himself a flick in the ear in return. I couldn't help but laugh, forgetting for just a moment about where we were and what we had signed up for. If I didn't look at the camp around me, I could almost picture the four of us sitting in my backyard, spending our summer in the heat, and chasing after girls, and having a bit too much fun for guys our age. We were supposed to be settling down into our adult lives, but I felt I had so much left to do. But with Lucinda, I didn't consider us declaring ourselves to each other as a settlement by any means. If anything, she was the one settling for me; I was certain there were far more appropriate suitors for her to wed and bear children with, but against all odds, she had chosen me. I would never take such a blessing for granted.

"As fun as this is, I think I'll take this inside," I declared, tucking it into the inside pocket of my uniform and giving it a swift pat for good measure. "You boys take care."

They let me go, but instead of heading back to my tent, which I shared with twenty other men, I went to the outbuilding where all the supplies were kept. We were allowed to help ourselves to anything we should want or need, within reason. I finished reading her letter then I grabbed a fresh envelope, a few pieces of parchment, and some ink and sat down at one of the only tables in there. To my luck, it was unoccupied, giving me all the time in the world to think of what I wanted to say back.

I had thought about it for so long that now the words had somehow disappeared from my mind. How was I meant to sum up everything I'd been feeling with just a few mere sentences? There were not enough words in the English language that would ever feel grand enough to convey how I felt, but I knew I had to try:

> My love, I have dreamed of the day I would hear from you, and now that I have, I can say for certain that I have never felt joy like I had when my fingers touched your letter. I see your face every night when I close my eyes, and even during those times when sleep would not come, I'd remember all the times we shared. Our time together was cut short, and I'll never quite forgive myself for leaving you behind, but please know, it was the hardest decision I've ever made. My only hope is that you understand my loyalty to the army will be short-lived, but my devotion to you will last a lifetime, if you'll allow it. I have every intention of doing what you wish, to get down on one knee the second my feet touch Montana soil.
>
> Please, take this letter as my undying dedication to you, Lucinda Carney. One day, you will be Mrs. Lucinda Anderson, this I swear. I will give you anything your heart desires. I promise to come home at a decent hour and take care of you in every way you need. I will be the man to make you a mother, and I will spend the rest of my time on this earth making sure that you get the life you deserve. We will be happy together, and while I may face dark days ahead of me in this place, the thought of coming home to you is what will guide me through the darkness. I love you, Lucinda, always hold onto that. It doesn't matter how much space is between us, that love will never fade, not across oceans or through time.

I double checked that the address matched the one she had written on her initial letter and attached the appropriate postage. I would not let something like a missing stamp come between her and this letter. All there was left to do now was wait.

Chapter 15

March 2005

I had come at a crossroads in my life, and as much as I wanted things to return back to normal, there was a voice inside my head telling me that I had to see this through. It didn't make sense, not to me, to my husband, or children, or even mother for that matter, but there was some greater force at work here. The truth had long since been locked away, thanks to the lost letter, and it was my job to help shed some light on it.

Even if that meant putting my marriage on the line. Deep down, I didn't think Justin would ever truly leave me over something like this. While he might never understand why I do the things I do, he still loved me, and I knew that. None of us were ourselves lately, with Amy packing up and leaving the house, Brenda on the verge of a mental breakdown because of school, and my mother's accident, our white picket fence life was not so picture perfect anymore. Perhaps it was best for us to stop trying to maintain such a standard; it wasn't healthy. Try as we might to uphold the expectations of society, that wasn't who we were—we were always a little broken, but there was nothing wrong with that.

With everyone off in their own little worlds, not paying me much attention these days, I had plenty of opportunities to pull at a thread that had been taunting me for some time. I didn't think anything of it at first, but there was something about the look in my mother's eyes when I made the remark about her only having one child, so she didn't understand the troubles of having to deal with two hormonal teenagers at once.

My initial thought was that it had been regret. Regret that she and my father only had one child and that she really wanted more. I'd never really talked with my parents about why they only had me; it didn't really seem like my business at the time. Most families after the war were just trying to keep their heads above water, and I could only imagine the burden of having more than one mouth to feed while the world was still recovering from the many losses it faced. My father was able to give us a good life, one filled with love, laughter, and happiness, and things might've been more difficult if they had a bunch of little kids running around the house.

The more I thought about that dark and gloomy look in her eyes, the more I felt that it wasn't regret at all... but guilt. Such an emotion had become my constant companion; I knew it quite well. What didn't make sense to me was why she was feeling guilty, or rather, what about. Again, was it the fact that she only had one daughter? It was possible that she was unable to bear more children and that my father may have desired more, and she just wasn't capable of fulfilling that for him. I thought about asking if she had any fertility issues but didn't think it was exactly an appropriate question to ask one's mother.

Then one night it dawned on me—the reason that she had that guilty look in her eyes wasn't because of the lack of children in her life, but rather, the possibility that there was another, but she'd lost it. I had to know for sure. I had to rule out the possibility, and in the event that I was wrong, I would allow myself to move on.

Even with that proclamation in mind, it had still taken me days to pluck up the courage to begin my investigative work. I had no idea what other family secrets I might stumble upon; what if there was something more nefarious going on that I unveiled? I would never be able to forgive myself if I brought shame onto our family.

I had to treat this as a delicate matter, which meant involving as few people as possible. I refused to bring Justin into it; not only would he likely try to talk me out of it, but I feared that he would seriously begin to question my sanity. Brenda was too young and too impressionable ever to understand, and well... I didn't think I could just ask my mother what the heck was going on, and why she was being so secretive all of a sudden; over the last few days, she had shut down any more talk about the past.

"Mom? Are you home?" Brenda asked.

I had been planted in front of the family computer for the better part of an hour, but the internet search bar remained empty, mostly because I wasn't sure where I should even begin.

"In here," I called out.

When she rounded the corner, I watched as her eyebrows pinched together, and she crossed her arms over her chest while she leaned against the doorframe. "What are you up to?"

"Oh, just some stuff for work. There are only a couple more months out of the school year, and that means it's crunch time for us teachers," I fibbed.

Brenda nodded, as if she somehow understood what I meant. I supposed in a way she did, but from the other side of things. She had lived and breathed school since she was old enough to walk and talk. While she had not settled on a profession quite yet, I knew in my heart she would go on to do great things with her life; my only wish as her mother was that she would also take the time to enjoy the simpler pleasures that it had to offer. The saying "you're only a kid once" could not be more true; I feared she would go on to regret her decisions when she was my age. I know I had a few buried deep within the back of my mind.

"Right, well, I was thinking of having a sleepover with a couple of friends from school. Do you think that would be okay?"

I could hardly contain my excitement that she was interested in something else other than studying. "Of course!" I cheered. "Absolutely, I think that's a marvelous idea. Do you want me to drop you off anywhere? I don't mind."

"No, it's alright, Erin's mom is coming to pick me up. She'll be here in the next half an hour. I just wanted to know if you had a chance to do my laundry. There are a few things in there that I wanted to pack."

I was grateful I had at least stuck to my motherly duties so I wouldn't be a complete disappointment to my daughter. I had been failing in other aspects of our relationship, but at least she would always be able to count on me to handle the chores when things got tough. "Yes, they're washed and folded in the basket in the laundry room. Do me a favor and bring them up to your room for me, will you? And bring the basket when you're done, I have a few more loads I have to do over the weekend."

"No problem," Brenda said before disappearing down the hall.

I waited until I heard her bedroom door close before returning my attention back to the computer. It was now or never; Justin would be home soon, and he'd for sure know something was up if I was glued to the monitor.

I typed two words into the search engine: Lucinda Davenport. A few hits popped up, but nothing all that promising. My parents' wedding was featured in the newspaper way back in the day, which I gave a quick read. It was short and sweet, letting everyone in Whitefish know that the young couple had tied the knot after only a few short months of courtship. Other than that, I didn't have much success finding a clue to what I was looking for. I had to try something else.

Next, I tried her maiden name. *Lucinda Carney.*

That produced several more articles, and there was one in particular that caught my eye. It was the link to a website called *The National Archives for Children's Homes*. My heart beat furiously in my chest. This was what I had feared the most: finding out something that would change my life. The only problem was I didn't know if it would be for the worst or the better.

Haunted by curiosity, I continued reading, even though there was no turning back. With a few more clicks, I was redirected to a different website, one with all the physical scans from back in the day. It was a bit difficult to read, as they were photocopies, and not all legible, but I worked with what I had available. My mother's name popped up in February 1943. The blurb read:

> Lucinda Carney—admitted to Montana's Maternity Home for Unwed Mothers in October 1942. She was cared for by Mother Superior Esme and Sister Elizabeth during her stay at the

home. She gave birth to a daughter, Charlotte, in February 1943. Charlotte was dropped off at the local church, where she was later put up for adoption. Records state that she was adopted by a young couple, Dorothy and Earl Fletcher. The adoption was closed, and there was no further known contact between the two families. No more information available.

I stared at the computer screen for what seemed like hours. Brenda had slipped out of the house; I barely remembered her saying goodbye from the front door before she disappeared for the weekend for some much-needed relaxation with her friends. I knew it must have been quite some time because what had snapped me out of my trance was Justin's footsteps walking through the house.

"Marina?" He rested a hand on my shoulder, his face paled as if riddled with concern. "Is everything okay? You look like you've seen a ghost."

Grounded back in reality, a few tears slid down my cheeks, but I made no effort to wipe them away. Justin yanked the chair out from under the desk and whirled me around so I could face him. He cupped my face with his hands, his eyes moving back and forth at rapid speed as he studied me closely.

"Honey, talk to me, please. You're scaring me. Is it Amy? Has something happened to her? Where's Brenda? I looked upstairs but her room's empty, and she's always in there—"

"Brenda's staying over at a friend's house this weekend," I whispered. The words barely made it out of my throat. It came out all hoarse and scratchy as if I hadn't had a sip of water in ages. "Amy's fine, or at least I think she is. I haven't actually heard from her in a while, but that's not exactly unusual."

"Then what is it?" Justin pried. "You can tell me anything, you know that. Don't you?"

For the first time in over a week, I looked at my husband, really looked at him. His eyes were rimmed with dark circles, no doubt the aftereffects from sleeping on the sofa most nights. I understood respecting my space the first night of our little spat, but he'd been distant ever since. I hadn't realized how much I had missed him until now. Even so, I was still careful with my words, not wanting to face his judgment or wrath, despite what he had just said.

"Can I? It seems like lately all I've done is upset you."

He pouted, and if I didn't know any better, I thought he was on the verge of tears too. "Aw, honey. I'm so sorry, I never should've made you feel like that. We're supposed to be a team, and I guess I haven't really been holding up my end of the bargain much."

In all honesty, I hadn't either. Marriages and relationships require compromise, understanding, love, and respect, and we'd been in a muddled state for some time. Now, more than ever, we need to remain united. We both had a few things to work on, but I knew that we would be stronger when we came out the other side.

"What I'm about to tell you requires wine and whiskey," I huffed. "Trust me."

Slipping his hand into mine, he guided me toward the kitchen and placed me in one of the chairs at the table. He silently gathered a wine glass and a whiskey glass, first pouring some white wine into my cup. He made quick work of making himself an old-fashioned before he slid into the chair opposite to me, tentatively sipping, waiting for me to begin.

"I know I probably shouldn't have done it, but I wouldn't have been able to stop obsessing over it unless I had."

"What did you do?"

"I just had this feeling that my mother was lying to me about something, it just took me a while to put my finger on it. She never lies to me. We have a pretty good relationship, her and I. Not like what I have with the girls, but I wish I did. I wish they could come to me with their problems instead of shutting themselves out of my life. Amy's tactic is to run away from her issues, and Brenda, well, she has somehow convinced herself that my love is conditional based on her success in life."

My chin bobbed, and tears pricked my eyes again, as all the emotions I had forced myself to bury deep inside were beginning to resurface. It was only a matter of time, and with what I had just learned, now was as good of a time as any.

"I'm not following, Marina," Justin said.

"I Googled my mom," I blurted, burying my face into the crook of my elbow, overcome with shame.

I was plagued with regret that I hadn't respected my mother's privacy, despite her obviously not wanting to share intimate details with me about her past. I felt stupid, foolish, and selfish, and I had absolutely no idea how I was going to make up for what I had done.

"I take it by your reaction that it's not good news?" Justin murmured.

"I don't know, honestly. I'm still sort of processing it myself. I just wanted to see if there was anything more about my mother and Dwayne out there on the internet, and what I found, well... it's life-altering stuff."

"Go on," he urged.

"For a few months between 1942 and 1943, my mother stayed at a place called Montana's Maternity Home for Unwed Mothers."

I paused, allowing my words to seep into his skull. I could see the wheels turning in his brain as he worked it out for himself. It didn't take long; Justin was an intelligent man, not that he really needed to be to figure it out. The name of such a place didn't leave much room for the imagination.

"Considering you were born after that, I doubt she was admitted there because of you," he began. "Not to mention that she and your father were married at the time."

"I know."

"What else did you find?"

"That she had a daughter in February 1943. Her name was—is—Charlotte. There wasn't any information about the father, but based on the timeline…"

"It had to have been Dwayne," Justin echoed my thoughts. "But he would've been serving overseas at the time, would he not?"

"My guess is that she got pregnant just before he left. That's the only possible explanation. I doubt my mother was going around town sleeping with guys she didn't have a serious connection with. Dwayne is the only other man in her life that she ever admitted to loving; it has to be his child."

"Back up, honey, you're getting way too deep into this. We don't even know if this is her, I mean, there could've been another Lucinda in Montana that was pregnant at the time."

"Really?" I tilted my head to the side. "What are the chances of that?"

"Slim to none."

"I just, I don't know what I'm supposed to do with this information now that I have it. I mean, learning about the lost love letter was one thing, but this is something completely different. I mean, this changes things in our entire family dynamic. Who knows what relatives know about this pregnancy. Do you think my father would've known? What about my grandparents? I doubt she would've been able to keep such a thing a secret from the people closest to her."

"She was placed in a maternity home for unwed mothers, Marina," Justin hinted. "Obviously she was there for a reason. Times were tough back then, having a baby out of wedlock would've led to shame, especially in a small town like Whitefish. If this is your mother we're talking about, chances are, she didn't have much of a choice. The father of her child was fighting overseas, and without his letter, she would've never known his intentions to marry her. Without other prospects, there wasn't much to be done."

I tried to understand what he was suggesting, but it was hard for me to wrap my brain around it. Never in a million years would I have ever given my child up for adoption, not even if it meant I had to raise them by myself. Why would she do such a thing? But more importantly, *how* could she go through with it?

"I have a sister," I sighed. "Somewhere in the world, I have a sister, and her name is Charlotte."

"Don't do that," Justin warned. "Don't venture down that path until you know for certain it's true. You could end up hurting a lot of people, including yourself."

As usual, my husband was right. I couldn't very well go searching for every Charlotte in the area and begin reaching out and asking if they were adopted. I needed to confirm my suspicions with the source, even if it meant tainting our mother-daughter relationship for the rest of my life.

Chapter 16

October 1942

Time was a persistent thing; no matter how much you wanted to speed it up or slow it down, it remained as consistent as the sun rising each morning. It didn't matter if there was a relentless storm raining down, behind those thick, dense clouds, the sun waited to shine once more.

I had waited, waited for the love of my life to not only read the letter I poured my heart and soul into, but reciprocate it. Despite what the women in my life had been saying over the past couple of weeks—Mrs. Nelson at work, Edith, my mother from time to time, even Gianna and Madeline—I knew that he had little excuse to not reply with such haste. I know I had waited a while to send that initial letter, as I wasn't sure how to put such affections into words, but I had mailed it out at the same time that my best friends had sent off their replies. Both Dustin and Mark have returned their correspondence.

Twice.

Today was just a day, like any other before it, where I hadn't the faintest hope that my luck would change—not when my hunger continued to grow with each passing week. I was eating for two now, and even if my mind didn't want to eat, as the heartbreak I was suffering from was far too strong, the little one inside my tummy had a different opinion. I tore through breakfast like a ravenous beast, scarfing down an extra helping that my mother had loaded up on my plate. I was beginning to feel a lot like my older brother, but luckily, he hadn't made any snarky comments regarding my new eating habits.

"Did you sleep well?" Edith asked, taking delicate bites of her oatmeal, eyeing me from my left. Recently, she'd been obsessed with slimming down her figure, which made me feel even worse about myself. "I didn't hear you get up once last night. Has the sickness phase finally passed?"

"I hope so," I replied. I was getting really sick and tired of spending my days holed up in the bathroom with my head in the toilet.

"Please change the topic of conversation to something more appropriate at the breakfast table," Mother muttered.

"Alright," I obliged. "I think I'm feeling up to going to work this afternoon. I'm sure Mrs. Nelson has been having a difficult time keeping up with orders at the shop while I've been home. I think it's about time I get back into the swing of things. I'm going to need to start saving before the little one arrives."

Mother's eyes shifted between me and Edith, and the two of them shared a silent glance before my sister excused herself abruptly. I watched her leave, wondering what on earth she could possibly need to do at this hour to get up in the middle of a meal. It was one thing my parents were always adamant about—we sat down as a family, with a few minor exceptions. The boys had their excuses as they went off to work before daylight, but they were always home before dark, so we could eat dinner together. It wouldn't be long before our family of five became a family of six.

"I had tea with Mrs. Nelson earlier this week. We had a pleasant conversation about your, um," Mother paused, moving her mouth from side to side as she chose her next word carefully, "situation."

"My *situation?*"

"You must understand how having you there might affect the old woman's business. You're young, unmarried, and pretty soon you'll be starting to show. We've done all that we could by letting your dresses out at your waist, but now that you're in your second trimester, you're starting to put on weight, and your stomach is bulging more and more. You know we love you, but—"

"But what?" I demanded. I blamed my outburst on the pregnancy hormones, but it was a number of things. All I wanted was to have some shred of normalcy in my life, and now, she was taking it away. I wouldn't stand for it. "There are plenty of unwed mothers in town. What is so wrong if I am one of them?"

"Sweetheart… those women, well, they have a reputation, one that tarnishes their entire families for generations to come. While we might not be as grand or as popular as the Wilsons or the Baldwins, we must preserve what status we have. Your father and I have discussed at great lengths what to do, and we've come up with a solution to your problem. Since Mr. Anderson has not declared himself to you or made any indication to ask for your hand from your father, he's left us with no choice."

"Mother," I interrupted, my chin bobbing up and down. The tears streamed down my face, and I tried to work out what she was going to say next, but my mind was drawing a blank. "Please, whatever you think you've decided, it's not fair. This is my life, my choice, my decision to make. Dwayne and I, we're meant to be together. He's my soulmate, I know it, he's made promises and so have I."

"All he's done is put a baby in you!" she fumed. She took a moment to collect herself, taking a few deep breaths before her face returned to its typical stoic state. "There is a facility a few towns over, it's called Montana's Maternity Home for Unwed Mothers. You will live there for the remainder of your pregnancy, and once you've given birth and said your goodbyes, you will return home and find yourself a husband, fast."

My jaw dropped open as I tried my best to process her words. Not only was she kicking me out of the house, for months, but she and Father also expected me to give up my child? The last remaining connection I had to Dwayne?

"I don't understand why I'm being punished for one simple mistake…"

"It's not a punishment, sweetheart, but it's also not a tiny mistake you've made. This will affect Edith, even Leith too, if he ever decides to settle down and choose a wife. These are dark times, Lucinda. With the war, with the economy, with your father's injuries, we just cannot afford to have this hanging over our heads too. One day you'll thank me, I assure you, but until that day, you're just going to have to live with these consequences."

"What about my life here, in Whitefish? What about my friends, my job? I mean, you're asking me to just pick everything up and move away from you and my family, it's not right."

"Everything will be here when you come back." She leaned forward, moving to grab my hand, but I flinched, placing it in my lap, where she could not reach it. "You'll be surprised how fast time will fly when you're there. You'll blink and you'll be back here, and it'll be like none of this ever happened."

I didn't want it to be over that fast. I didn't want to forget the child growing inside of me, the one that was a direct link to the man I loved, who was halfway around the world. But like everything else in my life, it seemed that I had no choice in this matter.

"When do I leave?"

Mother sighed, and for the first time, she showed just the faintest glimmer of emotion. "Tonight, once your father comes home from work. He'll be driving you there himself."

***

I did not speak to my father the entire ride there. He tried several times to engage in polite conversion, but I simply looked out the window and cried. Shedding such tears was pointless as my parents had already made up their minds about their tainted daughter, but they continued to fall.

A few hours later, we arrived at the place I was to spend the next few months. It was difficult to make out its beauty as we were covered by nightfall, but from what I could see, it looked like any old house but bigger, and more secluded, and had a massive fence that wrapped around the property. A lump formed in my throat; if I didn't know any better, I thought they were sending me off to prison.

"I suppose this is it," Father exhaled. "Do you have everything you need? I mean, is there anything else I can bring for you?"

"I don't need anything else from you, thanks," I sneered.

I could see the pain in his eyes. I was his first daughter, his little girl, and all of a sudden, I had grown up and was soon going to be a parent myself. I could've been kinder, but it wasn't my job to make it easier for them; they were supposed to be doing that for me. I had no idea how to handle any of this, I needed their love, support, and guidance. But instead, they were shipping me off to be someone else's problem.

"I will be back once this is all over," he said. "You will get through this, and when you have, you will get the life you deserve. It will be filled with love and happiness; this I swear."

"It already was until you ripped it all away," I whispered. With that, I waved farewell, grabbed my only bag, and headed inside.

A group of women of all ages was standing in the foyer, tentatively waiting for my arrival. They all wore similar uniforms, which consisted of all black garments, save for the white collar around their neck, making their gold crosses visible for all to see. Every inch of their skin was covered, including the hair on their heads.

One stepped forward, separating herself from the rest. "Welcome to the Maternity Home for Unwed Mothers," she greeted. "You must be Lucinda Carney."

"Yes, that's me," I confirmed. "And you are?"

"Mother Superior Esme. I am the head nun that oversees the facility, both the other nuns as well as our beloved guests, which now includes you. This is Sister Elizabeth, and she will be directly looking after you during your stay with us."

Mother Superior Esme gestured to a younger woman with fair skin and few wrinkles. She didn't look much older than me if I was being honest, but it was hard to tell based on just her facial features alone.

"Thank you, but I can take care of myself, I have been most of my life," I stated.

"I apologize for any misunderstanding, but you can't exactly refuse our care," Mother Superior said. "I assure you, Miss Carney, you will be most appreciative of her help, especially as you progress in your pregnancy."

"Come," Sister Elizabeth waved, holding her arm out for me to take. She even offered to take my bag, but I clutched it tight. "I will show you to your room. You must be exhausted."

I seriously doubted I would be able to get a wink of sleep after everything that happened today, but I reckoned anything would be better than standing before a group of nuns who were judging me.

The house was void of frivolous decorations. The only thing hanging on the walls were either crosses or intricate paintings of churches, landscapes, or Jesus. We walked upstairs, which creaked under my feet, and I imagined the house was very old. They'd tried their best to make it feel homey and comfortable with a maroon stair runner to hide the worn-out wood, but I had no trouble seeing past the peeling wallpaper.

We walked to the end of the hall, where Sister Elizabeth gave the door a quick knock before letting herself in. I was surprised to see two beds, two dressers, and two vanities. I had been under the impression that I would at least have a room to myself, but apparently, I was not allowed such luxuries as a forsaken woman.

"Patricia White, this is who I was telling you about," Sister Elizabeth smiled. "Lucinda Carney, this is your roommate. We tend to pair up girls based on when their due date is, that way they can sort of go through their pregnancies together. It's nice, isn't it? To have someone to share in this experience with."

Nice wasn't the word I would've picked, but I nodded just the same. "I have a rough estimate of how far along I am, but I don't know exactly—"

"Don't worry, child," she assured me. "We'll help you figure it all out in the next couple of days. First, we want to focus on getting you settled and making you comfortable. Stress is not good for the baby. It's our mission to help you have a healthy and a happy pregnancy."

"I appreciate it."

"Well, I'll let you two get to know each other," Sister Elizabeth cheered. "Breakfast will be served at nine o'clock, so make sure you're up and dressed for the day before that."

Flashing us both a cheery smile, she excused herself, shutting our door on the way out. Once she was gone, I let my shoulders drop and exhaled a deep breath. Although I had hoped I would be alone, I wasn't afraid to cry in front of Patricia. Hot, angry tears flooded out of my eyes, and I flopped down in front of the vanity, appalled by my appearance.

I was surprised to see Patricia's face in the reflection. I hadn't even heard her get up from the bed, but there she was, holding a hairbrush, poised at the ready.

"I had the same reaction when I first arrived," she admitted, gently pulling at the ribbons in my hair until it fell around my face. "I cried for days and days. It's not so bad though. I hope you don't mind them shoving religion down your throat. We pray two times a day and have bible sessions once a week. I was not much of a churchgoer myself before all this, but it's part of the program."

I sniffled. "How long have you been here?"

"Two weeks, and we've got many months to go before we pop these babies out of us," she laughed. "My advice? Make the most of it."

I remained silent and let her work the brush through my tangled locks without making a fuss. She scratched her fingernails into my scalp, which put me at ease, and even though I had thought I wouldn't be able to sleep, there was something about her calming presence that made me think I could fall into a deep slumber the second my head hit the pillow.

"So, what's your story anyway?" Patricia pried. "You look like a nice girl with a strong head on her shoulders. How'd you get mixed up with the likes of us anyhow?"

I didn't know whether I should be offended or pleased that she didn't think of me as some trashy girl who was knocked up—not that I saw her that way at all.

"It's a bit complicated," I began. "I suppose this is what I get for getting involved with a soldier. It was doomed from the start. Anyway, we, you know, *did the deed*, and that night he received his letter in the mail that he was being called away to join the war. Shortly after he left, I missed my period, and well, here we are."

"A soldier? Shouldn't your parents be proud that he's the father of your child? I thought those guys were respected members of society."

"They are, usually," I said. "But only when they come with a marriage proposal. Without such a promise, I'm just a tainted woman, doomed to be a spinster if I don't play my cards right."

Patricia muttered something under her breath, likely an acknowledgment that she was in the same boat.

"What about you? Why are you here?"

She exhaled, placing the brush on the vanity before sitting on the edge of her bed. "It's far less glamorous than your story, I'm afraid. I don't even really remember how it happened, or rather, how I ended up in such a predicament in the first place. Anyway, I was walking home one night with a friend, or someone I thought was my friend, when he decided to help himself to my virginity. A few weeks later, I had become my mother's worst nightmare, and here I am."

"He took advantage of you?" I gasped.

I didn't know whether to hug her or cry. I had heard of such scum men from my older brother but never had I ever met someone like that or even knew someone who had. It wasn't a thing in Whitefish. At least, I didn't think it was. I guessed there were dangerous men everywhere, no matter where you lived.

"It doesn't matter much now," she whispered. "I just want to get through this chapter in my life so I can move on and never look back."

I couldn't say the same. The baby inside me was not born of a sinister act, but one of true love, or so I had thought. Maybe Patricia had the right idea all along; maybe I wasn't supposed to form any sort of emotional attachment to the baby. I hoped that it would make it easier when I had to give them up.

I yawned, feeling overwhelmed by the weight of the world hanging on my shoulders. Patricia took that as her cue to get settled in her bed, and I did the same. She blew out the candle on the nightstand between our beds, and our room fell into complete darkness.

"Thank you," I blurted out, pulling the blankets up to my chest. "For making me feel less lonely here."

"Wait until you meet Nancy Turner," Patricia beamed. "She's a real treat."

Chapter 17

March 2005

"I was beginning to think you'd forgotten about me here," Mom joked, gesturing for us to take a break at one of the benches outside of the hospital.

I'd felt a pang of guilt squeeze my heart. I had been neglecting my duties to my mother by not visiting her as often as I knew I should've, but I had been preoccupied with many other things, including digging around in her past. Now that my marriage was on the mend, and Justin and I had worked out the little kinks and were back to communicating as we once did, I felt like the pieces of my broken life were slowly coming back together. Not in all aspects, as the mother department was still up in the air thanks to my estranged daughter, but I would take what I could get for the time being.

"I know, I'm sorry, it's just been one of those hectic weeks where nothing seemed to go right."

As a mother and a wife, I knew she would understand where I was coming from. We nestled ourselves beneath a giant willow tree, and I fished out the little snacks I had packed so we could have a bit of an impromptu picnic. Her eyes lit up when I revealed all the treats I had brought, knowing that some of them were her favorites. Hospital food was not the greatest, and she had become accustomed to a certain lifestyle over the years. I was more than happy to give her a taste of her home life, even if it was just for an afternoon.

Hopefully, she wouldn't be holed up in the hospital for much longer. When I first arrived on her unit, one of the nurses informed me that she was progressing better than they had anticipated. She also told me a bunch of other things I couldn't exactly wrap my head around, but as long as she was recovering and there was no sign of any permanent damage, I was happy. I made a mental note to discuss with Justin about throwing a barbeque or a "welcome home" party when we got a finalized date of when she would be released. Mom didn't care much for any fuss or muss, but I, on the other hand, was the queen of throwing parties and events, no matter the occasion.

"I hope everything's alright at home. Have you had a chance to see Amy at all since the last time we spoke?" she asked.

I wished I could say yes, because that was all I ever wanted was to be able to reconnect with my child again, but sadly, I hadn't. I'd even gone around to her work a few times over the past couple of days, and every time she wasn't there. I'd been tempted to speak with one of the managers to see if she was alright, but I didn't want her to know that I'd been checking in on her.

"No, she's been busy," I said. "You'll never guess where Brenda is this weekend though. At a sleepover, where studying is prohibited. You'd think as a parent I'd be over the moon to have her be so dedicated to her schoolwork, but I'm afraid she's going to miss out on everything else if she doesn't let up soon."

"It's part of who she is," Mother explained. "She doesn't know what else to be, or that she can be someone else. With her older sister out of the house, my guess is she's just trying to focus all of her attention on one thing, that way she doesn't have to think too much about it. I'm sure your aunt did the same when I—"

Her eyes widened and she cut herself off, as if she didn't mean to say what she had just said. I could tell she was trying to come up with something else, but her mind had drawn a blank, and she was made.

"When you moved out of the house?" I finished, though I had a feeling she wasn't talking about when she married my father.

"Yes."

"Mom, I have to ask you something, and I want you to be honest with me," I began, nibbling on a baby carrot. "What do you know about Montana's Maternity Home for Unwed Mothers?"

All color drained from her face, and I feared she was going to be sick. She gripped onto the end of the table, digging her nails into the wood, steadying herself. "Where did you hear that name?"

"I'm so sorry," I whispered, shame washing over me. "I didn't know what I was going to find when I looked you up, to be honest, I think a part of me was hoping that I wouldn't find anything, but—"

"It's alright, Marina," Mom rushed, placing a hand on her chest, where she fiddled with the wedding ring on her chain. "It was, um, not the most prideful moment of my life, but I suppose it's made me who I am today. It shaped me into the woman who became your mother."

"So, it's true?" I asked. "You had a child before you had me?"

I was grateful that the nurses had let me take her out on my own, because I was certain she wouldn't feel comfortable confessing her past in the presence of strangers who might judge her. Not that my mother cared much about what people thought, but still, no one outside of our family needed to know her business. This was obviously a secret she had been carrying for some time, and I was a bit humiliated that I had been the one to make her confess.

"It was different when I was the girl's age. A young, unmarried woman carrying a child was a hot topic of conversation, and not in a good way. If the people in town found out that I was pregnant, it would've been a scandal that our family might've never recovered from."

"Did Grandma and Grandpa send you there? Against your will?"

She chuckled a bit, her eyes glossing over for a few moments as she lost herself in the distant memories. "It wasn't so bad, looking back on it now. I was furious at the time, and I'd said a few nasty things to my parents, and it affected our relationship for a few months after the fact, but as time went on, I began to understand why they did what they did. Had I gone through with the pregnancy and raised the child myself, I never would've had the same opportunities that I did. I never would've met Russell, I never would've had you, and that would mean that those two precious angels of yours wouldn't exist either."

I never really thought of it like that until now. It was strange how one simple decision could alter the course of history. That one domino could decimate an entire family lineage, and no one would be the wiser.

"I suppose it's safe to assume that the father is..."

"Dwayne," she interjected. "He was the only other man I've ever been with other than your father. We'd only been together the one time, right before he was deployed, but that's all it took."

I couldn't imagine how terrifying that must've been for her at the time. Not only had she lost her one true love and didn't even know if he would ever make it back alive, but she'd been alone, subject to ridicule and judgment, all for something as beautiful as creating life. It wasn't fair; it still wasn't. I knew plenty of women my age who sneered in a young woman's direction if she was out by herself. It didn't matter if they knew absolutely nothing about her life. Her husband could've very well been at work, at home, or just up the street, but the second their eyes land on a young lady by herself, with a child, they assume the worst. I prayed that my own daughters would never have to be subjected to such hate.

"Did he ever find out?" I inquired. I had my suspicions, but I wanted to hear it from her mouth before I let my imagination run wild.

"No. It was kept very quiet. The only people who knew were my parents and the ladies I spent time with at the house. You know Patricia and Nancy? I have lunch with them from time to time. They were my close friends while I was in the maternity house. Patricia was even my roommate."

"I had no idea," I breathed. So, maybe she wasn't so alone, after all. I was happy to know she'd maintained these friendships and bonds, even after all these years. "And Dad?"

"I never told him. You'll find as time goes by there are just some things that a wife doesn't need her husband to know, and vice versa. It's perfectly normal to carry some secrets to the grave."

"Were you worried that he wouldn't want you anymore? If he knew you had a child before him?"

She sighed and reflected on my question for a few beats before she settled on an answer. "Yes and no. Your father and I had a special relationship, one I viewed more as a lifelong friendship than some magical force of nature. But he was old school, very conventional and conservative, as was his family. I couldn't risk anyone knowing the truth about my past, because it might've taken away from your future, and as a mother, I couldn't let that happen."

"The sacrifices you had to make," I shook my head, at a loss for words myself. "How did you do it? How did you say goodbye to your daughter, knowing that you'd never see her again?"

"It was the hardest thing I've ever had to do," Mom confessed. "I was just happy I got to name her before they took her away. Charlotte," she smiled. "It means free. It was what I was giving her, freedom, a chance to have a better life than I would've ever been able to provide."

"And you never thought to reach out? Not even now?"

"It was a closed adoption, the only thing they told me was that she'd been adopted by a young couple. They told me their names, but... I don't seem to remember them now. I blame my old age."

"Dorothy and Earl Fletcher," I reminded her. "That was all the information I could find from the maternity home."

"She never really felt like mine," Mom murmured, tears pricking her eyes. "I knew from the second I walked through those doors that somewhere down the road, when she entered this world, that I wouldn't get to watch her grow up. I'd never know her smile, or her laugh, or get to witness her first words or her first steps. She belonged to someone else. It was just better for the both of us if I never sought contact."

"If you could see her again, just one time, what would you say? What would you want her to know?"

"That I loved her with my whole heart, and that I never forgot her. That it was my wish that she lived a long and happy life."

I left it at that, as I could tell my mother was on the verge of a nervous breakdown, and I would never be able to forgive myself if I had been the cause. Maybe, just maybe, I might be able to fulfill my mother's wishes, and she could get her chance to see her child once more. I had managed to track down the man responsible, who was to say I couldn't find their love child too?

***

I was right; it didn't take much for me to track down my half-sister. I was beginning to wonder if pursuing teaching was what I was meant to do with my life. I had become an expert in finding relatives with little to no information at all, and I felt maybe sleuthing was more up my alley.

With a little bit of cross-referencing and a trip down to the library to look up Montana's census from the last couple of years, I discovered that just over two decades ago, Charlotte no longer went by Fletcher, her maiden name. She married a man named Cory Tatum, but that was all I could find. With her last known address scribbled down in my notebook, I took the afternoon off work and drove a few hours to a little town called Helena.

Little was an understatement. Helena was the state' capital city and one of the most populated in all of Montana. Growing up in Whitefish, I didn't care much for big cities, fast cars, or skyscrapers. I preferred the simpler things in life, like farmer's fields and knowing everyone in town by name. I wondered if Charlotte even knew her neighbors, if she had any that were close by.

After getting lost half a dozen times, I managed to find the right street and was pleasantly surprised that they had enough grass to be deemed as a front yard. It was still very much a suburban neighborhood, and the houses were so close together you could touch them at the same time. They had young trees that lined the edge of the road, which I figured they'd planted when the houses were first built to liven up the place. I found her house and parked out front, not wanting to be rude and block the driveway, just in case someone was to come home while I was there.

It took me the better part of an hour to muster up the courage to walk up to the front door. Holding my breath, I rang the doorbell and was greeted by a woman who looked an awful lot like my mother. I stood there for a few seconds, my mouth ajar, as I memorized her face. She shifted her weight, visibly uncomfortable, no doubt thinking that I was a crazy person.

"Hi!" I waved, realizing that an excessive amount of time had passed since she opened the door. "Are you Charlotte Tatum?"

"Yes, I am, and you are?"

"Marina Wood, it's a pleasure to meet you." I attempted to shake her hand, but she tucked her hands into her sweater pocket, eyeing me suspiciously. "I was hoping we could talk. Do you have a few minutes?"

"What's this about?"

I didn't even know where to start. How do you tell a person that they're your long-lost sibling on a random Monday afternoon? What if she didn't know that she was adopted? What if this ruined her entire relationship with her adoptive parents, all because I was selfish and wanted to form a connection with someone I'd just learned about only days prior?

This is a mistake. Just turn around, get in your car, and drive home. No one has to know you were here.

Despite the voice in my head screaming at me to leave, I couldn't force my feet to move. I just had to swallow my fears and get on with it.

"Do you mind if I come in? This is a pretty heavy discussion."

"No, I think I'd prefer if we talked out here," Charlotte said. She waved me over to the chairs on the porch, and I sat down in one of them, while she took one as far away from me as possible.

So far, things weren't working out in my favor, but I had to press on. "Your parents, they're Earl and Dorothy Fletcher, correct? And you were born in February 1943?"

I could see that she regretted ever answering the door in the first place. In her defense, I would've too if some random woman I never met before showed up out of the blue and started spewing facts about my life. She must've thought I was some sort of stalker, which, in hindsight, I guessed I kind of was.

"Yes..." she said slowly, twirling her thumbs in repetitive circles. "How do you know all that? Who are you?"

"I know because I know your birth mother, Lucinda Davenport. But she was Lucinda Carney at the time. She's my mother too."

A weight was lifted off my chest as soon as the words left my mouth, but it came rushing back when Charlotte's face contorted with horror and confusion. I realized that I naively assumed she knew she was adopted.

"Birth mother? What are you talking about, my parents are—"

"Earl and Dorothy, yes, I know. They adopted you after our mother had to give you up. I know this is a complete shock, finding out that you were adopted, and I'm not trying to take you away from your family at all, I just—I wanted to know you, even if just for fifteen minutes. I've always wanted a brother or sister, and now I have one."

Charlotte stood up and proceeded to pace back and forth on the wicker carpet under our feet. She fanned herself, though it was useless, as her face had gone beet red, and little beads of sweat trickled down her neck.

"This is crazy," she wheezed. "How could I be adopted and not know it? I have a whole family, a whole life, and now you're telling me that it was all a lie? I mean, what the hell am I supposed to do now?"

"Nothing!" I stood up, hoping to offer her some level of comfort, but she snatched her hand out of my grasp. "I don't want or need you to do anything. This was for me, my selfishness, and I'm so sorry that I brought you into this, but I thought it was only right for you to know the truth. Please, don't blame your parents for not telling you. They probably were doing what they thought was best for you."

"Best for me?" she huffed. "By lying to me? I have other siblings you know. Are they adopted too? And what am I supposed to tell my kids? My husband? This is my family, the only one I've ever known." She threw her hands up in defeat, but something shifted, and her confusion changed into rage. "Wait, you know our mother? Meaning she kept you and not me? How old are you? You don't look that much younger than me."

This was what I wanted to avoid—her feeling like our mother had abandoned her and kept me.

"It's complicated. Technically, we're only half-siblings. She had you out of wedlock, and well, back then she just wasn't able to keep you. I'm so sorry, I know how that must sound, and believe me, she wishes she didn't have to, but she didn't have much choice."

"I'm glad she did," Charlotte barked. "Why would I ever want to have a parent that was capable of giving up their child? I'm certain I was far better off without her in my life, no offense."

"You know what, I think I should probably go," I blurted. Things had most definitely gotten out of hand, and it felt only right to stop things before either of us said something we might regret. "This is my contact information, if you ever want to talk. I'm happy to fill in the blanks if that's something you're interested in. Again, please accept my sincerest apology for dropping this on you."

She let me leave without saying another word, which I was grateful for. I had not only yanked on the thread of my mother's past, but maybe, just maybe, severed it entirely.

Chapter 18

March 2005

"Amy? Amy? Wake up. There's someone at the door."

There was nothing worse than getting ripped from your dream world, especially when it was far more glamorous than reality. I blinked, a lame attempt to ground myself and remember where I was. It took me a few seconds to realize Tommy was hovering over me, pointing toward the motel door. I didn't understand why he couldn't just answer it, seeing as he was already up, but what did I know?

Scratching the sleep from my eyes, I stumbled across the room, nearly knocking over the take-out containers in the process. Luckily, there were just a few scraps from the night before, and nothing that would cause any permanent damage, should it have fallen on the floor. I'd hate to have to pay a fee to have the room professionally cleaned once we checked out.

The second I opened the door I realized that I was standing there in my pajamas. While all my bits and pieces were at least covered, it still didn't leave a whole lot of room for the imagination if you know what I mean. The young man I'd seen a few times at the receptionist desk looked at me up and down before making it glaringly obvious he was staring at my face to avoid a wandering eye. I shut the door a bit more, hiding my body behind it, feeling my face flush an unflattering shade of pink.

"Can I help you?" I didn't intend for it to come across as rude, but the man was standing there at an ungodly hour, waking me from my blissful slumber. I had no patience for niceness.

"Miss Wood, right?" he asked.

"The one and only." *Well, that's not necessarily true, but the only one in this motel*, I thought to myself.

"You have a phone call. We can have it transferred to the phone in your room, but it'll be an additional surcharge, as it's long distance. If you'd prefer, you can take it downstairs, and it won't cost you anything."

"Free option it is," I declared. "Just give me one second to get dressed and I'll meet you down there."

I slammed the door in his face and nearly collided with Tommy, who was only standing a few feet behind me. I scolded him, but he brushed my attitude off, following me into the space we'd deemed our bedroom, though the motel was an open concept.

"Well, what did he want?" he pried.

"Said that I have a phone call waiting for me downstairs," I repeated the man's words, though I was certain he must've heard them himself.

"Did he say who it was?"

I yanked my sweater on and was about to leave when he stepped in my path, crossing his arms over his chest. Something told me he was expecting it to be a call from a not-so-distant lover by the name of Kemp.

"I guess there's only one way to find out now isn't there?" I fired back, hitting him with my shoulder on the way out.

"Do you want me to come with you?" He called after me.

"No!" I shouted.

I felt bad raising my voice, knowing there were probably other people on our floor who were trying to get some sleep, but sometimes, Tommy just got under my skin. Not just under it, he seeped his way into my blood and bones, practically poisoning me from within. Sometimes I didn't know why I was still with a guy like him, but then I brushed a hand across my stomach and remembered that I didn't want to be alone.

I walked up to the receptionist's desk and found him doodling on a few scrap pieces of paper. "Hello? I'm here for the phone call."

"Ah, yes," he fumbled to cover up his pathetic little drawings, which looked a bit graphic in my opinion. "First door to your left. It's a conference room, I thought you might want a bit of privacy."

"Thanks for the consideration," I acknowledged before following his instructions.

I found the room without any issue and put the phone to my ear without even contemplating who it might be.

"Amy Wood speaking, who's this?"

"Oh, thank god," they said.

I recognized the voice on the other line immediately. It had been the bane of my existence my entire childhood, but now that I was away from home for the first time, it brought me an unusual sense of comfort. Maybe Kemp had been on to something when I ran errands with him, and he said that I just needed a little time and space to collect my thoughts before I found my way back to my parents. I thought he'd been a fool for suggesting something so ludicrous, but now? There was a slight possibility there was some truth to his words.

"Mom?" I gasped. "What the h-how did you find me?"

"You'd be surprised who I can track down with a little motivation," she murmured. "I went by your work a few times last week and you weren't there, so last night I asked your boss when you'd be in next because I really needed to talk to you. He said you were taking a short leave of absence from work, and that you were going on a vacation with your college boyfriend. What the hell are you doing in Idaho? You know what, don't answer that, because I think I already know."

"Mom," I groaned. "It's not that big of a deal. Besides, I don't live with you anymore, so you don't really have a say in how I choose to spend my time."

"Please tell me you haven't told Mr. Anderson about your grandmother. Things are really complicated, Amy, this is something you shouldn't be wrapped up in."

My mother had a history of blowing things out of proportion, but now didn't feel like one of those times. Her voice was shaky, and if I didn't know any better, I thought she might be pacing back and forth, which was never a good sign. While she had a neurotic personality, she did know how to keep it together, for the most part.

"What's the matter?" I asked.

"There's been some... revelations since you've been gone. It's adult stuff, but please, just come home and we'll talk about it as a family."

"No." I was putting my foot down on this one. For too long, I let my mother push me around and do what she wanted me to do. If we were ever going to mend our relationship, there had to be some sort of compromise, on both sides. "I'm not a child, Mom. Just tell me what's going on. I can handle it."

"They have a child together," Mom confessed, and I swore my heart skipped a beat. "A daughter. Her name's Charlotte."

"W-what?"

"Dwayne doesn't know. She never told him. She got pregnant just before he left for the war, and she had the baby well before he ever returned."

I had to sit down for that one. Luckily, the conference room had plenty of chairs to choose from, and I picked the closest. I remained silent for a few seconds, nibbling on the corner of my thumbnail.

"Grandma told you this herself? You're not just pulling at strings here?"

"Yes, she told me. My grandparents had her sent to a maternity home when she was a little bit older than you. She had a baby girl, but she had to give her up because she was unmarried, and it would've ruined her reputation in society if she'd kept her."

I was not someone who often expressed their emotions in such a manner, but I felt tears well up in my eyes. I held my stomach once more, running my fingers across my bare skin, closing my eyes and picturing what that must've felt like. I had no idea what the future held in store for me, or my little one, but I knew that I would fight tooth and nail for them, for the rest of my life. There was no chance I would ever give them up, even if the entire world turned against me. I didn't hold a grudge against my grandmother though; if she really said she didn't have any other choice, I had to believe her.

"I've met Dwayne, but he doesn't know who I am, or should I say, who I'm related to. His caretaker doesn't think it's the right time. He recently lost his wife, Connie, and he's still mourning her death."

"Aw, that's awful," Mom sniffled. "Are you planning on ever telling him the truth?"

"Soon, I hope. He deserves to know the reason why Grandma never waited for him was because she never got his letter. Their love was real, Mom. I can feel it in my bones. It doesn't matter if it changes things, he has a right to know. He's a good person, a great person, in fact. I've never met someone so loyal and dedicated in my entire life."

Other than Kemp. The two of them have given me hope that there are good men still out there in the world. Unfortunately, the father of my child didn't fit into that category, and I had no idea what I was going to do about it. At least he didn't know about the baby growing inside of me. No one did.

"Well, when you do, all I ask is that you don't mention Charlotte. I think it might break his heart. Your grandmother was pretty shaken up about it, and she's been the one to hold onto this secret for decades. I just don't think this is something where you should be the one to tell."

"I'll keep it to myself, I promise."

Mom fell silent for a minute, but then I heard a series of sniffles on the other line. "I miss you terribly, Amy. I don't want to go years without speaking to you. I don't want you to shut me out anymore."

Maybe it was the thought of soon becoming a mother myself, but I genuinely felt pity for her. She's raised me, given me a roof over my head, three meals a day, a warm bed to sleep in at night, and anything and everything under the sun. And how did I repay her after years of unconditional love? I ripped her heart out and stomped on it.

"I know you might find this hard to believe, but I miss you too. And Dad, and Brenda of course. How are they?"

"Your dad is trying to remain the strong pillar of the household, but I know he's torn up inside. You were his little girl, and he'll always see you that way. Brenda... she's coping the only way she knows how."

"By burying her nose in books, I presume." I knew my younger sister well. She didn't know how to handle change all that well, and I wasn't making any of this easier on her.

"I know you told me never to ask for you to come back home, but just know that the door will always be open if you decide it's the right thing for you. We love you, Amy, and we just want you to be happy."

"Thanks, Mom," I cried, wiping my snot and tears on the inside of my sleeve. "I love you too."

***

The last thing I wanted to do after that phone call was go back upstairs and pretend like it didn't happen. I knew what Tommy would say, that she didn't have any right to contact me and to go against all of her wishes. He didn't have the greatest relationship with his parents either, and I think he sort of fed off of the negativity in my life. He was like a leech; he latched onto things and wouldn't ever let them go.

I needed to talk to someone who didn't have a personal vendetta against the woman who gave birth to me. Since I was pretty much alone in a new town, such options were limited. But there was no one else I'd rather confess all my sins to than Dwayne Anderson himself.

He was an excellent listener and had years of wisdom and experience to back himself up with. If there was anyone capable of giving me life advice, it was him.

With what little money I had on me, I took a cab to the house and was grateful that the driver let me off, even though I was a few dollars short. He must've seen how red and puffy my eyes were and realized that I wasn't looking to take advantage of him.

I'd just made it up the last steps of the porch when Kemp walked out but stopped in his tracks when he spotted me. We didn't have anything scheduled for today, so there was no reason that I should've been there. I didn't want him to see me when I was such a wreck, but there was little I could do about it now.

"Amy?" He stepped forward, brushing a hand across my shoulder before cupping my cheek with one hand. He brushed a few stray tears away with his thumb and puffed his bottom lip out in a pout. "Is everything alright?"

"I just really need to talk to Mr. Anderson," I blubbered.

"Do you want me to stay and make you a cup of tea? I was just on my way out to run some errands, but I really don't mind—"

"No, no, go, I can manage the tea myself," I assured him. In all honesty, this was a conversation I wanted to have with Dwayne alone. I would feel embarrassed and self-conscious if Kemp stuck around to listen to the worst things I had done to the people who loved and cared for me.

"Are you sure?" I could see it was killing him inside that he had other things to tend to, but more importantly, that I didn't want him around at that very moment.

"Yes. I'll be fine. We'll catch up later, okay?"

With a flicker of hesitation, he walked down the porch steps, looking over his shoulder not once, but twice, before he got into the truck and pulled out of the driveway. I watched him go before I let myself inside, wandering the halls until I found Dwayne sitting in the sunroom out back. It looked like it was going to pour any second now, and the temperature in the air had changed drastically. It was as if the world was embodying how I felt on the inside.

"Amy dear? You don't look like your usual chipper self," Dwayne stated.

I broke down right then and there. It was the kind of cry where your walls come crashing down, your world is shifted, and there's nothing you can do to stop it. I didn't want to; this needed to happen. I'd been bottling up too many things for far too long. I joined him on the wicker bench, nestling my head on his knee, and he proceeded to brush back the hairs from my face, letting me cry for as long and as hard as I needed.

"I talked to my mom today," I confessed, letting out a deep sigh. It felt good to talk about it. "I didn't expect it to affect me as much as it did. I think I had acted like I didn't care for so long I had started to genuinely believe it. But hearing her voice, it just made me feel small and little again, and I missed her more than I ever thought I could."

"The heart doesn't always make sense, take it from me," he admitted. "Sometimes your head will tell you one thing, while your heart says another. It's taken me years to realize that at the end of the day, your heart will always win, so it's best to just give in to it and save yourself the time and effort."

"My heart has done nothing but cause me trouble," I hiccupped.

"How so?"

"I thought I had found love. It felt so real at the time, I was willing to uproot myself and my life just to make him happy. I cut ties with people, both family and friends, just to please him. But now that I've gained a bit of outside perspective, I'm afraid such efforts have gone to waste, at least on someone like him."

"And you're sure it's not true love? You'd be surprised that even the truest, most pure love can still cause you pain."

I sat up straight and wiped my face before hugging one of the couch pillows to my chest. "Is that you speaking from experience? From what you had with Lucinda?"

Sorrow washed over his face, and I felt a pang of guilt that I had brought it up when we were supposed to be focusing on me and my heartache.

"Yes. I know a thing or two about disappointment when it comes to love. I don't hold any resentment though; there's really no point when you're my age. You learn to live and accept the decisions that others have made."

"Whatever happened between you two anyway?"

I couldn't recall my grandmother ever telling me the whole story, just that it never worked out between them. I assumed they simply lost contact because of the war and him never going back to Montana, but I had a feeling there was something else, a tidbit she didn't have or was neglecting to share.

"The war happened," he sighed. "I'm afraid she just couldn't wait around forever, not on the slim chance I'd ever make it back. She had her whole life ahead of her, and what kind of man would I be if I was the one to keep her from doing everything she wanted? Even though she went on to live life without me, I'm happy to know she didn't waste it waiting around for someone as simple and ordinary as me."

"You're a lot of things, Dwayne Anderson, but plain and ordinary are not them. In fact, I'd say you're far from it. You're one of a kind."

He pinched my chin and held it in place, looking me in the eyes and into the depths of my soul. "As are you, Miss Amy, and to hell with any man who makes you think otherwise."

Chapter 19

March 1943

Just as Mother Superior Esme and Sister Elizabeth told me during the first few days of my arrival at the maternity house, my pregnancy had come and gone in the blink of an eye. It felt like one day I was the size of a balloon and feeling my precious little angel wriggle around inside me, and the next, nuns and nurses surrounded my bedside, guiding me through labor.

Luckily, I had a bit of experience under my belt, thanks to Patricia. She had her baby boy only a few weeks prior to me giving birth, and I had witnessed the entire thing firsthand. I'd been by her side the entire time, dampening her face with a wet cloth, letting her nearly break the bones in my hand as she squeezed with every ounce of strength she had inside her, and consoling her once it was all said and done. She didn't even want to hold him, not that I blamed her. He was the product of sexual assault, and although it wasn't the baby's fault, she was still haunted by that night. They whisked him away without trying to change her mind, which I thought was awfully nice of them. You'd think a room full of nuns might try to shove the concept of motherhood down one's throat, but they were surprisingly understanding of a woman's wishes not to see her child before they were put up for adoption.

Sadly, watching her go through all the pain and suffering didn't seem to prepare me all that well for when I had to go through it. What made matters worse was the fact that Patricia had moved out of the house by that point, as she was no longer pregnant, and no longer under their care. It was my understanding that she had moved back to her small town, though she made it abundantly clear that she had no intention of living with her parents again, not after how they treated her when they found out she was with child. I had no idea where she was going to be staying until she could get on her feet and take care of herself; my only hope was that she didn't get mixed up with anyone dangerous ever again.

Thus, the only companion I had at my bedside was Sister Elizabeth. While I definitely didn't have as strong of a connection or bond with her as I had with Patricia, or even Nancy for that matter, I still appreciated her comforting ways. The labor was long and excruciating, but not once did she complain or make a fuss. She hummed sweet lullabies in an attempt to calm my nerves, always kept a dry towel underneath my neck to catch my sweat, and stoked the fire every now and then when the room got too cold.

After two long days, my baby girl entered the world. She was the most beautiful and perfect little thing I'd ever laid my eyes on. I bawled the second I heard her tiny cries, fearing that something was wrong, but the nurses assured me that she was perfectly fine, and it was normal for them to cry. They asked if I wanted to hold her, and I did, but only for a short while. Those 10 minutes of her nestling up underneath my chin and falling asleep were the most precious moments in my entire life. I'll never forget them. But I knew they were doing me more harm than good. I was beginning to grow attached, and that was a dangerous game to play. The longer I held her, the more difficult it would be for them to take her away.

I had no choice but to let her go. I told myself I was doing the right thing, not just because my parents didn't want a daughter associated with such shame, but because I knew I couldn't give her the life she deserved. With no husband, and no prospects of one either, I would never be able to support the two of us. My mother and father were barely scraping by as it was, and I couldn't burden them with my child.

I was beyond grateful that they let me pick her name—Charlotte—and they promised me they wouldn't let her new parents change it.

Just like that, they took her away, and I never saw her again. I cried myself to sleep that night, and despite Sister Elizabeth offering to stay, I shooed her away, wanting to be left alone. She obliged, leaving me to wallow in the most heart-wrenching loss any woman might ever experience.

I had a daughter, but to everyone else, I didn't. I had just gone away on an impromptu vacation for the last several months, or at least, that was the lie my parents had told.

***

"Mom! She's home!"

I had barely stepped out of Father's truck when Edith came barreling out of the house, where she flung herself in my arms. Luckily for her sake I had fast reflexes, or else she might've eaten the dirt at our feet. She hugged me tight, burying her face into the crook of her neck until I practically had to peel her off me. She took a step back, and I got a good look at her. It was as if she'd blossomed into a young woman overnight.

Then again, it wasn't exactly overnight since I'd seen her last, but several months. I didn't expect so much to happen while I was gone, but time stands still for no one.

"Look at you," I breathed, brushing their hair off her shoulder and flicking it behind her back. "You look like a respectable young lady of society now."

"As do you."

She gestured to my stomach, which was no longer bulbous and stretched, but returning to its normal size. I was told by the nuns that it would take a few more weeks before I looked like myself again but wearing loose dresses would do the trick until then. I didn't mind the style of a more relaxed waistline; I think it suited me just fine. I considered adopting it permanently, even though my mother would surely have something to say about it.

Speaking of, she joined us out on the front yard, with Leith in tow. He looked the same as he always did, though a bit cleaner. I figured he'd just had a shower, because there was no way he'd come home from work looking like that. He hugged me too, brushing a gentle kiss on the top of my head. The action alone made me feel like I was home again.

"I missed you terribly," he said. "Talking to Edith just isn't the same."

"Hey!" our little sister protested, sticking out her tongue for good measure. "I can be fun."

"Fun, sure. Wise? Not so much," he teased.

"Now, now," Mother interjected. "Why don't we take this inside before the neighbors start peering out their windows. We don't want to give them something to talk about, now do we?"

Any fool could read between the lines. She was absolutely petrified that one of us might let it slip that I was at a maternity house for unwed mothers, *not* some exotic vacation halfway around the world with some half-cousin no one knew about.

We followed her inside, and I was surprised to see she had set up the sitting room with some tea, freshly made biscuits, and a few other delicious looking treats. I hadn't expected such a warm welcome now, not when I was supposedly off disgracing our family name, but my family clearly missed my company just a tad to go through the trouble. I wish they hadn't, knowing that my loss of income over the duration of my pregnancy must've burdened them more than they were willing to admit.

"What's all this for?" I asked, taking a seat in my usual spot, though it felt strange now. The entire house felt strange, like it wasn't my home anymore.

"What else?" Leith punched my arm, which earned him a quick smack from our mother. He rubbed his cheek tenderly before plopping down next to me, stealing two cookies off my plate.

"I've got to step out for a few hours, so don't wait up for me," Father declared. The room fell silent, and me and Leith exchanged a look, silently asking if he knew anything about Dad's odd behavior.

"I just got here," I blurted. "Don't you want to at least know how I've been? We barely spoke a word the entire ride home."

"I've got work—"

"The mine is closed at this hour," I raised my voice.

"You think that's the only job I've got now?" he fired back.

There it is—I knew it. I just didn't think any of them had the gall to come right out and say it. They blamed me for their shortcomings.

"Frank—" Mother started, but it was no use. She was talking to his back as he walked out the front door. "Pay him no mind, Lucinda. We're all just adjusting to our new circumstances, that's all."

"When can I go see Mrs. Nelson?" I asked.

If things were really that bad around here, I wanted to do my part and help lighten the load. It was the least I could do for all the trouble I had caused them.

"Tomorrow," she confirmed. "She's expecting you in fact. Can't wait to hear about all your travels. Try not to go into too much detail. It'll be difficult to remember them all when you're talking to everyone in town. Best to keep it simple so you can keep your story straight."

"Will do," I said.

Edith disappeared momentarily but returned with a small stack of envelopes. My heart fluttered in my chest as she dropped them into my lap. "These came for you while you were gone. They're mostly from Gianna and Madeline. They came around the house once a week asking when you'd be back. I think there's also one in there from someone named Patricia. Who's that?"

I ignored her question and turned my attention to Mother. "Any from him?"

She knew exactly who I was referring to. She couldn't hold my gaze for more than a few seconds. With a single shake of her head, my heart sank into my stomach. I knew I shouldn't have expected anything at this point, but there was still a small part of me that was clinging to the hope that he might reach out and apologize for his lack of response. It was too late for that now. I had no choice but to pick myself up and move on. Clearly Dwayne Anderson wanted nothing to do with me, and so, I no longer wanted anything to do with him. Pretty soon, his face would just become a distant memory, and if luck should have it, I might find myself someone far more suitable.

One could only hope.

***

Mrs. Nelson was overjoyed when I stepped into the store the next morning. She was not always the most affectionate woman, but she made the exception just this once. With a small peck on my cheek, she pinched the other for good measure, and returned once more to her disgruntled state.

"Do I need to refresh your memory on how we do things around here, or do you think you can manage to catch yourself up as you go?" she questioned.

"I can handle it," I assured her.

She certainly put me to the test. That afternoon, she informed me that she was going to be stepping out for an hour to gather some necessities from our supply shop across town and left me in charge to run things. It wasn't like she hadn't done it before a hundred times, but it still caught me off guard. I took the responsibility quite seriously, not wanting to disappoint her during my first few days back as a single woman out in society.

At least she had assigned only a few simple tasks for me to do while she was gone, including hemming a few skirts for a returning client. I'd been so wrapped up in my work that I didn't hear the bell chime over the door, only the sound of a man clearing his throat to get my attention.

I nearly jumped out of my skin when I saw him standing there. He was attractive to say the least, with his dirty blond hair styled to perfection. He wore a cream-colored suit, which was clearly tailored to fit his body, and not something he merely purchased off the rack. This man obviously knew a bit about style, more than any other boy I'd know, as the colors he'd chosen complimented his complexion quite well. Leaning his elbows onto the counter, he stared at me with his baby blue eyes, and I couldn't help but feel I was standing there naked and exposed.

"Hi," I stammered. "Is there something I can help you with?"

"Fabric," he said. "I need fabric, and I hope that you have some on hand here. I'd hate to have to travel across town."

"What do you need fabric for?"

"Clothes?" he chuckled. "Why else."

My cheeks burned. "I meant what type of garment. A shirt? Trousers? Pocket square? You look like the type that has one for every occasion."

He lifted his chin up, but a smirk played at the corners of his lips. "Oh, do I? And what type is that?"

Rich. Abundantly rich.

"You're not from around here, are you? I think I would remember a face like yours if I'd seen it before."

Once again, he smirked, and I realized I must've boosted his ego with a comment like that. I silently cursed myself for participating in such a flirtatious encounter with a total stranger. I couldn't help myself; he was very charming and made it so easy. I blamed it on the fact that I'd been surrounded by nuns for the last six months.

"You're correct. I moved here a few months ago. My uncle left me his estate and business, and since I'm my father's second son, it was a blessing to be bestowed such a gift. I'm doing my best to not take it for granted, but there are certain perks that come with the title... nicer clothes for one thing. It seems to have captured your attention, has it not?"

He was so forward with his intentions, I didn't know what to make of it. "I take it subtlety is not your strongest suit," I remarked.

"Neither is it yours," he winked. "Tell me your name. I've been in here dozens of times, but not once do I recall seeing you behind that counter. Surely Mrs. Nelson doesn't have a pretty face like you hiding behind closed doors. You attract customers."

"Oh, do I?"

"You enticed me to come inside just now." He waved to the massive windows of the storefront before looking back at me. "I was just minding my own business when I saw you standing there. I dare say I couldn't help myself."

I extended my hand out across the counter, and he took it, planting a delicate kiss on my skin. "Lucinda," I said. "Lucinda Carney."

"Russell Davenport. It's an honor to make your acquaintance, Miss Carney. I do hope to see you again soon, if you'll let me."

Indeed, I had. I told myself I was just curious about this handsome stranger, but deep down, I knew it was something else. Russell was my ticket to getting over Dwayne, as cruel and as selfish as that might sound. Not that he seemed to mind. We'd spent nearly every day in each other's company. He would often come to the shop and get his finest suits tailored, and then later that night, he'd taken me out on the town. I rather enjoyed his companionship. He was funny, energetic, charming, and he knew how to treat a lady well.

I couldn't help but feel like I didn't deserve it, but it was nice to be swept off my feet for once. I tried to not let my heart get too attached though. A man like Russell Davenport seemed too good to be true. There was a chance that I was just some form of temporary entertainment for him; that one day he might wake up and find someone else prettier and more suitable to his needs. He was a wealthy businessman after all and required a wife that would uphold his status, not bring it down. While no one in town knew about my secret affair or child, I still felt like they were judging when they looked at us too long. It was a feeling that would take some time to shake.

Weeks passed and still Russell had not grown tired of me. One night, he surprised me by taking me out to the most expensive restaurant in town. I was grateful I had dressed for such a grand occasion. Quiet nooks in town were more my style, but he enjoyed the finer things in life now that he had the money to pay for it. I told him on numerous occasions he didn't need to impress me with what he had in his wallet, but he assured me it wasn't for my sake, or his own, in fact. His only goal was to build up a reputation so that he might soon settle down and start a family without causing any alarm within the community.

"You look radiant," he breathed, looking at me with something resembling love in his eyes. "You'll make the moon jealous from how bright you shine tonight."

"Oh, stop," I blushed. "You probably stole that line from a romance novel, didn't you?"

"Did not. I just thought of it at the top of my head. That's what you do to me, Miss Carney. You've taken my heart and run away with it."

"Have I now?"

"Yes. And I feel it is only fair if I get the chance to do the same." He wiped his mouth with his napkin before sliding out from underneath the table and onto one knee. I thought both my head and my heart were going to explode.

This is going too fast, a voice whispered in my head.

"Lucinda, you are a remarkable young woman, and I know we haven't known each other for very long, but that doesn't matter when you know something is right. I plan on loving you for the rest of my life. Would you do me the greatest honor by becoming my wife?"

Too fast. This is too fast. But what if you don't get another chance? Russell is an excellent choice, even if he will always be second in your heart.

"Yes."

Chapter 20

June 1943

I barely remembered what happened the night I almost lost my life.

One minute I was deep in the trenches with my brothers by my side, the next, I was waking up in a hospital with nurses standing over me. At first, I thought it had all been a dream, that I would soon wake up back in the horrors of war, but that never happened. I did not take the news well. Some call it shell shock, others PTSD, but for me, it was something along the lines of being thrust back into a world I had seriously contemplated I would never go back to.

They told me I was a war hero, and I didn't quite understand what that meant either. Members of my platoon showed up, the ones who had lived anyway, to pledge their loyalty to me and thank me for saving their lives. I was happy to see Dustin and Mark were among the survivors, and they filled in all the gaps that my mind had forgotten.

"Bullets," Dustin murmured. "There were bullets flying everywhere. One snagged my jacket, but luckily, it didn't break the skin. We were cornered; there was no place else for us to go. It wasn't looking good for us. Some of the other guys had started saying their prayers and clutched the photographs of their beloved wives and girlfriends, desperate to see their faces one last time."

"We were ambushed, you see," Mark continued. He cowered in the corner of the hospital room, visibly shaken. I doubted any of us would be able to truly recover from what we'd seen and done any time soon. "It was like raining death from above. We were just a bunch of sitting ducks in that trench. There wasn't the faintest hope."

"But you got us out," Dustin jumped in. "Took the blow for us by causing a distraction long enough we could escape their line of fire. To be honest, you were as good as dead. It was a noble sacrifice. Granted us enough time to cut the bastards down, once and for all. We weren't able to get to you right away. Sergeant Matthews was worried they'd planted a bomb or a landmine or something, so he had a couple guys from another unit that were trained in that sort of thing to come check it out. Once they gave us the all clear, we all jumped in, not an ounce of hesitation between the seven of us."

"You were buried beneath a thin blanket of dust. There was so much of it, you blended into the snow. You were lying there, so still, we knew you had left the physical world and were watching over us from the clouds, with everyone else we'd lost in the war. A lot of us figured you'd gone and rejoined your dad."

"You had quite a few bullet holes in you," Dustin said. "But there was something in the way your mask had come down over your face, the plastic meant to shield your eyes, it was tucked over your nose. That's when I saw it—you'd fogged up the glass just enough from your faint breath. I thought it was just my eyes playing tricks on me, so I rushed down to your side, pushed some of the other guys out of the way and placed my hand on your chest. Sure enough, it was rising and falling, not by much, but enough for the platoon to spring into action."

"We screamed for a medic to come get you out of there, and they did. They brought you here, and they patched you up real good. You might be missing about five percent of your body when you first left, but I'm sure Lucinda will manage just fine, though the doctors do recommend holding off on any love making for the next couple of weeks, as you're still in recovery."

I slapped my best friend on the wrist for being so vulgar, but the three of us laughed it off. She was the only thing I remembered from that night; whether it was a dream, or a vision, I'd seen her face, hovering in the clouds, telling me that everything was going to be fine, and that I'd see her again soon. I had held onto that dream, and now that I was awake, I couldn't help but feel she'd been partially responsible for me pulling through, despite the odds that were stacked against me.

"How long have I been out for?" I asked. I figured it had been a couple of weeks, if that. My friends exchanged a silent look, and my stomach twisted into a giant knot. "What? Has it been a while?"

"The blast was in February," Dustin said slowly, giving me time to process what he was about to say. "It's now June."

I tried to sit upright, but my entire body ached, preventing me from doing so. One of the nurses who had been fiddling around with some medicine at a nearby table rushed to my side, insisting that I lay back down until the doctor came in to do a full examination. As tempting as it was to try and resist her suggestions, the truth of the matter was that I was exhausted beyond recognition. My bones hurt. My muscles ached. My head pounded, even my blood felt heavy, if that made any sense. The only thing that remained strong and true was my spirit, which never faltered, not once.

"That's almost five months," I breathed. "What's happened since? I mean, the war, is it..."

"Still raging on? Yes. We've made some successes here and there, but our platoon has been discharged. Most of the men have returned home, except your brother. He's around here somewhere. He hasn't left your side since you were admitted. None of us have."

"When can we go back?"

Dustin shook his head. "You've received half a dozen medals for what you did that forsaken night. You're a decorated war hero. They're going to be talking about you for generations to come. But they've also given you an honorable discharge, along with the rest of us. We get to go home, Dwayne. You get to go back to Montana soil, see your girl, marry the poor thing, and have lots of babies, like you've always talked about. Consider this a blessing from above."

"But..."

"You've done your time, my friend." Mark patted my shoulder before giving it a tight squeeze. "Now it's time for you to go live the rest of your life, in peace."

I didn't know what to do or think. All I managed to do was nod, and they left it at that. It wasn't long after the doctor came in and gave me the all clear. I was going home.

Whitefish looked the same, but then again, so different. I believed a small part of it was because I'd been gone for so long, I'd been accustomed to seeing canvas tents, dug out holes in the ground, and filthy men as far as the eyes could see. But not here. Here was clean, vibrant, and full of life. It was only just the start of another summer, but even so, the sun was blazing down on me from above.

I had been in my hometown for all of five minutes, but the only thing I could think of doing was seeing Lucinda's beautiful face. I knew I probably should've gone to see my mother first, as she no doubt was dying to hold her baby boy again, but I'd sent Ethan to go see her instead, promising I would swing by a little later, once I had my blissful reunion with the love of my life.

Still in my uniform, I walked across town, her home the light at the end of the tunnel. The driveway was vacant, so I assumed her father and brother wouldn't be home to welcome me, which was a shame, because I wanted to ask for his permission to ask for her hand in marriage. I suppose it would have to wait one more day. Surely, she could do that for me? After all, we did have a year of distance under our belts already.

I had not made it onto the porch before a tall man nearly plowed me over. I jumped back, cursing myself for still having the jitters, but sighed with relief when I realized it was only Leith. He looked different too; his hair was longer, and he seemed to have filled out his clothes a bit more. He was always so skinny, but I'd seen the way he ate and knew it wasn't from lack of food.

"Can I help you, Mr. Anderson?" Leith asked, nudging me back down onto the driveway and blocking my path with his body. He crossed his arms over his chest and loomed over me, and if I didn't know any better, I thought he might be angry with me.

"I'm here to see Lucinda," I said.

"I'm afraid I cannot allow that."

My throat tightened, and I started to sweat, not just from the heat, but from my increasing anxiety. "What are you talking about? Step aside, Leith. You don't get to decide who she can or cannot—"

"Actually, I can," Leith interrupted. "When my father is not around, I am the man of this house. You're not welcome here, not now, not ever. Don't you think you've caused her enough grief over these last twelve months?"

I shook my head a few times, trying to make sense of what he was suggesting. Lucinda and I, we knew that it was going to be a while until we saw each other again. She'd made promises to me in that first letter, just as I had done in my response. We were on the same page about our love story, so why was her older brother standing in front of me, refusing to let us pick up where we left off?

"I think there's been some misunderstanding here, Leith," I began. "She'll be expecting to see me, especially once word gets around that I'm home. Please, I'm begging you. She's all I've thought about for the past year; she's what has kept me alive all this time. I need to tell her thank you for that. I need to tell her that I love her and that not a day went by that I didn't think about her."

"That's all and well for you, Mr. Anderson, but I'm afraid I cannot say the same about her. She's moved on. She's found someone more suitable to her needs, a respectable gentleman that has devoted himself to her, mind, body, and soul."

"Lucinda!" I shouted, an act of pure desperation. If he was not going to step aside and let me go in, I would do my best to make her come out and face me. I wanted to hear it straight from her mouth that she had moved on. That was the only way I was ever going to believe it. "Lucinda!"

"Enough, Mr. Anderson," Leith warned. "She's not home. She doesn't even live here anymore."

"What?" I blinked. "What do you mean?"

"Did I not make myself perfectly clear? She found someone else. They're married and have been for a few months. She's very happy now. They live in a big house across town, and she has everything she could ever want." Leith paused, composing himself, and even took a step down off the porch and joined me at my level. "I do apologize, I'm sure this must come as a shock to you, and I do want to say thank you for serving this country well, but things are different now. Whitefish is different, Lucinda is different, as I'm sure you are."

I felt like I was on the verge of losing consciousness, but somehow, my legs managed to hold me upright long enough for me to turn around and walk down the driveway. I half expected Leith to chase after me, but he didn't, and instead just let me go.

Let me go. A trait that seemed common in the Carney household. Was he telling the truth? Had Lucinda really forgotten about all the things we said to each other? Did they mean nothing?

I had to find out for myself. I headed back to the downtown district, hell-bent on finding this supposedly big house that she had moved into. I considered stopping into the fabric store and speaking with Mrs. Nelson myself. She would have all the juicy details I needed to work out if her brother was just being overprotective or not.

That was when a beautiful angel caught my eye on the other side of the street. It stopped me in my tracks.

Her. My Lucinda.

Standing there in the flesh, her hair pinned up with pearls and ribbons. She looked so perfect, so ladylike, as if she'd just stepped out of an oil painting. She wore a light purple dress, one of her signature colors, that complimented her skin tone quite well. I was about to throw caution to the wind and dart across the street, even with cars whizzing past us, but I stopped at the last second.

A gentleman stepped out of the ice cream parlor and handed her a cone, and she planted a fat kiss on his cheek. It was not one of mere friendship, or gratitude, but that of love. They laughed as he dotted a snippet of ice cream on the tip of her nose before licking it off.

They walked in the opposite direction that I had just come, not a care in the world. She never even noticed that I had been standing there, not even as I trailed behind them for a mile or two. They were so absorbed in their own little world; it didn't matter what was going on around them. That was when it hit me: this was not the Lucinda Carney I once knew. I supposed that was the god honest truth, she wasn't a Carney anymore; she had a new name, her husband's name, though I had no idea what that was.

I didn't want to know.

Terrified that she might suddenly turn around and find me lurking behind them, I headed for my mother's house and never looked back.

"Mother?" I called out. "Ethan? Are you here?"

"Out back," his voice fell flat.

Something was off in her house too. I didn't notice it at first, only by the time I reached the back porch, and I realized there was a thin layer of dust coating the furniture.

Ethan stood on the deck, his back turned to me, as he stared at the unkempt grass. Mother was a stickler for keeping a well-maintained yard. There was no way she would've ever let it get that bad, not if she had anything to say about it. My heart hammered in my chest. I couldn't handle another loss, not today.

"What's going on?" I inquired. "Where's Mother?"

"One of the neighbors saw me come up to the house and bolted outside. They said she's been placed in a home, down by the lake. They said that she's got some sort of illness, a mental one, and that it got really bad in the last six months. They think it happened sometime after Father's death. She just didn't take it well."

"What are we waiting for? Let's go over and see her and tell her that we're home and that we're going to take care of her."

"No," Ethan said. "They said she won't remember us. She doesn't remember much of anything at all. Not even her own name, Dwayne."

"I don't understand, how can she just—"

"Grief does that to some people, I suppose," Ethan sighed. "It rips you apart from the inside out."

For the first time in my life, I let my emotions get the better of me. I grabbed the bottle in his hands and chucked it at the brick house, where it smashed into a million pieces. My brother didn't even seem the least bit fazed by my outburst—almost as if he expected it.

"Lucinda's married," I blurted.

Ethan's body tensed up. He obviously didn't expect those words to come out of my mouth unless I was talking about the two of us. "She told you that?"

"No." I shook my head. "Her brother. I went by the house, and he met me outside, and basically shooed me off the property. Said something along the lines of she wasn't going to wait around forever for me to maybe come home."

"That's bull. She loves you. I read that letter, there's no way a woman who could say those things would ever just—"

"I saw them in town, just now. Such happy newlyweds. Didn't even realize I was there, even though I stuck out like a sore thumb in a crowd with this uniform on. I didn't recognize her husband. He must be new in town because I've never seen him before. Anyway, I suppose it doesn't matter really. She's married, and all that's left for me to do is move on too."

"I'm sorry," Ethan murmured. "What do you want to do now? Name it, and we'll make it happen."

"I want to leave," I decided. "Whitefish, Montana. I can't stay here and watch them walk all over town, parading their love. That hurt more than the bullet holes did. If I'm going to settle down and start my life, it's going to be somewhere new. Somewhere no one else knows my name."

"When do you want to leave?" he asked.

"Tomorrow. Tonight, we'll stay here, in our family's house, one last time. Should give you plenty of time to take care of ownership, since I doubt Mother will be able to do anything with it before the sickness takes her."

Walking back inside, I headed for my father's study, stopping in front of the giant map on the wall. I swished my finger around a few times before placing it at random.

Twin Falls, Idaho.

It was settled; I would go to Idaho.

Chapter 21

April 2005

"I don't understand why *we* are the ones wasting our time shopping. I mean, isn't this the kind of thing that Kemp was hired for?" Tommy groaned.

I didn't reply right away, as it was taking all of my strength not to turn my head and snap at him. He knew why we were the ones doing it, it didn't take a genius to figure it out, he was just pissed that he was having to go up and down the aisles when he much preferred to spend his time in the motel room or at the bar. In fact, we had barely seen him at all at Dwayne's house since we started the kitchen project; he'd come up with every known excuse under the sun, and I was running out of patience to make him come with me. In all honesty, I preferred the days when he didn't. I felt like I could just be myself without worrying that he was going to make a snide comment about how much of a priss I'd become.

Not that I saw myself as such. I could just hear his voice in my head when I opted for tea instead of something with liquor in it. My only saving grace was the fact that he had yet to notice how much we'd drifted apart since coming on this trip. The last thing I needed was for him to leave me high and dry in a different state.

"First off, Kemp is employed by Mr. Anderson as his caretaker, although that's a bit of an open-ended title. He's more like a companion, I mean, he's more than capable of taking care of his basic needs, but he does get lonely from time to time." I realized I was getting off-topic when Tommy pretended to fall asleep and snored obnoxiously to the point some of the other customers stopped to see what all the fuss was about. "Anyway," I gritted through my teeth. "We were hired to help with the interior decorating of the kitchen. I am working on the design portion of our task, while you're here to be the muscle."

"This just feels like a huge waste of everyone's time. Don't you think? The man's got like what, a few more years left in him before he croaks? What's it matter what his kitchen looks like?"

I gasped, offended that he would ever suggest that Dwayne was going to die anytime soon. Not that I was familiar with his health, but he appeared to be in good shape, for someone his age. Maybe it was because I'd become so attached to him, but I had a hard time picturing this world without him in it. He'd brought such a light to mine, I wanted him to go on forever.

"What's wrong with having something nice to look at?" I remarked. "I wouldn't mind a beautiful house to come home to every night. It would be a step up from that dingy old college apartment we're staying in now."

Out of nowhere, Tommy pushed me up against the wall, his hand coming dangerously close to my throat. "I don't know where this snobbish attitude has come from, but I don't appreciate it. I work hard to put a roof over your homeless head, so it would be in your best interest to show a bit of gratitude instead of turning your nose up at it. Or do you all of a sudden think you're better than you are?"

People can see us, I wanted to scream in his face, but I held my tongue and nodded, hoping that response would suffice. It wasn't.

"Do you think you're better than me? Yes or no. It's a simple question," he growled.

"No, of course not. I'm just a runaway teen without a high school diploma. I'm nothing," I said.

He'd reminded me of it so many times that I had started to believe it was true. After a last long look, he shoved himself off me and returned to sauntering down the aisle as if that didn't just happen. I took a few deep breaths to compose myself and trailed behind him, shoving my trembling hands into my pockets. I refused to look anyone in the eyes as they walked past us, fearing they might take it as an invitation to make a comment on what they just witnessed.

"These ones," I declared, picking up a package of gold knobs and tossing them in the cart. "I think they match nicely with the white and blue paint I picked out. The color will really pop, don't you?"

"If you say so," he agreed. "Does that mean we can go now?"

I exhaled and was just about to roll my eyes at his childish behavior but caught myself just in time. "Yes. I'll meet you at the checkout. I just want to grab a few more bits and bobs for decorations to tie it all together."

"Waste the old man's money, what do I care," he chuckled before walking off.

I didn't see it as a waste. I thought Dwayne might enjoy a few nice additions to his shelves. I had gone around the house and gathered a few trinkets he had lying around, some that would remind him of his late wife and the time they shared in this world, but I wanted to also incorporate a few things that would represent me and Kemp. First, I found a tiny ceramic blue truck, one that looked an awful lot like the one he drove. Then I stumbled upon salt and pepper shakers which were two bluebirds that fit together like puzzle pieces.

That was the two of us. We'd spend many mornings and evenings out on the porch, feeding the birds, and I noticed there were two blue ones that always came back. My hope was that even after I was long gone, he'd see them and be reminded of our time together. I knew I would never forget him or the kindness he'd shown me over the last couple of weeks. The more I realized our spontaneous trip would soon be coming to an end, the more I realized how much I didn't want to go.

***

"These are fantastic, really. You've got such an eye for this kind of stuff, Amy. You should honestly consider making a legitimate career out of it someday," Kemp beamed.

I was not much for relishing in pride, but I made an exception, just this once. It was nice to hear that someone thought I was good at something. I certainly didn't want to spend the rest of my life working at Dunkin' Donuts. I had even started to consider going back to school and getting my diploma. I wasn't sure if I would physically go back to my old high school or figure out a way to take a couple of classes on the side until I was eligible to graduate. Either way, I wanted more out of life than what I had. I couldn't help but feel inspired by my grandmother's past; while she didn't feel like she had the resources or ability to take care of her firstborn child, I had options and could do better, no matter the cost. It was the least I could do for the life growing inside of me.

"Thanks, that means a lot. I really have been enjoying this entire project, even if it is technically a fake occupation," I giggled.

Tommy grunted, and I realized we were not alone and quickly returned to my grungy facade, the one he had helped me build. I could tell it made Kemp uncomfortable to see such a shift in my personality. He busied himself with another menial task, which conveniently took him into another room.

The only thing that brought me comfort was that Dwayne was not home to witness the two of them hash things out. He'd had a doctor's appointment scheduled today, one that was going to take up the better half of the afternoon. When I'd asked Kemp about it earlier, he must've noticed the fear in my eyes as he quickly assured me there was nothing wrong, it was just a routine checkup.

"Why do you have to be such an ass all the time?" I seethed, furiously ripping the tags off of the new kitchen towels I purchased.

"Why do you care if I hurt your precious boyfriend's feelings?" Tommy taunted.

It was always the same fight, over and over again. God forbid I talk to anyone of the opposite sex, he jumped to the worst possible conclusion. Every other time he'd been way out of line, but I couldn't say the same now. Kemp was everything that Tommy was not; he was kind, generous, loyal, charming, and just an overall good person. He was the kind of man that my parents would be more than happy to have me bring home and fall in love with. Kemp was the guy every girl ends up with at the end of the romantic movie. Unfortunately, I didn't see that happening for us. He was *too* good for me.

"Enough," I warned. "We're just friends, not even, we're colleagues in a way. He's been a huge help on this trip, and I would appreciate it if you stopped giving him such a hard time and be nice for once."

"I'm not nice," Tommy stated. "That wasn't part of the job description." Frustrated, Tommy threw down the unopened can of paint and grabbed me by the wrist. "The only reason I'm here is to keep an eye on you, and frankly, I'm getting real sick and tired watching you prance around this place acting like someone you're not."

I tried to yank myself free, but he dug his nails into my flesh and dragged me outside. I swore I almost broke my ankle on the way down the porch steps.

"Stop it!" I cried. "You're hurting me!"

"I don't care!" he shouted. He pulled me in close, our noses practically touching, as he glared at me with more rage than I'd ever seen before. This wasn't just anger or frustration, this was blood-boiling rage, and I had somehow managed to get caught up in the thick of it. "We're leaving. I'm done with this little charade you've built up in your head. We're going home and that's that."

"No!" I barked. "I've come too far to throw in the towel now. I'm so close, and I'm not going to let you take this away from me."

"You don't have any other choice, sweetheart," Tommy said. "I was your ticket to this god-awful place, and I'm also the only way you're ever going to get home."

"Please," I begged. "Don't do this. Not now. Just a few more days, and I promise we'll pack up and go back to Montana."

"You don't get to make any demands!" he roared. "I'm the one in charge here, not you. I'm the adult in this relationship, not you. I'm the one with the car, the money, the place to stay. The only thing you're good for is keeping half of the bed warm at night and that's it."

Hot angry tears welled in my eyes, and I let them fall. Just then, the screen door of the porch swung open, and Kemp stood there, though he didn't say anything. But his mere presence sent Tommy over the edge.

"This doesn't concern you," he grunted. "Go back inside."

"I think I'll stay." Kemp stood his ground, and I envied his braveness. I certainly didn't have any when it came to Tommy, though something resembling courage stirred in the pit of my stomach.

"Leave him out of this." I stepped to the side and planted both hands on my hips, letting him know I meant business. "This is between you and me."

"Ever since you met this guy, you're not the same. He's changed you, not for the better, I might add."

"Oh really? You think him encouraging me to have ambitions and dreams in life will do more harm than good?" I laughed, but it was the kind of laugh that should seriously disturb the person on the receiving end. "I should've known from the second you suggested I move out of my parent's house that you were not right for me. All you want is a sad, naive little girl for you to take care of to make yourself feel better. Now that I'm growing wings of my own, you feel threatened by me."

"Threatened? By you?" Tommy cackled. "You've damn near lost your mind, Amy. I think it's about time you learned your lesson."

He raised his hand, and for a split second, I thought for sure he was going to strike me. Maybe he was, maybe he wasn't, but Kemp didn't give him the chance. He flew down the stairs at lightning speed and knocked Tommy to the ground with one well-aimed punch to the gut. He went down like a bag of bricks, cradling his stomach as he rolled around in the grass. I stared, gobsmacked, not only that he had the strength to knock him down, but that Kemp actually had the gall to hit someone. I didn't peg him as the violent type.

"I want you off this property in two minutes or I'm calling the cops," Kemp demanded, standing over Tommy as he continued to roll around in agony. "And don't you ever raise your hand to Amy again."

"He won't ever get the chance," I muttered.

Kemp looked over his shoulder at me, and we shared a brief moment of silence while Tommy pushed himself to his feet.

"Isn't this cute," he spat. "I knew there was something going on between you two. I'm not an idiot."

"This is your final warning. Leave, and don't ever step foot on here again," Kemp said, using his body as a human shield to protect me from any more stray punches. I nestled in close, feeling comfort from his touch, even if it was just my hands on his back. I knew as long as he stood between us, no harm would come to me.

"Good luck getting home," Tommy scoffed. "And you can bet your ass I'm changing the locks on the apartment when I get home. Your stuff will be thrown in the trash."

"That's fine," I waved, feeling a sense of relief as I watched him back away toward his car.

My only hope was that I'd never have to see his face again, but more importantly, that our child would never have to know him either. I would fight him in court to make sure he never got a single visitation. I could even ask Kemp to speak on my behalf, say that he stopped a physical altercation between us, to show that Tommy was not fit to be a father.

I will do whatever it takes to keep you safe, little one, I thought.

"Maybe our friend Mr. Anderson will get an anonymous phone call tomorrow about how Lucinda's granddaughter has been snooping around his house. I'm sure he'll love that."

I took a step forward. "Don't," I pleaded as Kemp put his hand up to stop me in my tracks. "Don't involve him in this."

"Why not? It's what started this whole mess in the first place," Tommy pointed out. "If we'd never come here, you'd still be serving coffee and donuts, and everything would be as it was. You brought this on yourself, Amy, and now it's time you suffer the consequences of your actions."

With a final salute, he got into his car and sped off. Once his car disappeared out of sight, I fell to my knees, sobbing uncontrollably. Kemp knelt by my side, pulling me into his arms. I didn't fight it. I tucked my head underneath his chin and grabbed a fistful of his shirt and cried. He rubbed my back gently, muttering something under his breath, though I couldn't hear.

Things had really gotten out of hand. The worst part of it was that Tommy was right; it was my fault. We'd taken it too far, and now, people's feelings were going to get hurt, no matter the outcome. What if Kemp and Dwayne's relationship was never the same? All because I was selfish and wanted to mess with people's lives because I was bored with my own.

"We have to come clean to Dwayne," I sniffled, pulling myself free of his arms and looking him in the eyes. "It's the right thing to do. Not just because Ace is threatening to do it himself, but because he deserves to know what we've been doing behind his back."

Kemp nodded. "I know. I've been thinking about it for a few days now. I just... I don't know how he's going to take it."

"I'm sorry I got you mixed up in all this drama," I frowned. "It was never my intention. If I could, I'd take it all back."

He cupped my cheeks in his hands and pressed his forehead against mine. "Don't say that. I'm happy to have met you, and I'm sure Dwayne is too. You brought light and laughter back into the house, and I know we're both better off because of it."

"I'm a walking disaster. I ruin everything I touch. No good will come of this, nothing ever does—"

"Amy," Kemp cut me off. "Those are his words, not yours. They don't mean anything now, not if you don't want them to. They only have power if you let them."

My chin bobbed up and down again, and tears threatened to fall once more, but I fought to keep them at bay. "But what if they're true? What if I was never meant to do anything special with my life?"

"I may have only known you for a short while, but I know with a hundred percent certainty that you will go on to do great things. Just look at what you've done in the short time here. I would really love to be there when it happens, if you'll let me."

I nodded, a smile spreading across my face, and he brushed a quick kiss against the side of my temple. It was such a simple gesture, but it was the glimmer of hope I needed to know that everything was going to work out in the end.

Chapter 22

April 2005

Kemp and I had managed to piece together the last few bits of the kitchen before Dwayne returned home from his doctor's appointment. I was quite proud of our accomplishments, not just because it turned out so well, but because it was the first real thing I had finished in a long time. But with the project now complete, I had no more excuses of why I should be hanging around at the house. Surely Dwayne would begin to question why the interior designer was showing up after her job was done. The time had come for us to break the news to him about my real intentions, and the thought alone made me queasy.

"I grabbed take-out so we didn't have to cook tonight," Kemp said, plopping down a few Chinese food containers on the island. "I hope you're hungry."

"Starved." I nearly started to drool just from the smell wafting from the bags.

Dwayne disappeared for a moment to his bedroom, claiming he needed to change out of his clothes and into something that didn't smell like a doctor's office. With him out of hearing range, Kemp cozied up next to me, his breath warming my cheek from how close he was standing.

"Are you sure you want to do this now?" he whispered. "It's not too late to back out. We can give it a few more days."

"No."

It had to be done. He knew it as well as I did, but I figured he was just nervous about how his old friend was going to take it. So was I, but at least I didn't have as high of stakes as he did. They were so close

Dwayne considered him a grandson, and I couldn't bear the thought of shattering such a bond.

"Alright," he nodded. "But whatever happens, I'll be right here beside you." He squeezed my hand, but at the sound of footsteps returning to the kitchen, he promptly let go.

"Smells delicious, Kemp." Dwayne gulped in a deep breath and sat down at the dining room table. Normally, we'd eat out on the porch, but with the clouds rolling in, we'd figured it was best to just stay inside. "Let's eat."

I loaded up my plate, but my nerves got the better of me, and I found myself unable to swallow even a single bite. I pushed the food around in circles, not engaging in their conversation. It didn't take Dwayne long to notice something was up.

"You wanna tell me what's going on?" he questioned, glancing between the two of us. "Y'all are acting like someone's died."

Someone might once I spill the beans, I thought. "There's something I've been wanting to tell you," I murmured. "I, uh, I don't know how you're going to take it though."

Dwayne sighed and placed his chopsticks down beside his plate. He dabbed the corners of his mouth and knitted his hands together as if preparing himself for a story. "No sense in dragging it out then. Go on."

"Remember when we first met, how you said I looked like someone you knew? Lucinda? There's a reason for it."

"Which is?"

I closed my eyes and prepared for the worst. "I'm not from Idaho, Mr. Anderson. My family lives in Whitefish, Montana."

Although we were inside and none of the windows were open, there was a shift in the air. I was afraid to open my eyes because I didn't want to see the disappointment on his face. But I knew I couldn't hide forever.

"But that would mean…"

"I look like Lucinda because she's my grandmother," I confessed. "I'm so sorry, Dwayne. I didn't want to deceive you all this time, but we were worried that you wouldn't take—"

"We?" He glanced at Kemp, who sank lower in his seat, shame washing over his face. "You knew about this?"

"She showed up out of the blue; I didn't know what else to do. It's been less than a year since you lost Connie, and you're still coming to grips with that. I remembered the stories about this other woman, even if you never went into great detail. I couldn't put you through that, with the wounds of your heart so fresh."

"It's not his fault," I insisted. "I take full responsibility for this little charade. But you need to know that I didn't have any ill-intent on coming here and disrupting your life. There's a reason for all of this."

"Which is?" he said.

"Your letter," I breathed. "It was dated August 1942. I believe it was the first one you ever wrote to my grandmother. Do you remember it?"

Dwayne nodded.

"It showed up a couple of weeks ago. It turns out that she never received it, at least not when you first sent it. The post office was doing renovations or something and found it lost behind an old cupboard. It's been there, in Whitefish, all this time, only a few blocks away from its recipient." I paused, giving him time to follow along so that there wasn't any confusion. "She didn't think you had responded to her love letter."

His face paled, and I was tempted to reach across the table and grab his hand but thought against it.

"So she… she thought… that would explain why… all this time…" he fumbled over his words, unable to form a cohesive sentence. He clenched a fist and held it to his eyes, lowering his head for a few beats before sucking in a deep breath. "All this time, she thought it was I who abandoned her, not the other way around."

"Please don't blame yourself for what happened," I implored. "It was a freak accident."

"Freak accident? I lost the love of my life, all because some fool managed to lose my letter to the woman who stole my heart and never gave it back."

"I know it sucks right now but think about what wouldn't have happened if the letter made it to her. You never would've come to Twin Falls and met Connie. You wouldn't have shared a life together."

"Connie and I were close companions, friends, but we didn't share a passionate love for each other. She knew that as well as I did. What you're telling me is that I could've had my chance to be with my true love, to know life's happiness, and the only reason I didn't is because she thought I didn't love her back."

"But she knows now," I chirped. "She read your letter, and she told me all about you, about your love story. Her feelings were real and genuine back then, you must know that. I'd hate for either of you to never know that there was no bad blood all along."

"It's a little late for that!" Dwayne shouted. He stood up so fast that he knocked the chair out from underneath him. Kemp shot up as well, ready to assist, but Dwayne held his hand up to stop him in his tracks. "I need to be alone. Please excuse me."

I waited for him to retreat to his bedroom before I got up too. "I think that's my cue to head out."

"Where will you go?" Kemp asked. I could see that he was afraid for my sake, and it broke my heart to see him like that. "Ace is probably long gone by now. You have nowhere to stay or sleep for that matter."

I shrugged. "I'll figure it out." *I always do.* "I just know that it doesn't feel right to stay here, not right now anyway. He needs time to process this, and he can't do that with me right around the corner, not when I look like an exact replica of his lost love."

Kemp followed me outside until we reached the road. I looked both ways, wondering which way I should go, but he grabbed my hand, pleading for me to stop. "I can't in good conscience let you go out there on your own. I know you're a strong, independent woman, but you're alone in a state you never grew up in. It's going to get dark soon, and the weather forecast said there might be a thunderstorm tonight."

"What do you want me to do, Kemp?" I threw my hands up in defeat. "I don't have a lot of options at this point."

"Stay the night at my place. I have a loft in my apartment, there's a bed and a bathroom up there that you can have all to yourself. It's for guests anyway, not that I have many friends who stay over. And before you start jumping to any conclusions, I assure you that I am a gentleman, and I will not make any advances on you. I probably wouldn't even if you asked."

I blinked a few times. Any man I knew would jump at the chance to take advantage of a woman. "Why's that?"

"You're vulnerable right now. You're not thinking straight, and I couldn't live with myself if I was part of something you would soon regret when the sun came up."

With no other shining prospects on the horizon, I agreed, grateful that Kemp was the type of guy who wouldn't categorize this as a favor that needed to be repaid in the future. He was simply helping a friend out of the goodness of his heart. It was one of the many reasons why I had started to fall in love with him.

***

It took me a few seconds to realize where I was when I opened my eyes the next morning. So much had happened the previous day, that by the time Kemp brought me back to his apartment and my head hit the pillow, I was out like a light. I didn't even remember if I had any dreams, or if I was just in a state of bleakness. Either way, I'd felt somewhat refreshed.

The smell of bacon wafting from downstairs is what truly roused me. I took a quick shower and changed into the clothes Kemp loaned me from his younger sister. At least we were about the same size. Everything I had brought with me on the trip had been back at the motel, and despite our efforts to go and retrieve them, the receptionist informed us that Tommy had indeed checked out, and the place was cleared out. So not only did I only have less than a hundred dollars to my name to survive on, I had no clothes, no toiletries, and no personal belongings other than what was in my purse, which was practically nothing.

Kemp greeted me with a warm smile as he set the table. "I take it you slept well?"

"Better than I have in ages." I had no idea how nice it was to have a whole bed to yourself again. I'd been sleeping next to Tommy for months and had almost forgotten how good it felt to stretch out and starfish. I was always the one curled up on the edge of the bed, at risk of falling on the floor each night.

"Hungry? I figured it might be nice to have a home-cooked meal for a change. I'm sure you haven't had that in a while," he joked.

"College kids tend to survive off pizza and wings alone," I snorted. "Thank you. This is very kind."

"It's the least I could do."

"No," I shook my head. "You could do far less, and no one would judge you for it. I messed up pretty big, and now I've got to try and piece everything together."

"We messed up. This was a team effort," he reminded me. "Now, eat up. I have something planned for us this afternoon that I hope you'll like."

"What about Dwayne? Shouldn't we go over there and try and apologize again?"

Kemp sat down at the table and poured himself a glass of orange juice. "We will, later on. I know he may come across as a bit brutish and unfeeling, but deep down, he's a softy like the rest of us. He just needs time, that's all."

I left it at that, figuring that Kemp knew best when it came to Dwayne's feelings. "So, where are we going?"

What I really wanted to know is if he was considering it a date or not, but I was much too afraid to come right out and ask.

He smirked, and I remembered how giddy I'd felt the first time he looked at me like that. It felt like almost a lifetime ago after everything that has happened between us. "You'll see."

***

"An art museum?" My eyes lit up as we walked inside and paid for our tickets.

They weren't expensive, so I didn't feel too bad that Kemp had offered to pay for mine. This was his idea, after all.

"I thought it might be nice for you to do something other than design a kitchen while you were here in Idaho. I know you don't like to talk much about your passions, but I've seen the way you talk about colorology and what things work and what don't. I think underneath all that teen angst you're an artist at heart."

He wasn't wrong about that, I just never expected he'd be able to work it out for himself just from the way I looked at things. Art had been the one thing I loved consistently throughout my childhood and teenage years, and I missed the studio back at the high school. While I had explored many different avenues of expression, I still had a soft spot for clothing design, as it always made me feel close to my grandmother.

"You know, you're much more perceptive than you let on," I mused.

We walked around the first room, and I stopped at every painting to admire the work, just as it deserved. A lot of the pieces were from local artists, and I let my mind wander a bit, dreaming that one day that could be me if I tried hard enough. Kemp let me take the lead on the museum tour. Most of the time, I caught him looking at me instead of the artwork, and I was going to comment on it, but I was afraid he might stop if I pointed it out. I rather enjoyed the way his eyes sparkled when they were looking at me.

"Can I ask you a question?" I said.

"You can ask, I make no promises on whether or not I will answer," he chuckled.

"Is this what you had pictured for your life?" We stopped in front of a black and white painting, and I felt particularly drawn to it. There was something about the heavy contrast that made me feel like it was a reflection of my life. "Taking care of Dwayne and working at the rec center?"

"Not necessarily, but I don't mind doing it if that's what you mean. I enjoy helping people, and I feel like seniors are often neglected members of society. People tend to forget they were our age once, and how debilitating it can be to lose basic functions. Not to mention how lonely it can be when everyone around you starts to pass away."

"If you could do anything, or be anything, what would you do?"

"Something in the realm of what I'm doing now. I don't know if there's a specific field in mind. I never really thought about going to college. It just wasn't in the cards at the time."

"Why not?"

"It's expensive, especially if you don't know a hundred percent what you want to do. Until I decide, I'm perfectly content with where I am in life."

"I'm beginning to regret dropping out of high school," I confessed.

I had never said it out loud, but it was something that had been weighing me down for a while now. Ever since I bumped into Olivia, and she was telling me all about her school project. It made me realize how much I was missing out, and for what? So I could work a dead-end job that didn't bring me any joy or happiness? For a man—no, a stupid boy—just because he thought it was a good idea? I ruined what might be the best years of my life over one impulsive mistake. While I still had months to go before my little one made their entrance into the world, I couldn't help but feel I was running out of time to get my life back on track.

"So, why don't you do something about it?" Kemp suggested. "There are tons of ways you can obtain your high school diploma. You don't have to go back and start over if you're afraid of what people might think."

I nodded and rested my head on his shoulder, letting out a deep sigh. "I think I just might."

We walked the rest of the museum, twice, even though we technically weren't supposed to, before we hopped back into Kemp's truck and headed for Dwayne's house. My legs bobbed uncontrollably, even with Kemp reaching over and placing a hand on my knee in an attempt to calm my nerves. I just didn't want him to hate me for what I had done.

I was tempted to tell Kemp to turn around and go back to his apartment, but when he pulled into his driveway and turned the ignition off, I knew it was far too late. Especially since our old friend was seated on the front porch and could clearly see us.

"It's gonna be fine," Kemp assured me. "You have nothing to worry about."

We walked up to the house, hand in hand, and I could've sworn I saw Dwayne smile at the sight of us. I lingered behind Kemp, holding onto his bicep with my other hand like I was a scared little girl.

"I just made a pot of tea," Dwayne said. "It's inside the kitchen if you want to grab a cup."

"Sure, that sounds lovely. Amy?" Kemp glanced down at me, raising an eyebrow. "Do you want anything?"

"Tea sounds nice, thank you."

Kemp disappeared inside, and I stood by Dwayne awkwardly, looking anywhere but at him. Dwayne chuckled as if amused by my discomfort, but quickly put me out of my misery. "Have a seat Amy, I don't bite."

"That's not what I'm afraid of," I grumbled, sitting on the opposite side of the sofa.

"I don't hate you either. I know you two were just looking out for me because I'm an old man and you were worried about how I might react to such… earth-shattering news, but I promise I'm fine. In fact, I'm better than fine."

"Oh?" That piqued my interest. "You're in better spirits than yesterday?"

"You could say that. I hardly slept a wink last night because I was up thinking about it. And you know what my mind just couldn't let go of? Love. Such a complex concept, but at the same time, the most simple and pure thing any of us will feel in our lifetime. Love is not something to trifle with; to be able to feel it is a blessing all on its own. But the strange thing about love, about real love—the kind that sweeps you off your feet or takes the breath right out of your lungs—it doesn't expire. Years could pass you by, decades even, and you'll still feel the same way as you did when you first fell in love. It's beautiful, isn't it?"

"I'll have to take your word for it," I sighed. "I've never had the chance to feel something so strong yet."

"You will," Dwayne acknowledged. "I can see it on your face, you're a lover not a fighter, despite what others might think."

"So, what do you plan to do with this realization?" I asked.

"I want to see her again, my Lucinda," he proclaimed. "I know that a love like ours will never truly die, and I'm determined to put it to the test."

Chapter 23

December 1943

Our lives had forever changed from the moment that we found out our family of two would soon become a family of three.

Russell had his fingers crossed for a boy, as it would mean an heir to pass his new legacy onto. I, on the other hand, was secretly hoping for a girl. She would certainly never replace the daughter I had to give up, but at least it would give me the chance to do right by her... wherever she was in the world. At the end of the day, we knew we would be happy as long as our child was happy and healthy.

The day I told him that we were going to be parents, he rejoiced and made it clear that I would be halting all responsibilities outside of the home. It was his belief that a mother's only duty was to her children, and since he made more than enough money to provide for our little family, my job at the store was no longer required. I didn't exactly agree with his philosophy, but I didn't argue with it either. My entire childhood I watched my mother dedicated herself to both, and we turned out just fine. Then again, it wasn't something she had much of a choice over; it was either that or we starve.

It brought me a sense of comfort knowing that I would never have to struggle the same way my parents did, not with Russell as my husband. I felt awful to think such things as his fortune was not what drew him to me, but I considered it a happy bonus.

Despite the wondrous news that I would be a mother, again, the days that followed were not all rainbows and sunshine. In fact, the weeks that followed were consumed by grief and despair. I knew Russell had picked up on my melancholy state, he just wasn't sure what he was supposed to do about it.

"Lucinda dear," he called out from the bottom of the stairs. "Why don't you come down for some breakfast?"

In the last two weeks, I had only come out of my bedroom a handful of times. I recalled a familiar sickness in the first part of my last pregnancy, but this was different. I wasn't just queasy from the child growing inside of me, but from the incredible amount of guilt that this time around, I would have the love and support that every woman needed during this time in her life.

"I'm not hungry," I shouted back.

I heard his footsteps pad up the stairs, and knew I was in for it now. He meant well, I knew he did, but that didn't make it any less annoying when he fluttered around like a mother hen.

"Sweetheart," he sighed, slipping into the bedroom and plopping himself down on the edge of the mattress. "You must think of our baby. You need to eat, to keep up your strength. Your mother said these first few months will be the hardest, but you just need to think of what we'll get once this is all over."

I wanted to tell him that I was quite familiar with how this process worked, as I had been through it before, but clamped my mouth shut. No one was ever to know about the shame I once brought upon my family, not even the man I had vowed to spend the rest of my life with.

"I'm tired," I yawned. "I need sleep. Food will have to wait."

"No, no, no." He stood up and grabbed both of my hands and hauled me into a sitting position. "You will put something in your belly first and then you can come crawl back into bed. Besides, your mother stopped by an hour ago and brought over your favorites. When I told her the other day that you weren't eating much, she said she hasn't been able to sleep a wink since."

"You told her?" I groaned.

Even though I was no longer her obligation to care for, she was the type of person who would bend over backward for someone if she was able. I only wished she could've gone to such lengths with my first.

Maybe then none of this would've ever happened. I seriously doubted that Russell would've wanted me for his bride if I had a baby on my hip, and it would've been slim pickings for a place of work. But maybe I could've done it, if only I had the choice.

"She's your mother, of course I confided in her about how her daughter's been feeling. She raised three children of her own, she's been through this before. I was beginning to worry myself; I didn't know what else to do. I'm not familiar in this department."

"It's not so bad," I said. "This feeling will pass, you'll see."

"How can you be sure of that if you don't eat?"

I merely shrugged, as I didn't have the energy to debate back and forth anymore. I let him take me by the hand and guide me downstairs, not bothering to change out of my sleeping gown.

My mother definitely delivered. The sweet smell of strawberry turnovers made my mouth water, and I was grateful to see not an egg in sight. It was one of the things I couldn't stomach with my first pregnancy, and she must've remembered all the foods I had craved last year. Anything with strawberries. The gesture made my heart swell, knowing that she went through all this effort when she has so much on her plate already.

With me gone, Edith was forced to pick up the slack, and I couldn't help but feel a pang of guilt that she was robbed of the rest of her childhood because I had become a wife.

"Sit, sit," Russell urged. "I'll make you a plate."

"Just a few things to nibble on, please. I don't want to overdo it and make myself sick. I'd hate for this to go to waste."

He obliged, placing a strawberry turnover and a few pieces of sausage on my plate before pouring me a cup of tea. It seemed my unborn child could smell the delicacies in front of me, as my hands moved to shove a forkful in my mouth before I could even give it a second thought.

I must've been hungrier than I thought.

Russell helped himself too and settled himself in the chair beside mine, placing a hand on my knee underneath the table. It was one of the many ways he showed his affections—through something so simple as a touch. I appreciated it, as the thought of being wanted and safe was all I ever truly wanted from a man. That, and perhaps a response to a love letter.

"I had an idea that I wanted to run by you first," he disclosed. "I was thinking of hosting a little party here at the house this weekend, with some of your closest friends. I'll do all the arranging, I'd just need your pocketbook so I can get everyone's contact information to send the invitations, but that's it."

"A party?" I pinched my eyebrows together, curious why he had the sudden urge to host an event. My husband was not much for frivolous things, despite the new reputation in town he had. "So close to the holidays? Do you think that would be wise?"

"It won't be anything extravagant. Actually, your mother had been the one to plant the seed in my mind. She mentioned that sometimes women get together before a baby is born and they bring gifts and share stories about motherhood. I know not all of your friends have had the pleasure of bringing new life into the world, but I thought it might be nice to uphold the tradition."

"As long as you don't make too much of a fuss, I don't see it being a problem," I mused. "It's been some time since I've seen some of my friends, I think it would be fun. Everyone's been too busy with their own lives and marriages, it feels like we've grown up overnight."

Russell kissed the side of my head and gave my knee a gentle squeeze. "That's what happens, my dear. Now, I must head out as I have a lot of work to tend to today, but you eat until you feel like you cannot take another bite and go get some more rest. Might I suggest even taking a bath to pamper yourself?"

"I'm not sure I'll have the strength for that, but eating and sleeping is something I can handle," I replied.

He kissed me once more, this time on the mouth. "I love you, Mrs. Davenport."

"I love you too."

***

Russell had indeed organized the impromptu gathering, with the help of Edith and my mother. They prepared the food, while my husband took care of everything else, from pulling out the fine china he'd inherited, along with some cute and cozy decorations to liven up the place. I hadn't done much of it myself since we married, mostly because I didn't see the need. Our house was fine enough as it was and spending extra money on something as silly as candlesticks or silverware just felt... impractical.

I was finishing up with the last few touches of my makeup when I heard some of the guests start to arrive downstairs. I heard my mother's voice echoing through the halls, so I knew she would handle the greetings while I put myself together.

"Knock, knock," someone called on the other side of my door. I recognized Edith's voice. In typical sisterly fashion, she didn't wait for me to give the okay but helped herself inside my room, regardless if I was decent or not. "Oh good," she said. "You're dressed. That would've been awkward."

My sister had recently acquired an affinity for a bit of an attitude, though I found it rather hilarious. My mother did not.

"I'm almost done, I'll be down in a minute."

Seeing that it was the first time she'd ever been upstairs at my house, she wandered around the bedroom, poking her nose into everything and anything in sight. I didn't bother to protest, as we didn't have anything to hide.

"There are quite a few people downstairs, all here to celebrate you and your baby," Edith said. "How are you feeling?"

I glanced at her in the reflection of the mirror and could tell by the look on her face she wasn't asking about my symptoms, but rather, how I was processing this all the second time around.

"It's a new and wonderful experience," I gritted through my teeth. "I'm grateful that I'm not going through it alone."

"This time," she murmured.

"Careful," I warned, whirling around in my chair at the vanity so I could properly scold her. "Someone might hear you and that would be difficult to explain."

"Sorry," she apologized. "I'm just worried for you, that's all. I overheard Mother talking to Father the other night. She said sometimes pregnancies can make women do and say crazy things, things they regret. You're not feeling anything like that, are you?"

"Just hungry, tired, and sick," I chuckled. "It's sweet that you're concerned about me, but you really don't need to be. I'm fine."

She nodded, putting an end to our conversation. "I guess I'll just wait for you downstairs with all the other ladies. Did you know that Russell even invited Mrs. Nelson?"

I had no idea who he had arranged to come to the party. He was in charge of it all, not me, so it was surely going to be a surprise. I figured it was just going to be Gianna, Madeline, and my relatives, but apparently not. Edith disappeared, and I quickly finished, not wanting to make anyone wait for the guest of honor. Once I was ready, I headed downstairs and was slightly overwhelmed by all the faces staring back at me in the sitting room.

Mother must've lent a hand earlier this morning to put up a few decorations. There were several trays arranged on the tables with little finger sandwiches, meats, and cheeses. They'd even brought up a few bottles of wine from the cellar, not that I could stomach the stuff myself.

"There she is!" Gianna shrieked, jumping off the sofa and wrapping her arms around my neck. "I can't believe you're going to be a mom!"

"I know what you mean," I giggled. "I can hardly believe it myself."

My eyes landed on another familiar face—one I never expected to see again; at least not in a formal situation like this.

Patricia flashed me a cheeky smile before quickly brushing her index finger over her lips, a subtle indication that she had every intention of keeping my secret, or should I say, our secrets. It didn't make sense what she was doing there though; the only contact information I had of hers was from her last known address before our stay at the maternity house, and she'd assured me she had no intention of going back there. Russell must've reached out to every woman he could find in my pocketbook. I started to sweat, nervous that he might've learned something that he shouldn't.

"You're positively glowing," Madeline chimed in, nudging Gianna to the side so she could get her turn at a hug. "You look beautiful as always, Lucinda, perhaps even more. You know what they say, it might mean that the little one is a boy!"

"Why's that?" I asked, sitting in the cushioned seat in the corner of the room. There was something about this pregnancy that made me not want to be too close to other people; the thought of touching anyone for more than a few seconds other than my husband made my skin crawl.

"Daughters steal their mother's beauty, even in the womb," Mother explained. "Sons have no need for looks, so you get to keep it all for yourself. For a little while, anyway, until you start to age like the rest of us."

"Don't listen to them," Mrs. Nelson interjected. "You've still got a ways to go before you sprout any gray hairs or wrinkles. Besides, that's what makeup is for."

We laughed and spent the rest of the afternoon sharing stories from when we were kids, and the older generation bestowed their parental wisdom, which only seemed to frighten me more about the prospect of having a child myself. We ate, drank, and ate some more, or at least I did. I was beginning to move past the sickness stage and had headed straight for the blind hunger that I somehow could never settle. After opening a few handmade gifts, which I shed a few tears over, most of the group said their goodbyes, which I was secretly grateful for. I was not all that experienced with being a hostess, and the thought of entertaining for more than a few hours tired me out.

"Please tell your husband thank you for thinking of me," Patricia said, briefly planting a kiss on both my cheeks. She looked down at my belly, which didn't look like much at this point, but she rested her palms on it nonetheless. "You are lucky, little one. Your mother is a remarkable, strong woman, and you will be blessed to have her watching over you for the rest of your life."

Tears welled in my eyes, but luckily, they didn't fall. With one last hug, she departed, and all that were left was Gianna and Madeline. Well, my mother and sister were puttering around the house too, but they were more preoccupied with tidying up than engaging in conversation.

"That was nice, wasn't it?" Gianna acknowledged, nibbling on a few scrap pieces of cheese before my mother took the plate into the kitchen. "You're so posh now, hosting afternoon tea parties and lady brunches."

"Oh, hush," I waved my hand in her face. "You'd do the same if Dustin could afford such luxuries and you know it."

"Fair point."

"How is married life treating you? Is it everything you dreamed it would be and more?" I asked.

My best friend was always a bit of a wild child growing up, and none of us actually thought she'd commit to someone. Dustin was different though; he challenged her in ways no man ever could, or would. They were a great match. I was overjoyed when I heard that he had come back to Montana after being discharged from the war, though that was the extent of such knowledge. I told myself time and time again that I didn't care to know any other details, but deep down, I'd been dying to know if he'd returned alone or with anyone else that we knew.

"Better than I could've imagined," she beamed. "We're not exactly ready to start having kids yet, and I'm glad we're on the same page about that. There's a few more things we want to do together as a couple before we start our family."

"Oh?" I tilted my head to the side. "Like what?"

"Travel. He's got a few places on his list. He's been itching to stop in Idaho ever since—" she cut herself off, and it didn't take a genius to realize that she'd let something slip.

"What's in Idaho?"

Madeline and Gianna exchanged a look. Bile started to rise in the back of my throat, and it took great effort to force it back down. I didn't like where this was going.

"Not a what, a who," Madeline murmured. "We weren't sure how to tell you. We didn't know if you'd be interested to hear about it to be honest, now that you have Russell."

"Interested in what?" I seethed.

"It's Dwayne, Lucinda," Gianna confessed. At least she had the decency to not beat around the bush anymore. "He made it back home, shortly after Dustin and Mark arrived. Apparently, he came back with his brother, but they didn't stay in Whitefish long."

"He moved?" I asked. "But why?"

"Dustin didn't tell me too much. I don't know if he promised Dwayne he wouldn't divulge his whereabouts, or if he just genuinely doesn't have all the details, but I believe he mentioned something about his mother moving into the old folk's home across town. She's not doing too well. Doesn't even know her own name anymore, much less who her kids are. They sold the family house and left Montana behind."

I was overcome with an unusual mixture of emotions. Relief, to begin, that I wouldn't randomly bump into him in the street while walking downtown. Confusion, as I had somewhat convinced myself that he'd been dead all this time. But mostly, I felt anger, and betrayal, that he had been alive all this time and didn't even think to come and see me before he left. Didn't I at least deserve an explanation? Did he truly think so little of me that he thought it was better for the two of us if he just pretended like I didn't give my whole heart to him, only for him to rip it to shreds the first chance he got? Rage simmered in the pit of my stomach, threatening to boil over if I didn't get it under control. I reminded myself that this was how it was meant to be—that we were just two people who once loved each other, but not anymore. Besides, I had Russell now, and he was a great husband. I didn't have to worry about him running off and leaving me behind.

"Good for him," I huffed.

Gianna grimaced. "So… you're fine with this? Even though he never replied to your letter?"

"What letter?" I replied, and she took that as a hint to never bring up his name in my presence again.

Chapter 24

"Are you sure you don't want to come to the supermarket, honey?" Justin asked. "I don't mind waiting a little while until you're done."

"No, it's fine, go on ahead without me. The flower beds out front are in desperate need of pruning, not to mention that I have to get a head start on the vegetable seedlings for the garden out back. I've got lots to do and not a whole lot of free time to do it."

"Is there anything specific you need me to pick up for dinner?" He followed me into the garage, where all my gardening tools were perfectly organized.

"I made a list. It's on the fridge. Make sure you get the snacks and stuff for Brenda; you know how she gets. She calls it her brain food."

Justin frowned. "Ah, so she's back at it again with the all work and no play? I thought for sure that weekend with her friends was going to do the trick and make her realize we don't expect her to be a shining student if she doesn't want to be. We were average people and look how we turned out."

"I was not *average*," I gasped. "I was at least a little above. You, on the other hand, almost didn't graduate because you were failing two of your classes."

"It wasn't from lack of trying. I just didn't like the teacher, and he clearly didn't like me. When it came to exam time, I had the highest score in the class." He smirked as if that was a proud accomplishment, which, in a sense, I supposed it was. "Now look at me—I work in a prestigious position at one of the top banks in the world."

"You do this family a great honor, Mr. Wood," I giggled, planting a fat kiss on his lips, which turned into a bit of a heavy make out session before I broke it up. The last thing I needed was to traumatize our daughter if she caught us fooling around in the garage.

"Alright, alright, alright, I will get the list and check it twice," he cooed. "If I do a good job, will there be a reward for me in the near future?"

"Only if you get everything I asked for," I teased. "Now go, you've got other things to do today other than wander around a grocery store for hours."

He bid me farewell, and after grabbing my shovel, weeding tool, and wheelbarrow, I headed out to the front yard first to assess the damage.

I cringed a little on the inside. I was rather fond of the garden I had, as it took me years to not only hone my skills, but to figure out what plants I wanted and where to put them. Some did not do so well close to others, so I had to be mindful of that when tentatively choosing my annuals and perennials. It was a labor of love, one I didn't mind getting my hands dirty for.

Metaphorically speaking, of course. I had a cute pair of gardening gloves because I hated the feeling of dirt beneath my fingernails.

Humming to myself, I was so wrapped up in the pruning process I didn't hear the car pull into my driveway. It wasn't until the door slammed shut that I realized I was not alone.

"Back so soon, honey?" I called out, yanking at a tough weed that just didn't want to give. "Did you forget something?"

"I don't think I'm who you think I am," a woman replied.

I whipped my head around and saw the last person in the world I ever expected awkwardly standing at the edge of my lawn.

"Charlotte?" I exclaimed. "What are you—"

"I'm sorry for just showing up like this, unannounced," Charlotte said. "But, in all fairness, you had done it first, so it only seems right that I get a turn."

She made a valid point.

Charlotte shifted her weight from foot to foot and refused to hold my gaze for more than a few seconds. If I didn't know any better, I thought she might be on the verge of a nervous breakdown, but since I didn't know her all that well, it was difficult to make assumptions based on one ten-minute conversation. I felt somewhat responsible for her current anxiety; had I not gone out of my way to reach out to her and reveal such a life-altering situation, she would not currently be so... afflicted.

"Can I offer you something to drink? I just made a fresh batch of lemonade."

"Sure," she nodded frantically, happy that I was taking charge of the conversation. "That would be great, thanks."

I offered her a seat on the porch while I ducked inside and poured us two glasses of lemonade. I wished I had something else to offer, but since Justin was currently out grocery shopping and we didn't have much more than a box of crackers in the house, the drinks would have to suffice. When I returned, she was muttering something under her breath, and her leg was bouncing up and down as if she needed to relieve herself.

"Here," I said, handing her the glass, to which she took a generous sip. "Better?"

"Much," she said. "This should be the other way around, shouldn't it? I am the older sister, after all. Isn't that how it goes? I'm meant to be taking care of you."

"I'm not the best judge of how sibling relationships are meant to go. I was raised as an only child, the only close sisters I know are my two daughters."

"You have children." She said it in such a way that it almost sounded like it could be a question, not a statement of fact. In her defense, the only thing she knew about me was my name and that we shared a mother. Everything else she would have to learn over time.

"Just the two: Brenda and Amy. Amy's the oldest, and Brenda the youngest."

"Are they here?" She nudged her chin to the house, but I shook my head. "I have three. Two boys and a little girl. Lucas, Oliver, and Emily. The boys are the oldest, and my little girl, well, she's the baby of the family. She's only eight, and they treat her like a princess," she chuckled. "My oldest is in his first year of college. Time sure does fly, doesn't it?"

It felt strange how natural the conversation felt. While it surely started out as awkward and uncomfortable, I found it easy to talk to her about my kids, and vice versa. I wondered if it was simply because we were technically each other's families, and there *shouldn't* be any awkwardness between us.

"I'm hoping Amy will end up there someday, but I guess it doesn't matter if she does go or not. As long as she follows her dreams, that's all I could ever want for her."

"Uh oh," Charlotte mumbled. "That sounds like something a parent would say when they've had a falling out with their kid."

"That obvious, huh?"

"I only know from experience. Lucas was dead set on joining some rock band and touring the world with his friends, but I managed to convince him that would be a poor decision. It took him a while, but he eventually found his senses and enrolled in college classes days before the deadline. He's the happiest he's ever been. Sometimes we have to be a little tough on our kids. I'm sure your daughter will come around, too."

"I'm not so sure. She takes after her grandmother. Those two are stubborn as mules sometimes."

Charlotte flinched. I regretted my words the second they left my mouth, but it was too late to take them back. "About that," she began. "I guess that's kind of why I'm here. But you knew that, I'm sure."

"I pieced it together when I saw you standing there. You looked like you'd seen a ghost."

"I've been in a bit of a daze ever since you showed up at my house last week. I can't say it didn't come as a shock to learn that I was adopted. My parents, my adoptive parents, they never told me. Even now, I'm not sure why they didn't. I have my suspicions, that they were afraid they might lose me when I was old enough to go out into the world on my own or just that they didn't see the need. From what they told me, I became their child the day I was born, so in a way, I've always been theirs."

"I don't know much myself. I kind of went behind my mother's back and found you on my own. She still doesn't know that I went out there to talk to you. I think she's ashamed about what happened. It was a dark time in her life."

"I can only imagine," Charlotte agreed. "Not even my parents know why she gave me up. The maternity house doesn't divulge that kind of information, for privacy reasons I assume. Since it was a closed adoption, there was no need for them to ever contact her again after the fact."

I remained silent for a few beats, wondering if I should ask her what I wanted to or not. "Do you want to know the reason? Or would you prefer to remain in the dark?"

Her face twisted, but it wasn't of anger or remorse, but something along the lines of curiosity. "You know?"

"She wanted to keep you. It broke her heart that she had to part with you, but she'd convinced herself that it was the only way to be able to give you your best chance. She'd gotten pregnant from a soldier who had just been deployed overseas and didn't even find out until a couple of weeks later. Unfortunately, since they were unmarried, my grandparents were worried what people might think or do when they found out she was with child. It wasn't exactly an acceptable thing for a young woman to raise a child without a husband. So, they sent her away."

"That's awful," Charlotte sighed.

"That was just how it was back then, I'm afraid."

"My parents were furious when I asked them about it last night," Charlotte confessed. "They're pissed that my birth family reached out without their consent. They said you never should've been able to find me. They were even threatening to go to the maternity house and give them a piece of their minds, but I talked them out of it."

I didn't know what to say; I understood their fears, and if we were younger and she was still a kid, it would make sense they'd want to protect her. But we were all grown up now, with families of our own. They had nothing to worry about. They would always be her family, no matter what.

"I hope they know we're not trying to take you away from them, or that we're trying to tarnish their roles as your parents. They are your family, they're the ones that raised you as their own."

"They don't exactly see it that way. My mother has somehow fabricated these crazy ideas in her head that my birth mother is going to swoop in and jeopardize the relationship we have. I told her that was ridiculous, but there's no convincing her otherwise."

"You know, the human heart is capable of expanding to make room for more people in your life. Even if you do decide to be present in her life, or mine, it won't take away from the love you feel for them."

Charlotte frowned. "I wish she'd see it that way."

"She just needs time. We all do; this is not exactly something that happens every day, and it'll take a while before we're all adjusted."

"I hope so."

Before we could dive deeper into our conversation, a van pulled up in front of the house, and I recognized the driver. She was the mother of one of Brenda's friends. My daughter jumped out, and in an instant, I knew something was wrong. Her face was blotchy, her eyes red, and cheeks tearstained.

"Honey?" I chirped, meeting her down in the driveway, where she threw herself in my arms and proceeded to sob. "What's happened? Are you alright?"

Jennifer's mother rolled the window down, her face riddled with concern. "Something happened at school, they wouldn't tell me what though."

"Thank you," I said, wrapping my arms around Brenda's shoulder and guiding her inside. "I'll be inside in just a minute, okay? Mom just has to say goodbye to her friend."

Brenda, horrified that I wasn't alone, shielded her face with her hands and disappeared through the front door, slamming it shut.

"I suppose that's my cue," Charlotte observed. "I hope you won't mind if I pop over again sometime in the near future. I think it's safe to say we have a lot more to discuss."

"You know where I live."

I didn't even wait for her to leave before heading inside to see what damage control needed to be done. I followed the sound of heavy sobs and found Brenda curled up on the sofa, wrapped in one of my mother's knitted blankets. She hugged a pillow to her chest, and I couldn't help but think back to when she was in grade school and some of the kids wouldn't let her play with them and how utterly devastated she was. Something told me this was something a bit more extreme than that.

"So, are you gonna tell me what's wrong or am I gonna have to tickle it out of you?" I giggled, motioning to grab her at the waist, but she shoved me off.

"I'm not a kid, Mom," Brenda huffed.

"No, you're not, but it's still my job to cheer you up. Tell me what happened, honey. Let me fix this for you."

"You can't!" she cried. "No one can!"

"Is this because of a bad grade or something? Because if that's the case, I'm sure we can talk with your teacher. It can't be that bad, you're always studying, so—"

"It's about Amy," Brenda admitted.

I wasn't expecting that, nor was I truly prepared to have that delicate conversation. Then again, after what just went down between me and Charlotte, I supposed I could handle anything right about now.

"Oh?"

"I overheard some of the older girls in the grade above me talking about her outside their lockers. I wanted to ignore them, but I just couldn't this time. I told them they had no business talking about my sister like that, or in any regard, but they just laughed in my face."

"There will be bullies wherever you go, sweetheart. It's best to not engage with them, only if they're doing something that might actually hurt someone."

"They hurt me," Brenda said. "They didn't just laugh or call me names. They said some really dark stuff about her, Mom. I can't help but wonder if they're telling the truth."

"What did they say?"

"That she's trashy. That the only reason she dropped out of school was so she could sleep with her college boyfriend whenever she wanted. They said she's going to wind up a teen mom if she's not using protection. Am I going to be an aunt before I've even graduated high school?"

I'd felt like I'd been hit by a bus with what she was throwing at me. I exhaled a deep breath and tried to dissect her fears one at a time. "First off, your sister's not trashy, or sleazy, or any other synonym that might pop in their little heads. She's just... having a bit of a tough time right now. She's not like everyone else, she doesn't follow the rules of society like you or me. She's one of the rulebreakers, and there's nothing wrong with that. She'll find her way back home; I know she will."

"Before or after she becomes knocked up?"

"It doesn't really matter, now does it? We'll love her regardless of what happens."

I won't let her turn out the way my mother did. I won't follow in my grandmother's footsteps. I will love and nurture her, even if the world's against her because that's what decent parents do.

"Why couldn't she just be like everyone else?" Brenda blubbered. "Then they wouldn't have anything mean to say about her."

"If it wasn't your sister, they would find some other poor victim to antagonize. Those girls will never be happy until they're tearing someone down. Take it from me, they're not worth your time, energy, or tears."

Brenda sniffled, but I sensed that she was listening to my words and letting them sink in. My only hope was that she wouldn't have to suffer too much at these girl's hands; I made a mental note to send a word to their principal about their rude behavior.

"What if she doesn't come back?" Brenda asked. "I don't want to grow up without my sister. I want her there for everything. I want to see her face in the crowd when I walk across the stage and get my diploma, when I go off to college and when I get engaged. I don't want her to miss out."

"She won't," I assured her. "You know, I spoke to her just a few days ago. It was a nice conversation, might I add. Neither of us yelled. I think it was the first time we'd actually listened to each other without jumping down the other's throat. It's a sign, honey, a sign that better things are on the horizon."

"If you say so."

"Why don't you go upstairs and have a nice hot shower? Wash away those girl's nasty comments down the drain and be done with it. Dad will be home any minute with groceries, and I'll make us some dinner and we'll just hang out and watch movies. How does that sound?"

Brenda's face lit up, and I breathed a sigh of relief that I was able to at least put out one blazing fire. The rest would just have to wait.

Chapter 25

April 2005

When Dwayne had told us that he wanted to return to Montana so he could speak with my grandmother after decades of silence, I didn't know what to expect. Declaring that we were to leave the following morning, well, that wasn't it. But who was I to stand in true love's way? If that was what they had all those years ago, I supposed it would still be true now, regardless of the lost time between them.

"Are you sure you've thought this through, Dwayne?" Kemp asked, handing his old friend clothing options while he frantically packed.

I'd never seen him so spry. It was as if he'd had a new fresh breath of life pouring out of him. He took over on closet duty, clearly having a set idea of what he wanted to bring in mind. He sifted through his dozens of hanging shirts and trousers, stopping only briefly when he came across his old uniform. It had been cleaned since the last time he'd worn it, but you could tell just from a quick glance that it was well used. Parts of the fabric were tattered and torn, and if I didn't know any better, I thought I spotted a couple of bullet holes in the jacket.

"Yes and no," he chuckled. "It doesn't matter much now; my mind's made up. I'm doing this, Kemp, and you're either with me or you're not."

"Where you go, I go, you know that." Kemp slapped a hand on Dwayne's shoulder and gave him a firm nod, indicating that no matter what happened, no matter the outcome of this spontaneous adventure back home, he'd be there to see it through until the end.

I couldn't help but feel a sense of pride for my new friend. Sure, I had gone on a similar journey only a few weeks ago. Traveling out of state with my rude and vile boyfriend was not something I had ever considered doing until I learned of their story. It was strange, how much their love affair inspired me to do something crazy and wild. I'd done my fair share of chaotic things in the past year, things that would surely bring on a wave of disappointment from my parents, but this… this was something I was incredibly proud of. For the first time in my life, I felt like I was a part of something bigger, something blessed by the universe. And who knew, when it was all said and done, maybe it would be my turn for an epic love story next. I could most certainly use a bit of tender romance in my life.

Looking at Kemp, I motioned with my chin that I wanted to speak to him in private in the other room. Luckily, Dwayne was much too occupied in selecting a pair of shoes to notice our brief absence.

I tiptoed down the hall and dipped into the front hall, the furthest from his bedroom. "What's up?" Kemp asked, picking up on my unusual behavior.

"Do you think I could borrow your phone really quickly? Don't tell Dwayne, but I think it's only right that I call my mom and let her know of our impending arrival. I'd hate to give my grandmother a heart attack because she couldn't prepare herself."

Kemp's eyes widened, no doubt from the sudden fear that he might be partially responsible for an old woman's departure from the land of the living if this all went south. He fished out his cell phone and handed it over, nudging me out onto the porch, where I wouldn't be seen or overheard.

I paced back and forth for a minute or two, clutching the phone in my hand, wondering how I would even begin to tell her what we were up to. The last time we had spoken, she'd phoned the motel, and by the end of the call, I'd felt like maybe things were on the brink of settling between us. The last thing I wanted to do was be the cause of our downfall, again. I just had to be honest—that was all I could do at this point. Besides, this was not a decision I had planted in his head. Dwayne had decided it all on his own, we were just helping him see it through.

With my heart pounding in my chest, I dialed the house phone and prayed that she was there to pick up. It rang three times, and someone answered.

"Hello?"

I thanked the heavens above that someone had been listening to my prayers, that it was her and not Brenda.

"Mom?" I replied. "It's me, Amy."

"Amy? Oh my goodness. I didn't recognize the number. Are you alright? Is everything okay?"

"We need to talk about, you know, the situation at hand. Dad's not around, is he?"

"He's downstairs on the treadmill, he can't hear us." I could tell she lowered her voice just a bit, in the odd chance that he *could*. "Should I be worried?"

"I'm not sure, to be honest. It's uh… things have taken quite a turn here in the last twenty-four hours."

"Is Mr. Anderson unwell? Oh no, Amy, I'm not sure you should stick around to witness that if he is."

"No, no, it's nothing of the sort. So, funny story, he knows who I am now. I told him the truth about everything, about the letter, about how Grandma never received it until only a few weeks ago, and that all this time she thought he'd abandoned her, and that was why she married someone else."

Mom remained silent on the other line for a few beats. "You didn't tell him about…"

"No!" I rushed. "No, absolutely not. I kept my word about that, and I intend to keep it that way. I only told him about the parts that I'm involved in."

"How did he take it?" she asked.

"Not well at first. I suppose it was to be expected; how would you feel if you learned the love of your life was only a piece of paper away? Not to mention the post office is what, a couple blocks away from her house? His dedication was sitting behind some dusty old cupboard all these years and she was none the wiser. Then, out of the blue, he's told that was the only real thing standing in the way of his happiness. He was crushed, devastated, every synonym you can think of."

"I can't say I could ever speak from experience on something like that," Mom whispered. "Your father is my soulmate. We've never been separated, not since we first started dating way back in the day. Our love has never truly been tested quite like theirs has, and I hope it never will."

I, myself, was a rookie when it came to love, too. I had been so convinced that what I felt for Tommy was love that I was willing to bend over backward just to hold onto it. Oh, how foolish that turned out to be. The only good news was the fact that I'd probably never have to see him ever again. I'd considered lying about the baby growing in my tummy. My luck, he wouldn't even want to be part of our child's life, even if he knew they existed. But that was a problem for another day; right now, all I had to worry about was getting my mother caught up on the drama that was currently our lives.

"We're leaving for Montana in an hour or two. We just have to stop at Kemp's apartment so he can get his stuff, and we're headed on the road. I know that's not a lot of time—"

"Today?" Mom gasped. "No, no, no, that's too soon! Your grandmother is going to have a coronary if he shows up and confesses his love."

"I know it's not ideal, but it's happening, whether you want it to or not. We knew this going in that things would soon be out of our hands. We messed with people's lives, not just yours and mine, but generations and other families. There was bound to come a point where we would just have to let things unravel as they were meant to. We've done our part, Mom. We shed light on the situation, now all that's left is to stand back and see what they make of it."

"I guess I should've expected this," Mom murmured. "I just wished we had more time to prepare, that's all."

"They've had decades to come to terms with their feelings," I pointed out. "And no offense, but they're running out of it as each day comes and goes. If they want to spend the rest of their time on earth together, who are we to hold them back?"

"I know I don't say this often enough, but I'm very proud of you, Amy, of the young woman you've become. You know that, don't you?"

A small smile tugged at the corners of my mouth. No, I didn't know that. In fact, I had convinced myself that I was the perpetual disappointment of the Wood household, and that no matter what I did in the future to make up for the mistakes of my past, those decisions would haunt me forever. But maybe they wouldn't. Maybe this unexpected trip down memory lane was not only favorable for Dwayne and my grandmother, but for the rest of us too.

"You have no idea how long I've waited to hear you say that," I sniffled.

"Well, the good news is, the stars must've aligned last night for this all to come to an end. I just got off the phone about an hour ago with the hospital, and your grandmother is being discharged this afternoon. She's in perfect health again, although she is advised to take it easy, so as to not wind back up there any time soon. She'll be back at the house by the time you arrive."

"See!" I beamed. "Fate works in mysterious ways."

"Let's hope it's fate bringing them back together and not something else. I'll be seeing you soon then, Amy. Drive careful. I love you."

"I love you too, Mom."

She hung up and I held the phone there for a few extra seconds, listening to the beep before clicking off myself. The words had come out so naturally, I didn't even have to think about it. I knew I always loved her, she was my mom after all, despite our falling out. But I hadn't said them out loud all that much, not even when we'd bump into each other from time to time around town.

I was counting on the fact that their offer for me to be able to come home anytime was still on the table, because I had every intention of cashing it in.

***

"Are you sure this is the right road?" Kemp questioned. I could hear the skepticism in his voice. "Here, let me have a look."

He tried to reach into the backseat and snatch the map out of my hands, but my reflexes were far superior than his. In his defense, he was also trying to keep one hand on the wheel so we didn't end up in a ditch.

"I don't think so!" I said. "Your job is to drive, mine is to direct. Besides, I've made this journey once before. I sort of remember the way back."

"Sort of brings me no comfort."

Dwayne chuckled in the passenger seat but did not involve himself in our little marriage spat. He must've known from experience to just let these things slide, for the good of everyone's sanity. He was a smart man; Kemp, on the other hand, still had much to learn. I was more than happy to help teach him about the ways of womanhood and which hills to die on. Directions was not it.

"We're already halfway there and we've had no issues," I pointed out. "Consider me a master at reading maps."

Kemp scoffed. "Um, I do recall a slight hiccup when we were trying to find the right exit on the highway. We almost ended up going south, not north."

"Okay, I steered us off course for a moment," I confessed. "But that's it. The rest has been smooth sailing."

"You know what," Dwayne piped up. "I am getting a bit hungry. I saw a sign for a truck stop just up ahead, why don't we—"

The truck made an awful noise, followed by an intense jerk that felt like we were being ripped off the road. Kemp gripped both hands on the steering wheel, frantically looking in all mirrors to make sure we weren't just hit by someone else.

"What in God's name was that!" I shrieked.

I felt my heart sink to my stomach. I didn't have many phobias or fears, but I most definitely didn't want to perish in a car accident before getting the chance to live my life. Reflexively, a hand flew to my stomach, acting as a shield for my child. I hoped none of them noticed.

Smoke billowed out from underneath the hood, and while I didn't know much about cars, I knew for a fact that wasn't ideal. Kemp cursed under his breath but remained calm and in control as he steered us off the highway and into the truck stop parking lot that Dwayne had just mentioned. He turned the ignition off once we had come to a full stop, and I breathed a sigh of relief when I noticed the smoke had begun to dissipate. At least that meant there wasn't something actively on fire and that the truck was about to blow up.

Dwayne cleared his throat, grounding us both back into reality, as we tried to make sense of what just happened. "Well, I guess the universe heard that I wanted to stop for lunch."

I forced out a laugh at his remark, mostly because I was still pretty wound up from the adrenaline of almost dying. Kemp, realizing that I was in a frozen state of shock, reached into the backseat and grabbed my hand, giving it a firm squeeze.

"We're alright," he stated. "Why don't you get out and go for a bit of a walk, shake the nerves off."

I liked that suggestion. Slipping out of the truck, I wandered around the parking lot, and within a few short minutes, I felt like myself again. I parked myself at one of the picnic benches on the grass, where a few families were scattered about, eating their packed lunches before heading back onto the road again. I remembered my parents used to do the same thing when we'd take a trip anywhere, not that we ever did any cross-country travels back in the day, at least none that I recalled.

Kemp headed over, but I could tell by the way he was shaking his head that things didn't look too good.

"I come with bad news," he grumbled. "Looks like we might be here for a while. I don't have the right parts on hand to fix what broke underneath, nor do I have any tools with me to even take it off. I was thinking of calling a local mechanic, or a tow truck, but I don't have a phonebook either, and neither does the truck stop. The waitress said my best bet would be to wait around for a few hours and see if anyone shows up for a hot meal, but that's our only option at this point."

"I have a better idea," I interrupted.

Flashbacks burned in the back of my eyes, when I was packing up my room that fateful night, before I left the house for good. My dad had come to say his goodbyes, and when he hugged me for what he must've feared would be the last time, he said no matter where I was in the world, or what time it was, if I called and ask for him to come get me, he would drop everything and make it happen. I wondered if our situation would qualify in his books. The only thing I could do was try.

"Care to share?"

My eyes flickered to the phone booth at the side of the building, knowing he had run out of minutes on his phone just as we were leaving the house. I held my palm out and said, "Got a couple of quarters I could borrow?"

He gave me a sufficient amount I needed to call home and was gracious enough to let me do it on my own. I supposed it wasn't technically a private conversation, but still, the gesture alone made my heart flutter. It was that kind of instinctual kindness that had me flailing head over heels for Kemp. I was beginning to think it was becoming much more than just a silly little crush, and something far more raw… and dangerous.

This must've been some sort of new record, I had now called home not once, but twice within the span of a few hours. Dropping the coins into the machine, I held the filthy phone to my ear and waited.

"Woods residence, how may I help you?" he said.

I always found it funny how he answered the phone; it must've been a hard habit to shake after years of working at the bank and talking to clients.

"Dad? It's—"

"Amy?" His voice cracked like he was on the verge of tears just from me saying a single word. "Your mother said—"

"I'm coming home," I breathed, my chin trembling just a bit, but I composed myself, feeling exposed with all these families around. "Well, I'm trying, but we've run into a slight issue."

"Uh oh, that doesn't sound good. Anything I can do to help?"

"Actually, yes, that's why I was calling. Remember the night I moved out you said that if I ever needed your help, you'd drop everything to make it happen?"

"Say no more," he declared. "Just tell me where, and I'll be there as fast as I can."

I loved my dad for his promptness, not to mention the fact that he was always a man of his word. I figured that was one of the many reasons why my mother fell in love with him in the first place; he was not only reliable, but loyal to a fault, and today, I was beyond grateful for those things.

Since he was still a couple of hours away from us, we decided to make the most of our unfortunate situation and grab a bite to eat. Dwayne said he'd cover for us, as that was the least he could do to repay us for accompanying him on this adventure. I told him that repayment was not necessary, but he wouldn't take no for an answer.

With our bellies full, it didn't take much longer before I recognized my father's SUV pulling into the truck stop. As if I were a young girl again, I dashed outside, tears spilling from my eyes as I launched myself into his arms. He hugged me tighter than he ever has before and brushed a kiss on the top of my head, just like when I was a kid and had come home from school.

"I've missed you so much," I muttered, wiping my tears on his jacket before pulling away and fixing myself up.

"Oh honey." He cupped my cheeks with both hands and frowned. "Words will never be enough to explain how much I've missed you."

"So, this must be the man of the hour," Dwayne bolstered, raising his arms above his head in gratitude. "Thank you for coming to our rescue."

"And you, the writer behind a famous letter I've been hearing so much about," Dad winked. "And this gentleman is?" He nudged his chin to Kemp, who awkwardly lingered behind us.

"Kemp," I introduced. "He's Mr. Anderson's caretaker. He's joined us for the long haul."

"Pleased to meet you, sir." Kemp shook his hand before taking a step back. "I'll have to let you two go on ahead without me, though. I really should stay back with the truck and figure out a way to fix it or get it out of here."

"Don't worry about your truck, young man," Dad assured him. "I have a couple of clients at the bank that I work with, and I called in a favor. I gave them our location and they're on their way now to come pick it up and bring it back to the house."

"Oh, but sir, I can't—"

"The cost is covered." He slapped a hand on Kemp's back, in typical fatherly fashion. "I told you, it's a favor. I'll always take care of my girls, and my girl's friends, so today, that includes you."

"Thank you," Kemp sighed. "I appreciate your help."

"What do you say we get back to Whitefish then, shall we?" Dad suggested. "Mr. Anderson, your chariot awaits."

"I like you," Dwayne laughed. "You remind me of one of my old friends, Dustin. He was sharp as a whip too."

"Yes, I'm familiar with his antics," Dad said.

Dwayne stopped in his tracks. "You are?"

"Of Mr. Burton? Of course. He and my wife's mother knew each other quite well, they both grew up in Whitefish, but I suppose you already know that. He's still around, as is the other one..."

"Mark Sherman," I remarked.

"Wow." Dwayne's eyes lit up, as if he were transported back in time to when he was a teenager, and everything was pure and right in the world. I'd never seen them sparkle like that before, only when he spoke of my grandmother. "I can't believe it. They'd come to visit me a few times after I moved to Idaho, but we lost touch over the years. I'm happy they're still kicking around."

Dad smiled. "I'm sure they can't wait to see you again. It's about to be one hell of a reunion."

Something deep inside told me that was the understatement of the century, but we were about to find out.

Chapter 26

April 2005

It felt as if I'd traveled through time. I made a vow to myself all those years ago, 62, to be exact, that I would never step foot in Whitefish again. It was to remain in my past until the end of my days, but here I stood, at the west end of town, where some of my greatest friends once lived.

It looked different, but not by much. The trees were taller, more luxurious at the top, offering plenty of shade to the houses here. They too, looked different, the white picket fences now gone, and only vibrant green lawns remained. The Woods' house was beautiful, both on the inside and out, as Mrs. Wood took me on a lovely tour of their property. She was quite proud of her garden, which reminded me of my own mother before the war. What happened to her after her boys and husband left, well, it changed her, and she never recovered.

A few years after my brother and I settled in Twin Falls, we received a call from the home she'd been staying at that she passed in the night. It was the best death I could've asked for—nothing painful or frightening. I wondered if she'd dreamed of my father that night, kind of like I had when he died in battle. Were they reunited once more? Were they watching over us? I had faith that they were and that they were happy wherever they might have ended up. They deserved it more than anything. My mother had been a strong, remarkable woman, caring for Ethan and me all those years, while my father worked tirelessly to financially support us. We struggled as a family, more than I would ever truly admit to another person, but it somehow brought us closer together. Not a day goes by where I am not thankful for all the sacrifices they made for us growing up.

Going back to Montana stirred a lot of feelings, things I was prepared to take to the grave. I was beyond overwhelmed, but I put on a brave face, not wanting to concern my hosts, who had been beyond helpful in getting me settled. They refused to let me stay at a hotel in town, and graciously offered up their guest bedroom for me to sleep in while I stepped into the next chapter of my life. I wasn't exactly sure how long I'd be staying in Whitefish; I hadn't thought that far ahead in the game. I guessed it all depended on how Lucinda was going to react to my unexpected arrival.

If she made it abundantly clear that she wanted absolutely nothing to do with me, then I supposed I had no choice but to go back home with my tail between my legs. I had no idea if I would ever recover from losing her not once, but twice in my lifetime, but it was a risk I was willing to take for another chance at love.

She was worth it. She was back then, just as she was now.

If only I had fought a little harder when I was discharged from the war, perhaps we could've saved ourselves six decades of lost love, confusion, and heartbreak. I'd felt a pang of guilt even thinking such thoughts, knowing what it would've meant for the life I shared with Connie. But as much as I had loved and cared for her in my own way, it was nothing compared to what I felt for Lucinda. It wasn't even in the same galaxy. Our love existed across all universes; I mean, it must have, for how strongly I felt after just that first night of talking to her. The weeks we shared were some of the best in my life, and I would cherish them forever. There was nothing she could do or say to me now that could ever take that away.

While my fears of rejection weighed heavily on me, I knew there was a slight possibility that it would work out in my favor. I knew I had hurt her deeply, not intentionally of course, but I hurt her all the same. I couldn't imagine the pain and suffering she must've endured during those months of silence, wondering why I had not responded when she poured her heart and soul into that letter. It broke my heart just thinking about it, but now that I knew the truth about what happened, it was my job to make amends. If it were the other way around, I hoped that she would have the decency to do the same.

"Dwayne?" Kemp's deep voice broke through my thoughts, viciously yanking me out of the past and bringing me back to the present. "How are you feeling?"

It was just him and me at the house, as the rest of them had gone ahead to bring Lucinda back from the hospital. I was told that she'd been there for weeks now after having a bit of a fall and injuring her hip. I had so many questions to ask, but they assured me that she was in the best care there and that it was more of a precaution than anything else due to her age. I reckoned as long as she was not in any real pain, I should just take their word for it, but my nerves had been unsettled since.

"Fine," I said.

Kemp made a face. "You don't need to lie to me. I know you better than that."

"Alright, I'm terrified. But admitting so out loud is pointless, so I'm trying not to think too much about it."

"It's gonna work out," Kemp murmured. "I know it in my heart."

"Since when are you such an expert on love? Could it possibly have something to do with a remarkable young lady that's been staying with you ever since that daft imbecile left—what was his name again? Ace? Who even name's their kid that?"

Kemp laughed, letting his shoulders relax. "I thought the same thing at first, and when I asked Amy about it she said it's a nickname. Something to do with his expertise at poker."

"Ah." That explained it.

"But to answer your question," Kemp continued. "There's nothing going on between me and Amy, at least I don't think there is. We haven't really talked about it. I don't want to rush her into anything, not after just getting out of a relationship. I would hate for her to think I was taking advantage of her when she's in a vulnerable state. Not to mention she's in the middle of trying to get her life back on track with school and with her parents—"

"Oh, boy." I shook my head, knowing all too well what he was feeling at the moment. "You've got it bad, son. Take my advice: don't wait 60 years to come clean about how you feel. It'll save you a lifetime of anguish."

"I don't know what you're talking about," Kemp muttered.

"You will." I paused, deciding now was probably not the best time to be dissecting his love life when I was in the midst of salvaging my own. "I take it you know where I'm supposed to be going to meet her?"

"Ah yes," Kemp recalled. "Marina wrote down the address. She figured since you lived here when you were a kid you'd be able to find it no problem."

I swore my knees buckled slightly when I read the piece of paper. I chalked it up as my old age catching up to me, but I knew in my heart it was something else. "Are you sure this is correct? I was told that she moved to—"

"It's right," Kemp said. "She lives in her parents' house. After her husband died, she sold their estate. Amy said that the size was just too much for her to maintain by herself, and all she really wanted was to go back to the place she grew up."

I couldn't help but smile at the thought that she got to go back to the place where we fell in love. I would've thought the house would have gone to Edith, her younger sister, but there might've been a million reasons why that didn't happen. It didn't matter much now—my heart would lead the way.

***

As I stood at the edge of the driveway of her parent's old house, I felt tears prick my eyes. I remembered the last time I stepped foot on the property. Before I even made it up to the front door, her brother had come barreling outside and demanded that I leave. I didn't understand why he'd been so harsh at the time.

For the most part, he and I were on good terms. He knew how much I cared for his sister, how much it tore me apart inside that I had to leave to join the army. There was only so much I could do at the time. It wasn't like I could simply back out of my word. I had already enlisted before we were properly introduced, and I'm a man of honor and code... not to mention it was somewhat of an obligation of all men— young and old, unless they had a viable excuse—to serve their country with pride.

He was different that day; I could've sworn there was hatred in his eyes, and I didn't think Leith had a hateful bone in his body. He wasn't like all the other young men I knew. He was one of the good ones. He'd made more sacrifices back home than some did fighting overseas, and that was saying a lot. It just didn't make sense to me why he would be so harsh and hostile, especially after I had confided in him just days before I left that I wanted to spend the rest of my life with Lucinda.

I wondered if he ever told her that we'd met and talked about what the future held. I supposed he didn't, as that alone might've swayed her to stick around and wait for me, with or without a letter. He probably did what he thought was best for his family at the time, and I couldn't judge him for that. I only wished that he would've given me a chance to explain myself, maybe then things would have worked out between us. I didn't care if she was married to another; our love was strong enough that we would have found a way.

Go back, a little voice in my head said. I didn't know where it had come from, but I was tempted to listen. *Save yourself from a world of hurt and turn back before it's too late.*

"No," I muttered under my breath. "Only cowards run when things get tough. I've faced far worse than this."

Not wasting another minute, let alone a second, I walked right up to the porch and rang the doorbell, ignoring the sick feeling growing in the pit of my stomach. I heard shuffling inside the house and prepared myself mentally to lay eyes on the only woman I ever truly loved with every piece of me. The door swung open, and I let out a small breath between my lips realizing it was only Marina.

She smiled at me, as if she were pleased to be in on a little secret, before waving me inside. "She's in the sitting room. It's just down—"

"I know where it is," I chirped. "I've been here before."

Marina snapped a finger, our conversation from earlier returning in the blink of an eye. "Right, of course, how silly of me. Well, we'll be out back if you need us. My husband thinks it would be rude of us to sit in on such a private conversation, but what does he know," she laughed. "Anyway, good luck."

She disappeared through the sliding door, and I waited a few seconds until I was certain that we were alone. I didn't know why I was so afraid all of a sudden but sweat started to pour down the sides of my face, and my hands jittered at my sides. The soft melody of a song from our youth played from somewhere, the sitting room, I figured, where she was waiting for me.

Swallowing the lump in my throat, I pushed onward, knocking on the doorframe, though there was no door between us. I stopped in my tracks the second I laid my eyes on her.

For a split second, all I saw was the Lucinda Carney I had fallen in love with when we were teenagers. She had her hair pinned half up like she always did when she was on her way to work, a subtle shade of red lipstick to brighten up her face, and the purple dress she wore more times than I could count. She thought the color suited her best, and I couldn't agree more, though I figured she'd look great in almost anything.

I blinked, and that image faded, but the woman sitting before me was just as beautiful. Her hair fell around her face and was mostly white now. She had wrinkles around her eyes, which made me smile as that meant her life was full of laughter and happiness—or so they say. I spotted little hints of makeup, though not much, and she wore light blue trousers with a white top.

"My, oh my," I gawked, slowly removing the hat off my head and holding it to my chest. "You haven't changed a bit."

Lucinda snorted, but she cracked a smile all the same. "I'm certain that's not true but thank you for the compliment." She looked me up and down, analyzing me from the tips of my boots to my eyebrows. I felt exposed standing there but didn't think it would be appropriate to help myself to a seat without her offering first. "You don't look so bad yourself."

"My caretaker keeps me active," I explained. "I don't see the point of it, but he insists, and it's too much effort to object."

She nodded slowly, absorbing my words. An awkward moment passed between us, but she motioned to the small sofa to her left with the flick of her wrist. "Well, don't just stand there, have a seat."

I did and tried to remind myself not to stare for too long, as I didn't want to make her uncomfortable.

"So," I began. "I don't think there's really much of a point beating around the bush. You know why I'm here."

She fiddled with the hem of her shirt for a second before lifting her gaze to me once more. "You're referring to the letter that just came into my possession. I can't say it didn't come as a surprise. I'd waited so long for it that it didn't even feel real anymore."

"Lucinda…"

"I suppose I should've known there was some logical explanation as to why nothing arrived while you were away. I mean, we'd said so many things, exchanged promises, I never thought in a million years you of all people would be the one to break such sacred vows. But your silence spoke when your words did not. You have to understand what kind of position you put me in. Had a letter arrived, I would've been able to justify waiting for your return, if it were to happen. I'm ashamed to admit it now, but I would've preferred to find out you'd died in battle."

"I know, I know," I breathed, looking down at the carpet, as it hurt too much to see the pain reflecting in her eyes. "What makes matters worse is that it wasn't a short time later when I really did almost die, so I had no way of knowing you didn't get it or that you hadn't replied back."

Her face shifted when I mentioned the part about almost dying overseas. If I didn't know any better, I thought maybe she was overcome with guilt, but it wasn't necessary. It wasn't like she was the one who had put a bullet in me... or several for that matter.

"What was it like?" she whispered, holding a hand to her mouth. "I briefly heard a story from Gianna when Dustin and Mark came back, but I told them I wasn't interested in knowing what happened to you while you were over there. I wasn't interested in knowing anything that might've justified your absence."

"It was surreal. I still remember it like it happened yesterday. One minute everything was fine, or as fine as it could be when you were cowering in the freezing cold trenches. The next, our station was ambushed, and then in another, I was waking up in a bright hospital room surrounded by wires, bedsheets, and nurses. The smell is what brought me back from my dreamlike state. The scent of bleach and freshly washed bedding was so overpowering it woke me up."

"How long were you out for?"

"A few months. To this day, I'm still not sure how I managed to survive. More men died from something as simple as a cold, and here I was, several bullets in me, but I managed to see another day in the sun. It felt a bit like a cruel joke."

"Perhaps someone thought you still had something to do with your life," she murmured, shifting on the sofa to get a little closer to me.

"I came to see you when I returned to Montana," I confessed. "I came to this very house back in June '43. I had so much to tell you, so much that I wanted to say. I thought for sure we were about to spend what would be the rest of our lives together, but then your brother sort of crushed all that."

She tilted her head slightly to the left, her jaw moving from side to side. Suddenly, I wasn't sure if I should've mentioned that part. "Leith? What does he have to do with this?"

"He was the one who told me you were married, that you had, in his words, moved on and it was time for me to do the same. I can't say that hearing that didn't break my heart, because it did, but I also didn't want to come between you and your happiness."

Lucinda frowned. "I can't believe he did that and never told me."

"He was just looking out for you."

"Yeah," she sighed, "he had a bad habit of doing that."

"Where is he now?" I was afraid she was going to tell me he was dead too. I'd hate to speak ill of the dead.

"He's still around but not in Whitefish. He and his wife moved out of town shortly after they were married. My mother and father died when Marina was in her teens. Edith is still in town, but we don't see each other as often as we should. She changed after you left, she became more... closed off. She had a lot of dark days."

"I'm sorry to hear that."

"And you?" she asked. "I take it you settled down and got married yourself?"

"Yes, I did. Connie. She had a lot of love in her heart, enough to take care of me all these years. She passed away from cancer not too long ago. I'm grateful it wasn't a long fight, I never liked to see her in pain. She was my best friend."

"Russell was mine too," Lucinda revealed. "Sometimes he felt more like a friend than a lover."

My head snapped up, and she gave me a perplexed look, as if she didn't understand my reaction. I'd never met another person who considered their significant other to be more of a friend than anything else, but then again, everyone I'd ever known was convinced they'd married their soulmate. I couldn't say the same.

"I never would've left you high and dry, you have to know that," I said. "If that's all we get out of this reunion, I'm fine with it. I don't expect anything else, not after everything you've had to—"

"I was pregnant," she interrupted. My jaw dropped, as I tried to piece together what she had said, but more importantly, what she was implying. "I found out shortly after you were deployed."

"You mean..."

"We have a daughter."

I looked in the general direction of the backyard, but Lucinda was quick to clarify what I was thinking. "No, it's not Marina. Her older sister, Charlotte."

I could hardly wrap my head around it. I had a child? I never thought I would have a baby to bestow my wisdom and knowledge on. Connie was unable to have children, and adoption just didn't feel right to us. If we couldn't conceive the way God intended to, then maybe we weren't meant to have a child at all. It was a foolish way to think, and it was more Connie's philosophy than my own. But as her husband, it was my duty to respect her wishes. And so, there'd always been a sort of hole in my heart, unfulfilled, but I'd come to terms with it. Now, it felt like I'd become whole for the first time.

Just as much as I was overjoyed by the notion of having a child, I could tell by the pained expression washing over her that things hadn't necessarily worked out the way she'd hoped.

"No one ever told me that you had a baby, so that must mean that no one knew, at least not your friends."

"My parents kept it a secret, more for their sake than my own. Since I was unmarried, they were worried it would ruin my chances to marry and find work. My siblings might've been soiled too, had I gone against my parents' wishes and raised her myself."

"What happened to her?" I asked.

"She was put up for adoption the day she was born. I held her for a few minutes, kissed her, and that was it. I couldn't bear to look at her any longer because she was just a constant reminder of what I had lost. If there's one regret I have in life, it's that..."

Her voice cracked, and she stopped herself as the tears flooded from her eyes. I shifted to the edge of the sofa, close enough that I could hold her hands and bring her even the slightest bit of comfort. It wasn't much, but it was all I could offer at the time. I was still processing it all myself.

"I'm so sorry you had to endure that alone. I wish I could've been there, so you never had to go through that, but try as I might, I cannot rewrite the past."

She nodded, understanding that what happened between us is just something we're both going to have to live with.

"I never stopped loving you," she whimpered. "Even now, after all this time, I thought for sure when I saw you again that I would feel nothing, but it's like I'm a teenager again, and everything I felt for you back then is just as raw and real as it is now."

"I know what you mean." I rested my forehead against hers and closed my eyes for a second. What I was about to say next was surely going to change the course of our history, so I wanted to make sure I got it right.

"The last thing I want to do is diminish the life we shared with our respective partners, but I think it's fair to say that what we felt for them is nothing like what we feel for each other. I love you, Lucinda, I always have, and I always will. We've spent far too long apart and now that we're sitting here, face to face, I can't fathom spending another day without you in my life."

She sniffled and wiped a few stray tears with the back of her hand. "What are you saying, Dwayne?"

"You know I'd get down on one knee if I knew I'd be able to get back up," I chuckled, "so you'll just have to take my words as a gesture instead. Will you do me the greatest honor by becoming my wife?"

She looked at me with those bright blue eyes and it felt as if time stood still. "I thought you'd never ask."

Chapter 27

April 2005

It took more than a single night to get used to waking up in my childhood bedroom, but as the days turned into weeks, I was starting to adjust.

Everything had been the same just as I had left it, not even a thin layer of dust covered any surfaces. The bed had been made, which was the only thing that was different. I was a bit of a slob when it came to keeping my room tidy, at least to my parent's standards. I couldn't help but picture my mother coming in here once a week to do some cleaning, just to keep up the illusion that I was still living under her roof. It stung to think of how much damage my leaving caused my family, but there was little I could do about it now. All there was left to do was move forward and try to patch things up, whatever it took.

Brenda and I had exchanged all of 10 words since I'd been back. I didn't take any offense to her silent treatment; I figured she was going to have a hard time processing her old sister coming back, even if she'd been dreaming about the day herself. It was a lot of trauma and change to deal with, and I didn't pry or pester her to talk or work things out. I knew it would happen eventually, when she was ready to lay it all out.

The day after we'd come back to Montana, I went over to Tommy's apartment to see if he'd gone through with his word about throwing out all my stuff. Luckily, he wasn't there, although his roommate was. He begrudgingly handed me a garbage bag of all my clothes and sent me on my way. I was sure I had a lot more things than that but didn't feel comfortable barging in there to do a sweep myself. I supposed I just had to part with the loss of whatever was in there and move on to bigger and better things.

I even quit at Dunkin' Donuts. It probably wasn't the smartest move, given my situation, but I was cutting all ties to my past, and if that meant I had to spend the next month or so hunting down a new part-time job, so be it. Who knew, I might even get lucky and land something that I genuinely liked. I wouldn't turn a blind eye to something in the creative industry, so I kept my eyes peeled on the newspaper every day and scanned for any potentials that sparked an interest.

I had yet to have the heavy conversation with my parents about everything that went down between us, but knew it was on the horizon. I could only avoid it for so long. They were giving me a bit of a grace period, likely afraid that if they brought it up too soon, or at all, that it might spook me, and I'd take off again. I appreciated they were letting me come to them first, as I felt like I were the one in control and not the other way around. Now that the weekend had come, and everyone was puttering around the house doing their own thing, I felt like it was the right time to sit them down and hash things out—especially since Brenda was off at the library and wouldn't have to be subjected to us bickering if it came to that.

When I went downstairs, I found them each with a glass in hand and lounging on the couch. It had been a busy two weeks for the both of them, for all of us really, as we prepared for the impending nuptials of Dwayne Anderson and Lucinda Carney. She and my mother had sorted through all the necessary paperwork to revert back to her maiden name, although it wouldn't be long before she officially became an Anderson. As exciting as it was for us to have something to look forward to as a family, it was still a lot of work, regardless of how lowkey they'd asked it to be.

"Mom? Dad? Do you have a sec?"

They exchanged a quick glance, as if they were capable of reading each other's minds. Surely they must've known this was going to happen sooner or later.

"Of course." Mom took the lead, setting down her glass of wine and urging me to sit somewhere I felt most comfortable. I chose the carpet in front of the fireplace, so I could look at them both as we were about to have the hardest talk of my life.

"I, uh, I don't really know where to start," I laughed, but tears pricked my eyes none the same. They always said laughter was a defense mechanism, and it was true now more than ever. "I've thought about this a hundred times, maybe more, but still..."

"Just speak from the heart," Dad aided, flashing me a warm smile. "We're not here to judge or antagonize you. We just want to listen to your side of the story."

"I wish I could say there was one defining thing that led to my decision to leave," I started, picking at the skin around my fingernails. "It was more like a collection of really little, stupid things. Stupid in the sense that, looking back at it now, it just feels ridiculous that I ever let them get to me. But that's just the way it goes though, right? When you're a teenager, everything your parents do is meant to annoy you."

"We've been there, honey," Mom murmured. "We were kids too. We know that it's normal for a child to not always agree with the way their parents do things around the house. I just wished you would've come to us, as a mature adult, and we could've fixed things before they got too bad."

I could see the heartache in her eyes, the way she was pleading for me not to go away again, even if this was awkward and stressful. I had a bad habit of running away when things got hard, but I'd started to realize that was not the most effective way to deal with one's emotions. As selfish as it sounded, I would need all their help and support as I ended the next chapter of my life.

"I doubt this'll make you feel any better, but there's really nothing you could've done differently that would've changed the outcome. I think I had to leave for a little while, to gain some outside perspective before coming back. Without it, we'd probably just end right back where we started, and no one wants that."

"You're right, we don't want that," Mom said. "So, how do we avoid it in the future? I hope you realize we're not going to spend the rest of our lives walking on eggshells around you or cater to your every want or demand. The world just doesn't work like that. There's always going to be something or someone out there that you disagree with, and I don't think as a mother it would be right of me to shelter or protect you from such a harsh reality. Yes, it's my job to love you, and nurture you, and keep you safe, but I also need to prepare you for what's out there."

"I know," I nodded. "And I don't expect you to change who you are just to please me. I'm not that same childish little girl anymore. I've grown up, perhaps a little too much, since I've left."

My voice trailed off for a second, and I touched my stomach for only a few seconds, but it was enough for my mother's face to twist with sudden realization.

"I'm handling it," I whispered.

"Handling what?" Dad asked.

"How long?" Mom ignored him.

"I'm not exactly sure. I have a ballpark in mind, but I haven't been to the doctor's or anything like that."

Dad stood up, demanding our attention for once. He held his index finger up, and his hand trembled just a bit, as if he were on the verge of a nervous breakdown. "Alright, what's going on?"

I closed my eyes for a second and let out a deep sigh. "I'm pregnant."

He flopped back down on the couch, at a loss for words. Mom readjusted in her seat, and I wondered if she was tempted to come join me on the carpet, so she could hold me and tell me everything was going to be alright, but she hesitated long enough, knowing I needed my space.

"However you decide to do this, we're right behind you," she declared. "I will not let you go through this alone, do you hear me? There are plenty of options out there, and whatever you want to do, we'll do it."

I nibbled on my bottom lip, fighting back the urge to cry, again. I'd done so much of it lately I barely recognized myself. I was not a girl who was driven by her emotions; it was usually the other way around.

But pregnancy hormones were no joke, and I was forced to face things head-on now.

"I've sort of worked out a plan in my mind, I'm just not sure about the execution part of it. I know it's not ideal for me to raise a baby at my age, but I don't think I could ever give them up. I'm their mother, and just because I've made some mistakes in my life, doesn't mean they have to lose me."

"It's going to be a hell of a responsibility for you to take on, but if you're willing and able, I know you'll do just fine," Mom said. "My first suggestion would be to call a doctor and make a prenatal appointment. They'll walk you through everything you need to know, and we'll be able to get a more accurate date of when you'll be due to give birth."

"What about work?" Dad chimed in. "I know you just quit your part-time job, but are you still looking for something else? We don't expect you to pay rent or contribute to any bills while you're here, but it does cost money to take care of a baby, not to mention you'll have to see about getting insurance since you're not covered under our work anymore."

I blinked a few times, overwhelmed by the influx of information, it was difficult to process it all at once. There was so much I had yet to consider, but regardless, it didn't influence my decision to keep my baby.

"I'm going to figure it out. One step at a time."

"So, I take it you won't be returning to school?" he questioned.

"Not necessarily. I'm not going to be re-enrolling at the high school, but I have been doing a bit of research online, and I've found a few places where I can take night classes that'll contribute toward my diploma. It's not exactly the most conventional way of doing things, but when have I ever done anything according to normal society?" I chuckled.

"I suppose you're right about that. I know I might sound like a broken record but getting a high school education will most definitely open more doors for you in the future. You're not just thinking about yourself anymore, but your little one too. From now on, every decision you ever make is going to be in their best interest, trust me."

Oh, I knew that. I knew it the second I saw those two pink little lines on the pregnancy stick. It was why I had waited so long to tell Tommy that he was going to be a dad, and why I was grateful that I hadn't found the courage to do so. It was the one thing I'd yet to decide on— if and when I was going to break the news to him. He wasn't the most ideal partner, and I was never going to go crawling back to him now that I had freed myself from his cage, but I knew deep down that it wasn't right for me to keep our child from him. There would come a day when I would have to tell the truth. Today was just not that day.

"Can I ask a favor?" I paused, waiting for them to acknowledge my question with a firm nod. "Please keep this to yourselves. I don't even want Brenda to know, not yet at least. We're still on the outs right now, and I'd hate to add fuel to her fire. Besides, not everyone who's involved knows either."

Mom moved her mouth from side to side as if she wanted to make a comment but held her tongue. "You can trust us," she murmured.

"Thank you," I said. "And for what it's worth, I'm sorry for all hell I put you two through. I know an apology doesn't mean much—"

"It means a lot," Dad smiled. "We're sorry too. We're just glad that you felt happy enough to come back, because that's all we've ever wanted."

Happiness. It was still a concept I was trying to familiarize myself with, but if time was on my side, then I would have no issue finding it.

***

I knew that if I could face my parents and live to tell the tale, then I could do almost anything. While Brenda still had no interest in making up, there was someone else in town that I had wanted to clear the air with. It was going to be an awkward conversation to say the least, but he deserved to know everything he was getting himself into before he made the plunge.

That was, if I was reading our relationship correctly. We'd yet to discuss what was actually going on between us, but there was no denying that we had some chemistry. I knew it, I had a feeling he knew it too, we were both just too afraid to admit it out loud. A small part of me figured that he just didn't want to put me in an uncomfortable situation, not only because I had just come out of a relationship, but because I was in a foreign town with no real support system to rely on. I admired him for that, but now that I was back on Montana soil, there was nothing standing in our way.

Ever since Dwayne popped the question two weeks ago, he'd been staying with my grandmother in her house. Kemp too, though he was holed up in one of the old guest rooms. He probably didn't think he'd be staying here for such an extended period of time, hence the lack of clothes he brought, so I'd ventured into town with him so he could pick up a few more things before he eventually went home to his place. I selfishly hoped that he'd end up staying in Whitefish permanently, but I didn't have the gall to ask him flat out. This wasn't his home; his job as Dwayne's caretaker was null at this point now that he had his true love back, so in retrospect, he didn't have any reason to stay.

Unless I gave him one.

Ultimatums weren't my thing, I thought they were pretty toxic and manipulative if I were honest, which didn't make sense, since Tommy often gave them to me in our relationship. I chalked it up as I was blinded by my first love, but also, that he had me wrapped around his finger. The ball was always in his court— other than my job at Dunkin' Donuts, he was the one who put a roof over my head and made sure I had everything I needed. I cursed myself for ever falling for his stupid charms and empty words, but I'd been so drawn to his bad boy nature because I wanted to use it as an excuse to escape my mediocre life, that I ate up everything he ever said or did.

I promised myself I'd never fall for such lies again. I would approach relationships with caution, even if that meant taking things slow. I hoped that Kemp would understand that while I was no doubt interested in starting up something with him, it would take time for me to heal from the wounds that Tommy inflicted.

I'd arranged for him to meet me under one of the old bridges by the creek. It was one of my hideouts—or safe spaces, if you will—where I spent most of my afternoons sneaking off to avoid my parents. I didn't do anything nefarious there, no drugs or alcohol, but rather, tore through numerous sketchbooks. It was the one consistent way I'd managed to express myself, through art, and now that I had that itch back, I hadn't stopped sketching for two weeks now. I took it as an omen that good things were on the horizon, so today, I was feeling rather ambitious with enriching all the positive relationships in my life.

"Is this the part of the movie where you hold me hostage and eventually kill me?" Kemp joked, nearly scaring the daylights out of me as I hadn't heard him approach.

I held a hand to my chest, feeling my rapid heartbeat, willing it to return to its normal pace. "No murderer in their right mind would ever admit to such things," I teased. "It spoils all our fun."

"Hilarious," he smirked, joining me at the riverbank. We stared at the rushing water for a few minutes in silence, I'd almost forgotten he was there. "So, did you ask me here to watch the water go by, or was there something else weighing on your mind?"

"Yes, there was a purpose to you coming here, I'm just sort of trying to work out a way of going about it."

"Ah," Kemp chirped. He looked at me for a few seconds, and I felt my inside wriggle, not because his eyes always made me swoon, but because I could tell he was trying to interpret what I might be hiding behind mine.

"I know things have been a bit of a rollercoaster between us. We didn't exactly get along from the start, and I'm not offended that you thought I was some low-life teenager, because I kind of am—or was—but something changed the more we got to know each other. Right?" I paused for a moment to chew on the inside of my cheek. "I hope I'm not looking too much into your niceness."

Kemp smiled, the kind that didn't make me feel like he was about to patronize or look down on me. "No, you're not looking into it. You're different from anyone I've ever met. I wasn't looking for anything when you approached me that afternoon at the rec center. If I'm being completely transparent, I didn't think love or romance was in the cards for me. No relationship has ever worked out in my favor."

I found that incredibly surprising. He was everything a girl could ever want and more. Who in their right mind would let someone like Kemp Andrews slip through their fingers?

"I've only been in one, but I don't think I'm the most experienced when it comes to romantic relationships. My track record isn't looking the greatest," I chuckled. "But I'm hoping my luck's about to change."

This time when he stared into my eyes, I felt heat blossom in the middle of my chest. We leaned in simultaneously, and he brushed a tender kiss across my lips. It felt like my heart was going to explode. All the nerves in my body tingled, and I was tempted to pounce on him, but quickly reminded myself that I wanted to take things slow, so I held back.

"Wait," I breathed, not wanting to stray from the real reason I had called him here in the first place. "There's something I need to tell you."

"Oh?" He blinked a few times but pulled back enough to give me some space. "That sounds serious."

"Before anything starts between us, I need you to know what you're about to get yourself into," I declared. "You won't just be in a relationship with me. There's someone else you'll have to consider... someone who is not here in the physical world just yet."

His eyes flickered to my stomach. It didn't take a genius to work out what I meant. He remained quiet for a beat, and his silence nearly drove me over the edge.

"It certainly complicates things," Kemp acknowledged. "But that doesn't change how I feel about you. It'll take more than a baby to scare me off, Amy Wood."

I felt like I might melt into a puddle of happiness.

See, a voice in my head said. *You just needed time.*

"So, does that mean…" I began to ask, my voice trailing off as I moved my hands in circles, wanting him to finish my sentence.

"Yes," he purred. "I would love to go out with you."

"Does that mean you'll be my date to Lucinda and Dwayne's wedding?" I grinned, playing with the ends of his hair.

He planted a kiss on my cheek, and I blushed. "Do you even have to ask?"

Chapter 28

May 2005

The time had finally come when my grandmother and her future husband were going to share their vows and spend the rest of their days together, bathing in all the love and happiness they could offer. Although she'd already been through this once before, my grandmother had a case of the jitters, and when I asked her about it, she simply said that it was because she'd been waiting so long to walk down the aisle and see Dwayne standing there, that it felt too good to be true.

I reminded her again and again that it was very much real, and that in less than an hour, we were to head over to the place where it all began.

The town hall.

It felt only fitting since that had been where they first met, and the sparks of their new love first ignited. I'd heard the story about the officer's dance nearly half a dozen times since we settled on the venue. She gushed and gushed about how this strapping young man had walked right over to her and just started talking. My grandmother was a lot like me in the sense that she didn't do well in social situations or engaging in conversation with strangers. But it didn't take much for Dwayne to skip from strangers and go straight to lover status. When I asked her how she knew he was the one for her, she said it was something about the way his eyes sparkled. It wasn't just a trick of the light, it came from somewhere within, and only happened for her. I thought I'd seen something similar in Kemp's eyes before, so I clung to the hope that what she said was true, because that meant that there was a pretty good chance that he might be my soulmate too.

However, unlike my grandmother, I had no real reason to speed things along and settle down. It just wasn't how relationships unfolded these days; people took their time to get to know each other, not tie the knot and let things work out for themselves. Kemp and I still had much to learn about each other, not to mention the fact that I was going to be giving birth before the year was out. If what we had was real, it could certainly last a few months, or even years, before he popped the question if that was what felt right. It took Dwayne six decades to finally do it, so I had faith things would work out just like they were meant to, in their own time and on their own terms.

"Look what I've got!" Mom cheered, holding a cold bottle of champagne above her head.

Meticulously placing her thumbs beneath the rip, she popped the cork, and shouted with glee before pouring the ladies a couple of glasses. It was just the four of us, my grandmother, mother, me, and Brenda. She was never one to object to letting us drink on special occasions, and a wedding certainly fit into that category. Unfortunately, alcohol consumption was not something one did while pregnant, so I was quick to place a hand over my glass so she couldn't contaminate it.

Brenda shot me a quick glance, her brow arching ever so slightly. I knew exactly what she was thinking—that I was never one to turn down a bit of champagne when at a family gathering.

"I've got a bit of a stomach bug," I revealed. "I don't think having a drink will help much."

"Ah," she said, but it didn't exactly sound like I had convinced her.

I would have to be careful the next couple of days to not do anything suspicious that might lead to her finding out about a very important secret. It wasn't that I didn't trust her to keep it, because I knew if I asked, she would button up her lips and take it to the grave. It was because she had so much on her plate already, which my mother had gotten way too deep about the other day while we were out picking up our dresses for the wedding. Apparently, Brenda had several emotional breakdowns since I'd left, and our mother was growing more and more worried for her well-being. I suggested therapy, but she seemed hesitant about that, as if she didn't want my sister to feel like we thought she needed professional help.

Maybe all she really needed was a good talking to from her big sister. "Hey, Brenda," I blurted out, "can you come help me with my makeup in the bathroom? I just can't seem to get my eyeliner right. It's been a while since I got all dolled up."

Regardless of any tension that might've been simmering between us, she perked up at the thought of helping me with something and jumped at the chance.

"Of course," she beamed, and we slinked away, leaving mom to help Grandma get in her sophisticated, yet simple, white dress.

I jumped up onto the counter so that I was at the perfect height for her to do my eye makeup. First, she started with some eyeshadow, which I was never much of a fan of, but I let her go at it, just this once. Neither of us talked for the first few minutes, and I'd contemplated not bringing it up at all, as I didn't want to ruin the moment. I knew that I wasn't likely going to get another chance for a while, so I had to suck it up and rip off the Band-Aid. She would thank me for it later.

"So," I cleared my throat, "Mom was telling me that you had a run in with some mean girls at school. You wanna talk about it?"

Her eyes widened, and I knew I had caught her off guard. She pursed her lips, and I hoped I hadn't backed her into a corner too much with my question. The last thing our family needed was another daughter who ran away from her problems.

"It's no big deal," she muttered. "They're just bullies who have nothing else better to do with their time. Mom said it was best to just ignore them."

"She's right," I started. "But, if you need someone to kick their ass, well…"

"No," Brenda squealed. "I don't need you getting into any fights on my behalf, even if they were talking about you."

"They were, were they?" I already knew that, but I wanted it to come from her mouth. I had a sneaking suspicion that she didn't bother telling our mother the whole story anyway.

"It's not worth repeating, trust me."

"They think I'm some kind of harlot," I snickered at my use of the word. "That I'm just a wash out who threw her life away for some dumb boy. That I'll never amount to anything worthwhile because I dropped out of high school. But the worst part of it all, is that they compared me to you. They probably said that you were bound to follow in my footsteps, that it was only a matter of time."

Brenda's cheeks reddened, and I knew I had hit the nail on the head. She had not been distraught because they said all those horrible things about their older sister, she was upset because her worst fear was ever turning out like me. I knew I should've been offended, and a tiny part of me was, but I held no resentment over it. I had made mistakes, I had done stupid things, and they were things I prayed that my sister would never do. I guess in a way I was grateful that those mean girls had said something, because as long as it meant that she would steer clear of the rough path I stumbled down, she would do just fine.

"You probably think I'm a horrible person, don't you?" Brenda sniffled. "Most little sisters dream of one day becoming like their big sister. You were supposed to be my hero."

"I know," I murmured. "I turned out to be a terrible role model, and for that, I'm sorry. I wish I could go back and change it all, but that's not how the world works. I'm fine that you don't want to be anything like me, really, I hope that you won't make the same mistakes that I have. But—"

"Why does there always have to be a but?" Brenda sighed. "You were doing so well without it."

"But," I ignored her comment, "you need to stop trying so hard to be different. Mom tells me you barely sleep because you're up all night studying to get the best grades possible. There's nothing wrong with trying to achieve greatness in high school, but something tells me you have ulterior motives for this academic drive. You're so hell-bent on doing the complete opposite of what I did, you're losing yourself along the way. That's not healthy, Brenda, and I'd hate for you to miss out on important milestones."

"It's not just that," Brenda whispered. "I thought… I thought that if I excelled in school, that Mom and Dad would have a daughter to be proud of. Ever since you left, you were all that she talked about. I didn't understand it. You left. You left our family, and it was like we didn't matter to you anymore. You never came over, you never called, you were just gone in the middle of the night, and you never looked back. It hurt, Amy, it hurt that you were capable of doing that, but it hurt even more that despite all the pain you caused, they still loved you."

She buried her face in her hands and quietly sobbed, not wanting to alert our mother or grandmother. I pouted myself, not because I was sad, but more because I felt as if I'd done a lot more than fail her because of my life choices. I pulled her into a hug, and she nestled her head in the crook of my neck, and for the first time in a long time, I felt like I had my sister back. I never wanted to be the one to bring her to tears, but I couldn't allow her to walk around town with these burdens weighing her down anymore. It was time for her to let it all out, once and for all.

"Mom and Dad were just trying to make sense of why I had left. They didn't know how to process it, and neither did you. It came as a shock to everyone, and we all deal with grief and loss in our own unique ways. They did it by never letting my name fade for too long, and you did it by shutting out every other aspect of your life."

"I guess I never saw it like that before," she said.

"You should know you never have to compete with me for their love or attention. They love us both, equally, in spite of all our faults. And for what it's worth, I'm sorry I didn't come and check in on you. I know now that I should've. I just thought you'd be better off without me."

Brenda pulled herself back and wiped her face with her fingers before checking her makeup in the mirror. "I think I'll always need you."

It felt good to hear her say that. It meant that regardless of what had transpired in the past few months, she would always see me as her big sister, and that was all I could ever want from our relationship.

With all of that out of the way, she continued with my makeup, this time, with a smile on her face. I couldn't help but think of my little baby—I wondered if they were a girl, and if they were, how much fun it would be to help teach her all the things that we knew about life. Either way, Brenda was going to be the best aunt in the world, and I felt supremely lucky to have her in my life.

***

Despite my grandmother and her husband-to-be telling us over and over again that they didn't need anything fancy, that was not how my mother rolled. It was definitely more laid back than most weddings I'd been to, but I thought it suited the occasion just right.

The hall was separated into two parts—the backside of the room, which had the giant bay window, was where the ceremony was to be held. The wooden arch was adorned with fresh flowers and greenery, most of which had been handpicked by my mother herself. The colors were muted, more pastel, and were paired with deep greens, which complimented the atmosphere nicely. It was a spring wedding, after all, so anything floral fit the theme just right.

Along with the flowers on the arch, the aisle was also decorated with giant pots of flowers, which would be available for guests to take home if they wished. Two dozen chairs were neatly arranged, and people had already started to filter inside to get the best seats possible. I recognized a few familiar faces: Gianna and her husband Dustin, as well as Madeline and Mark, two couples that had grown up alongside Dwayne and my grandmother. It made me happy to see they were all still really great friends, even after all this time. I wondered if Olivia and I would still talk decades from now. I hoped we would. She was the only real friend I ever had, and I missed her terribly.

My Great-Aunt Edith had also arrived only moments ago, though she was not joined by her husband or her kids. There were a few other relatives I knew, as well as a few I didn't, and others that I figured were old friends from either side. The most important, and the only guest I really cared about was Kemp, and he looked more dapper than usual. His face was freshly shaved, and he wore a tanned suit with a white shirt underneath. His tie was the same shade as the purple in my dress, not just because he was my date and we wanted our outfits to match, but because he was the best man, and I was the maid of honor.

We'd only had minutes to go, and so Dwayne took his place up at the altar, along with the priest and Kemp.

"You look beautiful, Amy," Dwayne said before taking my hand and kissing the top of it. "Thank you for everything you've done for me."

"Oh, you don't have to thank me," I said. "It was a team effort."

"You should give yourself more credit. Had you not bravely traveled out of state to come meet me, we wouldn't be standing here today. I might've never had the chance, or the courage, to fight for my love, and I owe it all to you."

"We should really thank that postal worker who delivered the letter," I giggled. "That's what started all this. He could've just thrown it out and we would've all continued on with our lives just as they were. He made a choice to bring it to the house, not knowing how such a simple act would have colossal ripple effects."

"That's a good point," Dwayne nodded. "I should track down the lad and thank him myself."

"Mom caught his name, you should ask her after the ceremony," I suggested.

A bell chimed, signaling that the ceremony was about to begin. I stood tall on the left side of the altar, holding something very precious in my pocket. Kemp matched my stance on the other side of the altar, just a few steps away from the man of the hour. Dwayne faced the aisle, tentatively waiting for his bride. I couldn't help but smile at the pure joy radiating from his body, and how it grew exponentially the second Grandma stepped through the doors.

Although I had been there when she got all dolled up, there was something about seeing her with all the twinkle lights and the flowers that brought tears to my eyes. She beamed from ear to ear, my mother on one hand, and my father on the other as they escorted her down the aisle. Not once did their eyes stray from each other; it was like they were the only ones in the room, which I supposed was how it was meant to feel.

When they reached the end of the aisle, the music tapered off, and my mother kissed her on the cheek before taking her seat in the front row, my father in tow. Dwayne held out his hand, and she took it happily, joining him in front of the arch. But before the priest could speak, the side door opened, and five people stepped inside, rushing just a tad.

I glanced at Kemp, but he shrugged his shoulders, and he clearly didn't know who those people were. Mom whirled around in her seat to give the intruders a piece of her mind, but her face softened, and I knew she must've recognized them. She waved them up to the front, and that's when I noticed that the entire second row was empty, as it had been clearly reserved for someone special. They quickly took their seats, and the woman and my mother exchanged a few words before nodding at the priest to begin.

"Welcome friends and family of Dwayne and Lucinda. We are gathered here today on this marvelous occasion to bring these two together in holy matrimony. It brings me such pleasure to bring these two households together, as I think we can all agree it's something that should've happened long ago."

The crowd chuckled, as did I, knowing just how long both of them had waited for this moment. Once the room settled down again, the priest continued with his speech.

"Normally, I'd have the bride and groom repeat a specific set of vows to each other as part of the sacrament, but today, we are doing something a little different. Lucinda, if you would please take the lead," he urged.

She glanced over her shoulder at me, and I promptly slipped a delicate piece of paper into her hands.

My grandmother cleared her throat before looking out at her loved ones. "First off, I just wanted to thank you all for coming and celebrating with us today. I think I speak for both of us when I say that it means the world that you all have come to bear witness to the beginning of our love story. It's certainly been years in the making," she smiled. "In my hands, I have the words that I first wrote to Dwayne, over sixty years ago. It was the letter that sealed my love, so it only felt right to share some of those words with you all, as part of our vows.

"I love you, Dwayne Anderson, I love you more than I'll ever be able to show, but I hope you know that you have captured my heart and soul. I'll wait for you until the sun rises in the west and sets in the east. I promise that I will never love another again, not in the way that I love you."

Dwayne leaned forward just a bit, but stopped himself, realizing now was not the time for him to be kissing his bride. The priest motioned that it was his turn to read his vows, and so, Kemp stepped forward and offered the lost letter that had started it all.

"Please, take this letter as my undying dedication to you, Lucinda Carney. One day, you will be Mrs. Lucinda Anderson, this I swear. I will give you anything your heart desires. I promise to come home at a decent hour and take care of you in every way you need. I will be the man to make you a mother, and I will spend the rest of my time on this earth making sure that you get the life you deserve."

He choked on the last couple of words, and he took a few deep breaths to compose himself. "I'm sorry you had to wait this long for us to stand here today, but my words were true then just as they are now. You are my whole world, Lucinda, my heart and my life, and one day I will die a happy man knowing that we got to spend the last of our days together."

There were hushed sniffles throughout the crowd, and my mother was by far the loudest. We shared a quick glance before we returned our attention back to the happy couple.

"May we have the rings please?" the priest asked.

I fished out the piece of jewelry that my grandmother had picked out for Dwayne a few days prior. She hoped it would suit him well, which I thought it did. It was not your typical shiny gold, but a gunmetal gray, something that I figured was meant to signify his duty to the war, and now, his duty to his wife. She placed it on his finger and brushed a quick kiss against his hand.

Kemp handed Dwayne my grandmother's ring next. He told me about its history, how it belonged to his mother, and he had every intention of proposing with it the second he got back from the war. It had been in his pocket the day he went to visit my grandmother, and it had remained in its red velvet box ever since. He didn't even propose to his first wife, Connie, with it, as a part of him always knew it would belong on my grandmother's finger, so it didn't feel right. He placed it on her left hand and sealed it with a quick kiss.

"Now that Dwayne and Lucinda have shared their vows and exchanged the rings, which serve as a symbol of their infinite love, it is now my honor to bless this marriage. I wish the both of you a happy life filled with love, laughter, happiness, and joy. But know that even on the darkest of days, when your love is tested and challenged, I implore you to remember the words you exchanged here today, as they will be your constant reminder of the tender love you two share. I present thee, Mr. and Mrs. Anderson. Dwayne, you may now kiss your bride."

The priest did not have to tell him twice. He grabbed my grandmother by the shoulders and planted a fat kiss on her lips, and the room erupted in claps and cheers. Once they pulled apart, the music picked up again, and they walked down the aisle hand in hand, blowing kisses to everyone as they passed.

Kemp and I brought up the rear, where I looped my arm around his, and he snuck a quick kiss on my temple. I blushed but was grateful I had on a layer of makeup to hide it. My mother and father were not far behind, as the immediate family was asked to join the bride and groom in the adjacent room while the staff transformed the room for the reception.

"Congratulations, you two," I grinned, hugging and kissing them both. "I suppose now I can call you grandpa?" I teased.

"Grandpa Dwayne, it has a nice ring to it, wouldn't you say?" he remarked. "I never thought I'd hear such words come from someone's mouth."

"Speaking of…" Mom cleared her throat as the woman from before slipped inside, although she was alone this time. "There is someone I'd like everyone to officially meet. This is Charlotte, my sister," she paused, "and your daughter."

If I had been drinking or eating anything, I surely would've choked. Not in a million years did I see that coming, but the more I looked at her face, the more I could see the family resemblance.

My grandmother was on the verge of tears as they embraced, and Dwayne was too impatient to wait for his turn, so he joined in too.

"You have no idea how many times I've dreamed of this moment," my grandmother murmured. "Not just being able to marry the love of my life, but to get the chance to see our child again. For the first time in forever, my heart is now full."

"I'm happy that we got the chance to be here," Charlotte said. "And I'm looking forward to getting to know you both, now that I know you exist."

"Hey, that reminds me," Dwayne began. "Marina, I need the name of that post office fellow. I need to tell him exactly how many lives he's changed since delivering my letter."

Dwayne and Lucinda's love letter didn't just bring them back together but sparked a love story for a new generation. Stay tuned for Amy and Kemp's journey next.

www.ingramcontent.com/pod-product-compliance
Lightning Source LLC
Chambersburg PA
CBHW070546120726
47909CB00007B/2260